gargantuan

gargantuan

A RUBY MURPHY MYSTERY

MAGGIE ESTEP

 THREE RIVERS PRESS • NEW YORK

Published by Three Rivers Press, New York, New York.
Member of the Crown Publishing Group, a division of Random House, Inc.
www.crownpublishing.com

Three Rivers Press and the Tugboat design are registered trademarks of Random House, Inc.

Printed in the United States of America

Design by Lynne Amft

Library of Congress Cataloging-in-Publication Data
Estep, Maggie.
Gargantuan : a Ruby Murphy mystery / Maggie Estep.—1st ed.
        p. cm.
1. Women detectives—New York (state)—New York—Fiction. 2. Coney Island (New York, N.Y.)—Fiction. 3. Jockeys—Crimes against—Fiction. 4. Museums—Employees—Fiction. 5. Horse racing—Fiction. I. Title.
PS3555.S754G37   2004
813'.54—dc22
2004001802

ISBN 0-609-61033-3

10 9 8 7 6 5 4 3 2 1

First Edition

To John Rauchenberger, partner in crime

ACKNOWLEDGMENTS

THANKS TO Elizabeth Tisdale and Georgeann for companionship on all those bone cold afternoons at the Big A.

Joe Andoe for instigating the birth of Ben Nester.

Charlie Moran for the "sheets" as well as endless and fascinating Horse Talk.

Doug Koch and Tom Bush for letting me hang out with Sherpa Guide, a prince among horses.

Thanks also to Jane Smiley for her blessings in borrowing one of the greatest equine characters ever written, Justa Bob.

Many thanks to my mother, Nancy Murray, and my stepfather, Neil Christner, for a place to hole up finishing the book—as well as their equine expertise and access to Oat Bran Blues, Jack Valentine, and Darwin's Hiccup (who have been fictionalized slightly but hopefully will not mind since they are, after all, horses).

The Virginia Center for the Creative Arts and Byrdcliffe Artists Colony for peaceful places to work.

Meredith Maran, Patricia McCormick, and Meredith Trede, friends par excellence.

As ever, deep appreciation to my family, biological and non, Stew and Shahram, Princess Soraya, Beckett, Lion, and Ellen—and Jon and Chris and Jenny in particular for vital editorial input. Also, many thanks to my indefatigable friends and helpers, Kelly Sue DeConnick, Annie Yohe, Jennifer Dallas, and Thorpe the Gnome.

And of course, I'd be in deep trouble without the advice, support, and constancy of my agent, Rosalie Siegel, my editor, Shaye Areheart, and publicist Tim Roethgen.

Robert Small for all sorts of things, most notably his distress at being left out of previous acknowledgments.

Lastly, kudos to Almuhathir for going off at 95–1 on June 6, 2003, rallying to win, and enabling me to pay off debts accrued traveling to racetracks far and wide.

gargantuan

1.

The Jockey

I open my eyes and am startled to find a body next to mine in bed. I sit up and protectively pull the blankets all the way to my chin before realizing that the body is Attila Johnson's and that I've invited it to be here. My heart rate returns to normal as I glance down at Attila's form. His pale hair is glowing in the darkness and he seems painfully innocent in sleep even though, when awake, there is too much life in his face. I look over at the clock. It's four in the morning. I get up as quietly as possible, not wanting to disturb his sleep. Before meeting me three weeks ago, I don't think the man ever slept. Or ate. Right now he weighs a hundred and fourteen pounds, one pound less than I do. To him, of course, this is overweight. He's supposed to keep his weight under one-ten. This alone is an act of heroism, never mind the rest of his life that is devoted to rendering his body a light and muscular instrument meant to steer a thousand pounds of thoroughbred around a racetrack at thirty-five miles per hour. Which is a thing Attila does purely out of love. He got into riding too late to ever hope to be in the big leagues or do much more than work his tail off just to pay the rent. But the man loves and understands horses. This is part of why he's so compelling to me and why he's here, sleeping next to me when I still have unfinished business with another man, Ed, who up and left town just when I'd gotten to really liking the fact that he was around.

I put my robe on and walk into the living room, pulling the bedroom door shut behind me. Stinky, my large Buddha-like cat, looks at me from his post on the couch and, when I tell him aloud I'm not going to give him a snack, puts his head back down on his paws and sighs deeply. Lulu, Stinky's calico companion, is nowhere to be found and is presumably holed up in a shoe box somewhere, dreaming of murdering birds.

I go stand at the window. The snow has stopped for a breathing spell but the wind is howling its song along Stillwell Avenue, echoing through the snow-covered rides of Coney Island, the place I call home.

Lulu suddenly materializes and jumps up on top of the piano, forcing me to look at the instrument that I haven't touched in days. Above the piano hangs a small Bach portrait. Johann Sebastian appears to be scowling disapprovingly at me and my wanton musical ways. I didn't take up piano until age thirty-one and I have to work very hard for even slight improvement. My goal is to be able to play at least some of Bach's Goldberg Variations before hitting forty. I have a little more than six years to go but it's not looking promising right now. Between my newfangled *thing* with Attila Johnson and the blizzard that hit town five days ago, my whole life has been suspended. I haven't practiced the piano or returned friends' phone calls. The Coney Island Museum has been closed so I haven't gone to work. I haven't done much of anything other than lie around naked with Attila and I'm starting to get restless. I find myself seized with a need to talk to someone other than Attila or myself. I open the front door and look across the hall to see if Ramirez is home and awake.

My neighbor's door is open and he is in his customary position at the kitchen table, staring ahead, apparently doing nothing at all. He is wearing his outfit of choice: soiled white undershirt and faded pants. His arms are big but middle age is starting to slacken the muscle tone. His broad face is heavily lined, giving him a gruff look that's offset by large, kind eyes.

"Ruby," he states.

"Ramirez, what's up?"

"You want some tea?" he asks, as if visiting each other at four o'clock in the morning is the most natural thing in the world.

"Sure," I say, still standing in my doorway, suddenly hesitant about imposing on my neighbor.

"You can keep standing there if you want but maybe it's easier if you come in and have a seat." Ramirez indicates a chair.

I pull my door closed behind me and do as he suggests.

"Where's the jockey?" he asks sarcastically. Ramirez, like all my friends, seems to have his doubts about this liaison. I suppose it came on a little suddenly. For two months I was heartbroken over Ed's leaving for a job assignment in Florida—and our never having discussed exactly what was or is going on between us—then, suddenly, I was shacking up with Attila.

"He's sleeping," I tell Ramirez, tilting my chin up defensively.

"I don't want to know," Ramirez counters, putting up a hand as if warding off lurid sexual details that might involuntarily spout out of my mouth. Not that I've ever dreamed of telling my neighbor about my sex life—with Attila or anyone else—but there's something about Attila—or me *with* Attila—that seems to make people think I'm going to carelessly relay graphic details of our sex life. I think it's because he's small. Sometimes small people seem perverse to large people. As if a raging libido lives inside of them, making up for their diminutive stature.

"Elsie's still in Puerto Rico?" I ask, even though I know she is.

My neighbor nods his head and then, as if in homage to his absent girlfriend, gets up to start brewing tea. Ramirez was never a tea kind of guy as far as I could tell but Elsie knows about and uses herbal teas and medicines and, before heading down to Puerto Rico to visit a sick aunt, left Ramirez elaborate instructions on brewing certain teas for certain occasions. I don't know what she told him to brew should I visit before the crack of dawn, but I'm sure it'll be interesting.

"You hear from Ed?" Ramirez asks with his back to me.

"Not this week," I say through clenched teeth. Ramirez never seemed to approve of Ed while we were actually seeing each other, and it wasn't until Ed left for Florida that my neighbor took any interest in him at all. When I started this thing with Attila, Ramirez suddenly became Ed's strongest advocate.

"I told you we left things up in the air," I continue addressing Ramirez's back.

"I know what you told me," he says, finally turning around.

Ramirez is no idiot. He knew exactly how strongly I felt about Ed without my telling him.

"Why don't you like Attila?" I ask him.

"I like that jockey fine," Ramirez frowns.

"No you don't."

"I don't trust him, lady," Ramirez says, sitting down heavily.

"How can you not trust him? You don't know him."

Ramirez shrugs. "I just don't want to see you in any more trouble with men," he says, making it sound like trouble with men is my life's pursuit.

"Can we talk about something else?" I ask.

"Go ahead."

"When's Elsie coming back?"

"Soon I guess. Not sure. Aunt's still sick."

"Oh."

"There's something about those eyes of his. They're a funny color, Ruby."

"What? Whose eyes?"

"The jockey."

"His eyes are blue," I protest.

"They're a funny bright blue. I don't like it. I knew a dog with eyes like that once."

"You're comparing the object of my affections to a *dog*?"

"No, just his eyes."

This is disturbing. Ramirez has never poked his nose so firmly into my affairs. Elsie, yes. But not Ramirez. He stands up and goes to the stove to see about the tea.

"Drink your tea," he says a moment later, setting a cup in front of me.

He sits back down and frowns again, causing his dark eyes to disappear under folds of forehead. "I'm sorry to be in a mood, Ruby," he sighs. "It's the snow. It's getting to me."

"Apparently."

"Don't be mad," he urges, uncharacteristically patting my hand and squeezing it.

"Okay," I shrug.

I sip my tea and, as soon as it's slightly cool, drink it all down and bid my neighbor good night.

"You're sure you're not upset with me, lady?" Ramirez asks, escorting me back to my own front door.

"No," I sigh. "I understand."

"Understand what?"

"Understand everything," I say, not wanting to explain myself.

"That makes one of us," my neighbor says.

I go back into my apartment. Stinky is still on the couch and Lulu is now keeping him company—though she's sitting about a foot away from him, pretending she doesn't like him enough to get closer.

I walk back into the bedroom where I find Attila still sleeping but turned onto his side. He's bunched up, like he's riding a race-horse in his sleep. I get in bed next to him, prop up on my elbow and stare at him. His blond crew cut is growing out and some of his hair is mashed to the side of his head. His entire body is, even in repose, rippled with muscle. It occurs to me that racehorses and jockeys are similar in their impossibly lean but muscular physiques. Horses don't have to vomit up their dinner to keep to a certain weight though.

I rest my head on the pillow and look up at the ceiling which, for some reason, I recently painted leafy green.

"What are you doing?" Attila suddenly asks. I turn my head and find that his eyes are open.

"Nothing."

"I woke up and you weren't here," he says, reaching for me.

"Just went across the hall to say hello to my neighbor," I say, entwining my legs with his.

"That Ramirez fellow?"

"Yeah."

"That guy hates me."

"What makes you say that?"

"I just know. You spend enough time around horses, you develop a sixth sense. Mostly about horses, but about people too."

"I think he's just protective of me."

"So you admit it? He thinks I'm bad for you? He's got it in for me?"

"No, nothing like that," I protest, running my hand down Attila's forearm, kneading the muscles there.

"What, he liked your last boyfriend better?" Attila presses on.

"Not that either. He's a Vietnam vet, he's suspicious by nature."

"Uh-huh," Attila grunts, not buying it. "The man can't stand me," he declares.

To take his mind off this alleged hatred, I run my hands over Attila's compact chest and then down into his boxer shorts. He growls, wrestles me down, and pins me underneath him.

"Nobody hates you," I say softly into Attila's ear.

"That's not entirely true," he says, putting his mouth to mine. I didn't believe him. But I should have.

2.

Man on Fire

I woke up feeling like someone had ripped out my insides and replaced them with fire. I took a deep breath and turned onto my side but the view wasn't one to cool me down. Ruby was sprawled across two-thirds of the bed. Her black hair was coiled in snakes against the white sheets. Her red nightgown was unceremoniously hiked up over one hip, exposing her hind end. I reached over and lightly rubbed her thigh, my hands rough against her soft, pale skin. She let out a small sigh and tucked one hand under her cheek but she didn't wake up.

I got out of bed and started stretching. I felt the fire spreading from my internal organs to my limbs. When I fail to follow my customary physical regime of running several miles, doing hundreds of sit-ups and push-ups and riding at least a dozen horses a day, I pay a price. Where some athletes' bodies become stiff and half crippled, mine turns to fire. Not that I'm a traditional athlete. I got into all this a little late in life. I'm thirty-four and still an apprentice jockey. A *bug boy* they'd have called me in the golden days of racing. But the golden days of racing are gone and so are mine. Or so I thought. Until I met Ruby.

She was hanging over the rail looking down into the saddling paddock at Aqueduct Racetrack. She was standing next to a wild-eyed blonde and both women were staring at my mount, Ballistic, a less than stellar grandson of Native Dancer. A few months earlier, Ballistic had gone off as the favorite in an allowance race at Saratoga and hadn't finished in the money—he'd dropped down in class in each successive race and was now running for a tag at Aqueduct. The horse had bad luck just like me.

I don't usually look at the racing fans. At Aqueduct, in the middle of winter, most of them are either grouchy old white men clutching coffee-stained tip sheets or angry Jamaican guys prone to calling both jockeys and horses *blood clots*.

On that cold afternoon, something made me crane my neck and look up into the spectator area. And I saw her. She wore a red fake fur coat and, from that distance, her lips seemed as red as the coat even though it didn't look like she was wearing lipstick. Her long black hair was falling loose and wild and her eyes were searching for something. I found it difficult to stop looking at her. Although I'd already been given a leg up onto Ballistic, and had picked up the reins to make contact with his mouth, I wasn't really paying attention to the horse. The girl's eyes met mine and she smiled a little but it was hard to tell if she was smiling at Ballistic or me. Probably the latter since, for the first time in nine months, good ol' Ballistic won a race. I didn't have much to do with it. I just stayed out of the old guy's way and let him do his thing. Which, on this particular day, he did by an uncharacteristically large margin, crossing the finish line a half-dozen lengths ahead of the second-place horse.

Henry Meyer—Ballistic's trainer—was even more surprised by the win than I was. He looked stunned as he ran a hand through his thinning hair then took hold of Ballistic's bridle, steering the chestnut into position in the winner's circle. Ballistic stood proudly as the track photographer took the win photo. I hopped down off the horse's back, patted him on the neck, then took my saddle and went to weigh in. When I stepped off the scale, Henry came over and clapped me on the back. For better and mostly for worse, Henry had always had faith in me. Now, it had paid off.

"Glad to win one for you, Henry," I said, looking into his tired brown eyes. He offered a rare smile and, for the first time, I saw something other than weariness radiating from him.

When Henry had turned away, I looked up to the spectator area, hoping to find the girl in the red coat. She was hard to miss. I stared up at her for several seconds but she wasn't looking in my direction.

Ballistic was my last ride of the day so I went into the jockeys' room to change back to street clothes. A few of the guys congratulated me and slapped me on the back. I nodded and grinned but my mind was elsewhere. When I emerged from the jocks room, I found myself walking into the grandstands. I almost never do this. But I felt compelled to find the girl. Jockeys are a superstitious lot and I felt certain she'd somehow made the race come out as it had. She'd held good wishes in her heart for me and Ballistic and these wishes had influenced fate.

As I wove through small packs of spectators, I pulled a cap from my jacket pocket and put it on so that none of the horseplayers would recognize my noticeable blond hair and hurl insults at me. I was pretty sure they'd all bet against Ballistic and me and would no doubt heap unpleasantries upon me at the top of their lungs. A few old guys looked at me sideways, registering something, but I moved swiftly, darting around people until I finally spotted the girl. She was standing near the saddling paddock's indoor viewing area. She was still with the wild-eyed blonde; the two of them hunched over a computerized printout of the *Daily Racing Form*. They were oblivious to the fact that several men were eyeing them, which is a raging testament to their extreme attractiveness. Those guys normally wouldn't look up from their heavily annotated tip sheets if a tidal wave suddenly reared up from the not so distant sea and engulfed all of Aqueduct.

I stood about a foot away from the two women. My red-coat girl was frowning in concentration, chewing on the eraser of a little blue Aqueduct pencil. Eventually she felt my eyes on her. She glanced up briefly then did a double take and looked up again. This time she smiled. I felt that smile reach deep inside me.

"You're . . . you're . . . that jockey," she said.

"Attila Johnson," I said, extending a hand to shake.

"Nice job on Ballistic," she said. Her hands were even smaller than mine but she had a grip of iron. I noticed that her eyes were gray.

"No, actually, Ballistic did a nice job on me. I just tried to keep out of his way," I told her.

She grinned at this, as if I'd uttered a magical phrase.

"You ride?" I asked, because in that grin I thought I saw a girl who knew horses.

"Not really. Not like you mean. I walked hots once for a month at Belmont," she said, shrugging, "but I don't ride well. I'll get on a quiet horse given the chance but I couldn't do *that*," she said, motioning out at the track with one of her small hands. Her fingernails were unpainted though I'd have bet a hundred bucks right then that she had her toenails polished a strong red.

And I'd have won my bet. It was the first thing I checked two nights later when she took me home to her apartment in Coney Island. I hadn't even had to do much that day at Aqueduct. We'd talked a little more, she'd told me her name—Ruby—which I've rolled around like a good taste on the back of my tongue ever since. Eventually, she'd written her number down on a blank corner of her *Racing Form* printout and, three hours later, I'd called her. She immediately asked if she could come watch me exercise horses the next morning. I don't win many races but that's just dumb luck, I ride well. I told her it was fine. I'd leave her name at security.

The next morning at seven A.M., I was trotting one of John Troxler's three-year-old fillies along the rail when I noticed a girl standing there yawning. Ruby. She wasn't wearing the red coat this time but she still stood out. She was a little too well dressed to be a backside worker but too wild looking to be an owner. I smiled to myself, kept my filly going along the rail, then turned her around and, at the five-eighths pole, had her going full steam. The filly posted her best workout time to date, five furlongs in fifty-eight seconds and change. After handing the filly off to her groom, I walked to the rail and Ruby and I grinned at each other like idiots. Later, after I'd ridden six more horses, I took Ruby to the backside cafeteria and bought her dark, rich cups of coffee until she stopped yawning.

By the time she took me home to her place that night, I was elated. Expanded. Afire. There was lust, but something else too. We still hadn't kissed. Maybe we both knew things would quickly get out of control.

We walked into her place having just eaten lousy Italian food in Sheepshead Bay. A cat the size of a pony immediately launched itself at Ruby's legs, nearly tripping her. Evidently this was some sort of ritual Ruby was used to because she adroitly dodged the animal. I followed her into a small kitchen where I watched her take a packet of raw meat out of the fridge and mix strange-looking powdered crap into it, then set this down for the large cat and its friend, a tiny calico. As Ruby and I stood, transfixed by the sight of the cats devouring their meat, Ruby shed her coat, letting it drop to the floor. She was wearing a low-cut dark blue sweater and a pair of simple black pants that I'd been imagining ripping off her body throughout dinner. She stood one inch shorter than me, five foot four.

I studied her face, the small, well-made nose, and the lovely mouth that liked to laugh. She stared right back at me, her eyes mapping me, committing me to memory. After a few moments, I got down on all fours and unzipped her little black boots, making her lift one foot at a time as I removed the boots and the socks underneath. She didn't question this. I grinned when I saw her violent red toenails. She grinned right back, as if this were all perfectly understandable behavior. I stood up and leaned my whole body into hers, mouth against mouth, hip bones jutting into hip bones. She draped her arms at the small of my back, right above my ass. I shoved her toward the kitchen counter, startling the little cat who stopped eating and skittered out of the kitchen—though the pony-sized cat didn't move a whisker. I picked Ruby up and carried her out of the kitchen. She squirmed in my arms, adjusting her weight, like she didn't think I'd be strong enough to carry her.

"Don't squirm, girl, I gotcha," I told her.

I deposited her on the couch and she reached for me, roughly pulling me to her. Then her mouth was on mine again, her small hands searching my surfaces. And so on and so forth.

It was one of those things. Our bodies fit together perfectly.

Everything about her made sense to me, from the top of her ruffled black head to the tips of her luscious red toenails.

Two weeks into all this, I was over at her place one night when a blizzard came clamoring out of the sky, snow sliding down in sheets. We sat on Ruby's lumpy green couch. She had a CD playing, classical music by some Polish guy. The music was beautiful and sad. It made me think of all the things that had gone wrong in my life but it also brought the good to mind.

Ruby had the lights out and we were staring out at the night that was bright with snow.

"What'll happen to the track tomorrow?" she asked in a soft voice.

"Closed probably," I told her.

"So we can stay up all night?" she said, slipping her hand down my pants in that unceremonious way she had.

"Apparently," I said, putting my hands inside her fuzzy white bathrobe.

We spent the next day in bed. And the day after that. Five days went by and the snow was still coming down and we were both wrecked from sexual excess.

I FINISHED STRETCHING and sat down at the edge of the bed. Ruby's red nightgown was still hitched up, exposing her rear end. I ran my hand very lightly over her right hip and along her ass. She rolled over onto her back and opened her eyes.

"What time is it?" she asked.

"It's six. And it's still snowing. Sleep," I said.

"Are you okay?" she asked, sitting up and pulling the sheet all the way to her chin.

I wasn't entirely okay. I had a lot on my mind and most of it was unpleasant. I wanted to tell her, to come clean, but I couldn't. Not just yet.

"I'm fine," I lied, reaching over and pushing a strand of hair off her forehead, "everything is fine."

She frowned slightly and studied my face. I worked at keeping it relaxed, empty. I think she knew something was bothering me but she was tired and soon sleepiness won out. She lay back down. I pulled the blanket over her and watched as she slipped back into a sound sleep.

I went into the kitchen to get an apple from the fridge. I stared out at the snow while I munched the apple. The fire in my body was getting worse. I didn't know if I should go outside and run a couple miles or do three hundred sit-ups or what. I needed to get on a horse. I needed to feel an animal's spirit beating inside my own. But the weather wasn't cooperating. So I just stood there, on fire.

RUBY MURPHY

3.

Sherpa Guide

I'm starving but I'm terrified of taking out my box of Honey Nut Cheerios since the sight of it might give Attila a carbohydrate craving and cause him to eat several bowls of the stuff, then feel obliged to purge, take laxatives, and run ten extra miles to prevent the Cheerios from adding ounces to his riding weight. All of this would make me feel horribly guilty, and I have enough guilt in my life as it is. I feel guilty sleeping with Attila when Ed's still in my blood. I feel guilty because my father's dead and I'm alive. I feel guilty over Ratso, a cat I had back when I used to drink too much. I left the cat with a roommate when I got carted off to rehab and the roommate abandoned him while I was two hundred miles away and detoxing. It was the only time I had truly homicidal feelings for another human. Then it all just turned to guilt. And I don't need any more guilt. Right now or ever. I decide against the Cheerios and opt for making poached eggs. I know Attila will eat one.

I get the egg carton out of the fridge and, even though I fed the cats not ten minutes ago, Stinky thinks he's starving. He meows, then actually rises up on his hind legs and tries to swat my hand. This is quite a feat considering that he weighs close to twenty pounds and has an enormous belly. He looks like an acrobatic Buddha. I try to distract him from his alleged hunger by giving him a catnip mouse but he's not interested. He goes to lie under the kitchen chair and shoots me withering glances.

I boil water, then gently drop eggs into it. One of the eggs flops and the yolk breaks. I can't say that I have strong culinary skills. I grew up in a house full of animals, and my sister, Chloe, and I ran wild with the dog pack while our parents worked. As a result, Chloe and I are great at taking care of animals, but not so good at things like cooking or cleaning.

"You're cooking?"

I turn around and find Attila, freshly showered with a towel wrapped around his waist. His arms and torso are so stunningly fit that I nearly lose control of the last egg I'm attempting to drop into the water.

"I'm poaching some eggs," I say, turning back around and taking care not to let the egg break.

"You got a poacher?" he asks, coming to stand at my side.

"What's that?"

"You know, a gizmo you put the eggs in so they poach elegantly."

"No, I guess I don't," I say, contemplating the notion of poaching eggs elegantly.

Attila smiles and apparently finds it appealing that I don't have a poacher. He reaches for me and I drape my arms around his waist, savoring his narrowness. Ed is thin but nearly a foot taller than Attila. He doesn't feel narrow. In fact, I don't remember what he feels like and this probably isn't the moment to try remembering.

"The eggs will burn," I say, pulling back from Attila.

"I don't think poached eggs can burn, but okay," he says, relinquishing his grip on me.

I get plates from the cupboard and start scooping eggs out, managing to break another one in the process. Yolk oozes onto the cheerful floral motif of the plate which, I believe, was a hand-me-down from my best friend, Jane, who is perpetually upset by my lack of kitchen accoutrements. Jane is hardly the queen of kitchenwares, but she firmly believes in a certain amount of household civility that I just don't possess. Whenever there's a gift-giving occasion, Jane gives me kitchen items as opposed to the frivolous baubles I'm partial to.

"You're a veritable household goddess." Attila points at the oozing yolk then kisses my neck. "I'm going to get dressed," he adds.

I turn to watch him walk away. He has no ass to speak of, but that's fine.

I put the plates on the kitchen table, set cutlery and paper towel napkins out. Stinky is still scowling at me from under the chair so I get down on all fours and scratch him under the chin. After about ten seconds he gives a reluctant purr. I'm not sure what's distressing him more: not being fed again or Attila. Stinky doesn't approve of my boyfriends. Though he vaguely tolerated Ed, he has no use for Attila and refuses to come into the bedroom to sleep when Attila is around. I soothe the beast as best I can, then stand up to get the orange juice. Before opening the fridge, I glance at the photo of Sherpa Guide I have hanging there. Sherpa Guide is my hero. A diminutive bay racehorse who has a heart the size of an ocean. He's just a New York–bred gelding of humble lineage—and I adored him long before Derby and Preakness winner Funny Cide suddenly made being a New York–bred gelding a glamorous thing. Sherpa doesn't always win but he always runs his heart out. His owner thinks very highly of him and often puts him in tough races. A few months ago, Sherpa ran in a big stakes race and went off at odds of 60–1. Though he had a bad trip and got boxed in on the rail, he still managed to run fourth, earn his owner twelve thousand dollars, and beat the pants off several regally bred colts. I couldn't have been prouder. Ed used to encourage me to get in touch with Sherpa's owner and trainer and meet the horse but I never did. I'm afraid to. What if he doesn't like me? I'd have to kill myself. Instead, I keep a photo of him taped to my fridge and look at it whenever I need succor.

"Staring at Sherpa again?" Attila has come back into the kitchen, fully clothed now.

"Every day," I say.

"I don't know why you don't just go meet the damned horse and get it over with."

"I will," I say. "Someday."

Attila rolls his eyes at me. While Ed seems to understand my caginess about the whole thing, Attila just thinks I'm silly. I brood slightly over this as we sit down to eat our poached eggs. Three for me, one for Attila.

Outside the kitchen window, the snow is redoubling its efforts. Enormous flakes are sticking to the window, staring in at us before melting and sliding away like little ghosts. Attila takes one bite of egg, then looks out at the snow and frowns. I know he wants to get back to the track and ride. He likes me, he lusts for me, but, for him, nothing holds a candle to steering a thousand pounds of race-horse.

4.

Cool My Head Off

That morning, my kid had come into the kitchen and, before sitting down to his bowl of cereal, looked up at me and said, "Dad, I need a horse."

The kid's seven years old. And he hadn't asked for a pony, mind you. A horse. And now, a few hours after this request of his, I was standing on the snow-covered beach at Coney Island, staring at the lady who'd put horse notions into my kid's head. Ruby Murphy. Wearing that stupid red coat of hers.

I'd brought Ruby by to meet my family a few weeks earlier. The girl had been a little down, nursing wounds from a guy she was crazy about who had up and moved to Florida. She doesn't have any family in New York and I felt like she might benefit from being around mine. The day before coming by my place, Ruby had been out at Aqueduct, hitting exactas with her friend Liz, a good-looking but tough-as-tacks little blonde who probably packs a Magnum in her panties. So the night Ruby came by my place to meet my kid, and try to keep a pleasant look on her face as she ate my wife's cooking, she talked about horses horses horses. She works at the Coney Island Museum, but for a month last spring she worked out at Belmont walking off racehorses and she's been horse crazy ever since— even more so lately since taking up with a rider. That night at dinner, Ruby had talked on and on about racing and riding—and this horse and that horse and I'd seen a craving come into my son

Jake's eyes. But he hadn't said anything about it until this morning at breakfast, saying, "Dad, I need a horse."

"Yard isn't big enough for a horse, kid," I told him and he got thoughtful the way he does and said nothing more about it. I felt bad, I hadn't meant to silence him so quickly, but I didn't know where to go with such a request.

Now here was the girl responsible for my son's sudden horse fever. Ruby Murphy. Standing on the beach, knee-deep in the snow, staring ahead.

She hadn't noticed me yet so I called out to her: "Hey, Shorty. "

She turned toward me and smiled her crooked smile.

"What are you doing, Sal?" she asked.

"What's it look like I'm doing, lady?" I was naked except for my bathing suit and my boots.

"You coming?" I asked her, knowing full well her cutoff point is November. She loves the water and will go in when it's pretty damned cold. Which is how we'd first met. Both of us taking a dip in the Coney waters late October two years back. The girl doesn't mind cold water. Just not *this* cold.

"No way," she shook her head. She'd come to stand closer to me now. I saw that her long black hair was knotted and that she had bags under her gray eyes. She looked like she'd tumbled out of bed, put her coat on and come to the beach.

"I'm just waiting for Attila, he's running," she said, motioning toward Brighton.

"The jockey?"

"Yeah." She looked sheepish and I could see she had in fact just tumbled out of bed.

"I can't believe you're going out with that guy," I said.

Ruby and I had been talking about Attila Johnson one day just a few weeks before she'd met him. I like to play the horses now and then and Ruby and me were talking about some races. I'd noticed, as she had, that there was a new apprentice with an unlikely name. Especially considering he was a little blond-headed white guy.

Seemed to me *Attila Johnson* sounded like the name of a massive black guy, not a shrimpy little blond guy.

"I gotta go in the water, I'm freezing my dick off," I announced to Ruby—then immediately felt funny for saying it because Ruby is, after all, a lady. I've heard some foul phrases come out of her mouth and I've always felt at home with her the way you usually only do with a guy, but all the same, she's a lady.

She held my bag of clothes for me as I jogged ahead to the water. I stopped and took my boots off right at the edge, just where the snow ended and the water started. I ran in until I was waist high, dove under for a few screaming seconds, then raced back out.

"Good?" Ruby asked, handing me my bag.

"Very." I pulled my towel out and wrapped it around my waist. Took my bathing suit off like that, right there on the beach, with just the towel for cover. I started packing on layers of clothing. Ruby just kept gazing out toward Brighton.

"Coffee?" I asked her once I had my clothes on.

"Nah, gotta wait for Attila to get back," she said and, right on cue, a small blond man came running toward us. With him was a black guy, the two running in tandem, Attila's head barely chest high to the black guy.

Attila stopped in front of Ruby. His eyes were huge and he looked insane. He was also soaking wet. The black guy stopped a few feet back, looking a little confused. I realized the black guy was the guy Ruby calls Rite of Spring Man, a sort of lunatic job that walks around Coney with a boom box on his shoulder blaring classical music.

"Someone just tried to kill me," the jockey announced.

"What?" Ruby frowned, like she was hearing a bad joke.

"This guy saved my life," Attila indicated Rite of Spring Man. "Somebody was trying to drown me."

Attila's teeth were chattering and his lips were turning almost as blue as his eyes.

This was all a little too much for me. I'd come out here to have a quick dip, hadn't even planned on stopping by to see if Ruby was around. Was just going to cool my head off a little then go home and see what the wife had concocted for dinner because in eight years of being married to the girl, I still sometimes go home full of hope. About dinner being palatable, about her liking me a little.

Ruby had covered the jockey in her fake fur coat and was saying something to Rite of Spring Man, who didn't look particularly shaken about any of this and was just standing there looking mildly baffled under the steel-gray sky. I thought about just quietly walking away and heading back to my truck parked there in the lot near the Cyclone roller coaster. But at one point Ruby put her hand on my arm, letting me know she wanted me around. So I stayed.

I walked with Ruby and the jockey back to Ruby's place, witnessing an argument between the two about calling the cops. Ruby couldn't understand why Attila wouldn't let her call them. Attila, whose sketchy past was mapped out on his face, was getting tenser by the minute and the veins on his neck were turning into ropes.

"I just don't want to," he was telling Ruby. "This is something *I've* got to take care of." The jockey was talking with his hands, more like an Italian than whatever it was he was.

"Sal?" Ruby looked to me for support.

We were in her place by now, had come up the stairs, passed by her neighbor Ramirez's open front door and seen him, as usual, sitting at his kitchen table, staring down into a cup of coffee. Ramirez had nodded at us as we'd gone ahead into Ruby's.

"I don't know what to tell you," I said to the girl, "I take it your man's got his reasons for not wanting the cops involved."

"Well, what are they?" Ruby asked Attila. She looked angry. I noticed she was pretty when she was angry. It had never been like that with Ruby and me, she'd never radiated even the slightest bit of sexual something around me and, in return, I'd kept my engine tuned down. I'm faithful to my wife most of the time anyway, straying occasionally when she goes on a particularly long jag of not wanting me inside her—she's an adult student at Hunter College taking women's studies classes and sometimes she gets notions about not wanting a man inside her—but it's not like I've ever strayed emotionally. And Ruby's not my type anyway. I like my wife's flaming hair, her big, well-made chest and her ass that sticks out like a shelf a man can rest his troubles on. Ruby is too small and sort of reminds me of a ferret.

"We'll talk about it later," Attila told Ruby as he shot a dirty look in my direction.

"I want Sal here. He can help," Ruby said, though why she thought this I couldn't tell you. I guess she had the idea that between my being a Teamster and my Italian family going back a lot of generations in Brooklyn, maybe I knew how certain things worked. Which wasn't entirely off the mark. Though what with my back problems and being out on Disability for a while and my endless struggle trying not to take the Percocets the doctors had prescribed, it's not like I was in the prime of my powers.

"So what's up?" I asked Attila now. "Somebody got a hit out on you?" I was joking, but the way the guy's bright blue eyes went dark, I saw I'd hit the jackpot. Oh boy.

"Attila?" Ruby's head snapped toward him.

"I dunno," Attila shrugged. "I didn't think it was a real concern."

"Didn't think *what* was a real concern?" Ruby's face was knotting up.

"Well, there was a threat," Attila said, giving me another dirty look. He wanted me gone but he wasn't gonna come out and insist.

"I didn't think drowning was an approved method of offing someone though," the jockey added, trying to be funny.

Neither Ruby nor I laughed.

"Do you want to tell me what's going on now?" Ruby said. She had a small red splotch in the middle of each pale cheek—her anger, showing itself like that in two tiny patches. My wife, she gets pissed off, her whole body turns bright red to match her hair.

"There's a lot going on," Attila said, hunching forward on Ruby's green couch. "I've done some questionable things."

"Like what?" she asked sharply.

"It's a long story, Ruby." Attila sounded very sad. "You know I haven't had an easy time trying to make it as a rider. Some folks offered me a nice chunk of change to do some things I didn't really want to do." He fell silent, resting his palms on his small knees.

"You have to tell me what you're talking about," Ruby said, in a voice that made the jockey's sad eyes focus on her. We both knew she meant business.

"Nothing that bad," he sighed. "I held some horses back in a few races. Stuff like that," he said. "Now I don't wanna do it anymore. But it's hard to get out once you've gone that route."

"Oh," she said, frowning. "So what's wrong with calling the cops?"

"I call the cops, they call the Feds and the New York Racing Association, etcetera . . . I get my license revoked. I never ride again. I go back to a life of shit."

I didn't know what the guy had done before becoming an aging apprentice jockey and I had a feeling Ruby didn't know many details either.

Still, for some reason, this little guy with his bright blue eyes was growing on me. Or maybe I just wanted to help out. I offered my services.

"You want, I could watch your back," I said.

"Huh?" Both Attila and Ruby looked at me, not knowing what I was talking about.

"I could look out for you. I'm out on Disability right now. My wife's never home and my kid's off at school most of the day. I don't watch my ass I'm gonna lie on the couch all day popping Percocet. I could come with you to the track. Keep an eye on you."

"It's not just at the track. They seem to know my every move," the jockey said.

"Well," I said, "I can't be with you twenty-four/seven but just about. My wife hates me this week and my kid ain't home much. Maybe if I made myself scarce for a couple of weeks I'd get appreciated more."

Attila looked at me and blinked. So did Ruby.

It took a little more persuading and, to tell the truth, I don't know what I was thinking, why I was so gung ho on the whole idea, but after a while, Attila agreed to it.

Ruby went in the kitchen to tend to those cats of hers and Attila and I stayed in the living room, talking about it all, him telling me the way his schedule worked each day. He seemed a little suspicious of my motivation for doing this. I would have been too. But it was just something I wanted to do. I couldn't have explained it at gunpoint.

Eventually, I got up to go. I told them I was stopping next door at Ramirez's place to ask him to keep his eyes open. The guy's a piece of work. Never quite got over his tour in 'Nam. Which is to say, all these years later, he's one alert and paranoid motherfucker. Couldn't hurt to have him keeping an ear out.

After me and Ramirez shot the shit awhile, him telling me he was thinking of asking his girl Elsie to marry him, me telling him, What the hell, why not? And then asking him to keep an eye on Ruby, I went home.

Karen, my wife, was in the kitchen, doing terrible things to our dinner. Jake was in his room, doing his homework. The kid is studious. Makes me proud. I didn't interrupt him, just cracked his door a little, and saw him hunched over his desk, already looking like some professor at age seven. I smiled to myself. Then went to watch what my wife was doing to that poor meat loaf.

5.

After Near Death

I was sinking into the middle of Ruby's exhausted couch, turning my entire life over in my mind. Ruby was at her piano, sitting a little hunched, her small, not-so-graceful hands pulling beauty from the yellowed ivory keys. She was playing Bach. Her favorite. Sometimes I couldn't distinguish Beethoven from Haydn from Schubert. But when she played Bach, I knew it.

The female cat came over and bumped her head against my foot repeatedly, as if trying to shake an idea loose inside her tiny head. My own head was full of images. The cold beautiful freedom of running on the empty beach. Nothing ahead but snow, sand, and horizon. Then I'd sensed rather than seen someone behind me. Before I'd had time to think, I was being wrestled to the ground, face-first. I struggled and yelled as I was dragged into the icy water. I took in huge involuntary gulps of cold salty sea and felt my head freezing as someone held it under the surface. I was kicking but I could feel myself weakening. I was on the verge of blacking out when suddenly my attacker let go. I pulled my head out of the water and saw a seagull dive-bombing a spot just in front of me. For a moment I thought the gull had somehow saved me. Then I saw a man standing on the beach, looking at me. I wasn't sure if he was the one who had just been trying to drown me. I got to my feet and stood there, knee-deep in the water, looking at the tall black man.

"You okay, mister?" the man asked me.

"Did you just try to drown me?" I asked, feeling ridiculous, struggling out of the surf.

"Nope. That guy did," he said, motioning to the right. I looked and saw a figure running away. "I was just walking along here and saw something funny going on," he continued. "I yelled out, asking what the guy was doing and then he stopped doing it and ran off."

"What'd he look like?" I asked.

"Big white guy," the man shrugged.

It didn't mean anything to me. I knew a lot of big white guys that might have a reason to hurt me.

"What color hair?" I asked the man who'd just saved my life.

"Had a hat on," the man said. "You gonna be all right?"

I could tell the guy wanted to get going. He had done his good deed. I was shaken though and it showed. He offered to accompany me a ways and I didn't say no. We jogged together back toward Coney where Ruby was waiting for me.

I hated to see the pinched look on her face and the way her gray eyes turned dark. She was standing with a big guy who looked Italian. I was wary for a minute, but he had a nice face. Right away they both seemed to know I was holding out on her, and I knew the time had come to tell her. Some of it at least. I was already regretting how my problems could cloud up what had, so far, been simple.

Ruby wrapped me in her red coat and wanted to call the cops. As for my savior, after nodding at Ruby, he just took off. I never even found out his name.

A number of hours had passed now and all the fire I'd felt in my body earlier was long gone. In its place was a fear that I could taste at the back of my mouth, like someone had put a gun barrel in my throat and left it there to rust.

RUBY STOPPED PLAYING piano and turned to me. "Are you hungry?" she asked, frowning a little, like thoughts of my possible hunger had suddenly invaded and disturbed her.

"Always," I said.

"Let me rephrase that. Will you eat something?"

"Something, yeah. What do we have?" I asked, feeling awkward the moment the words left my lips, thinking that the *we* and its implication of lasting coupledom was grossly forward of me.

Ruby either didn't notice or wasn't jarred by it. She got up from the piano bench. "Let's see," she said, heading into the kitchen.

I wrestled myself from the couch and followed her.

"I'm a miserable failure at food procurement," she said, after opening and closing the kitchen cabinets a few times. She looked dejected and vastly appealing. She was wearing dark blue jeans and a long-sleeved red T-shirt that clung to her chest.

I ached for her even though she was standing right there.

"You shouldn't have to be bothered with mortal tasks such as those," I said, reaching for her hand and kissing the sweet spot on the inside of her wrist. She laughed.

"Protein shake?" she said.

"That's fine, yes," I said.

She pulled out the container of protein powder and put powder, juice, and bananas into an ancient-looking blender.

"You know what I think," Ruby said as she poured us each a mug of protein drink.

"About what?" I asked, sipping at the beverage and trying not to make a face. Her culinary ineptitude was such that even the protein drink tasted funny.

"About what happened on the beach."

"I don't want to go into it right now."

"Don't shut me out," she said, her face pinching slightly so that her mouth seemed smaller.

"I'm not, Ruby, it's just that I have some things to work out and until I've done that, I can't discuss any of this with you."

"That bad?" She drew her eyebrows together.

"No, not that bad." I lied. Things *were* that bad. But I wanted to keep her away from the kind of fear I was living with.

I steered the subject elsewhere, asking her when she was going to take me to hear some of her beloved classical music. I knew she occasionally went to concerts at Lincoln Center or Carnegie Hall. She'd even taken her friend Big Sal to hear some Bach in a church. So far though, she hadn't offered to take me to any cultural events.

"I didn't know you were that interested," she said, looking surprised.

I wasn't really but I was trying to share her passions.

Ruby started foraging through some mail on the kitchen table, producing a schedule for Lincoln Center. She read off details of several different concerts, explaining the merits of each.

"You decide," I said softly.

"Okay," she shrugged. She finished off her protein drink.

"I've got to get back to practicing now. Do you mind?"

"I couldn't mind less," I told her.

Her expression changed and she grew somehow remote. She had moved back to the world of music. She went to her bench, loosened her shoulders, and started playing.

I choked down the rest of my protein drink then returned to the malevolent couch. Ruby was already conjuring beauty from the piano and I felt a stab of envy. She was right there with her piano and I was miles from a horse. In spite of the obvious danger of even leaving the house, I needed to ride. I didn't know if they'd have cleared the track enough by tomorrow for actual workouts but I thought at least I'd put in an appearance on the backstretch, go see some of the trainers I ride for, offer to hand walk a few horses. It would calm me. All of which meant that, if I was to keep my bargain with Ruby and her friend, I had to call Sal and ask him to come with me to the track at the crack of dawn tomorrow.

Just as I started thinking about retrieving my cell phone and making the call, the phone beat me to the punch and rang, the sound of it a terrible shriek against the music-filled room. I jumped up and raced over to get it out of my jacket. I looked at the incoming number, got a slightly sick feeling at what I saw, and turned the phone off. I glanced at Ruby. She just kept playing her music, not seeming to miss a note, lost in her own world.

I went back to the couch, but now I was rattled. Not only was someone trying to drown the life out of me, but my insane wife, Ava, was calling. This the third call in the last twelve hours or so. Not that I'd answered any of them. Or even listened to the voice mails she'd left. But I'd seen her number in the call log. I didn't know exactly what her calling me meant other than she'd sniffed out the fact that I'd met a woman I liked. Ava would have smelled that from five thousand miles away.

I'd told Ruby about Ava. She hadn't seemed too shaken about my technically still being married, but she did question me.

"You love her?" she'd asked.

"Of course, love, sure, but not *in* love. She's insane."

Ruby squinted at this.

"A lot of guys I know, the pull of an insane woman is something they never get away from."

She was wise. And partially correct. I couldn't imagine ever completely cutting off from Ava, particularly given that we have a ten-year-old daughter. But I didn't want to be married to Ava anymore. I'd tried very hard for close to fifteen years. That had to be enough.

We'd met when we were young. Still both living in North Carolina. She was blond, taller than me and, a few months after I started seeing her, substantially heavier than me. The girl was bulimic. She went from one-fifteen to one-forty-five in the blink of an eye. I didn't mind that much. There was something sensual about having a large woman covering me with her body. She had a lot of male in her too. Would lie against my back and sort of hump me. As a kid, I'd experimented with my same sex maybe a little more than was common. I'd even sort of "seen" a man a few months before I'd met Ava. But this was Grinderville, North Carolina. Not a completely asshole-of-the-universe bigoted kind of place but close. The man's name was Jed and we'd had to be very discreet. He was forty-three and married. When I met Ava, I quickly lost interest in Jed and in the half-dozen or so women in Grinderville who chronically put themselves in my path.

When I met Ava, the whole infernal world stood still.

She was working at a geriatric home where I would go to visit my grandma. I was in Grandma Stevens's room one day, huddled with her over the tip sheets for the nearest bush track, because well into her nineties she was still playing the horses, which I didn't understand since at that point I'd never set foot on a track.

Grandma sent me out to look for a nurse. She couldn't find her glasses and was convinced her roommate, Nellie Nelson, had stolen them. Nellie Nelson was, according to Grandma, a notorious kleptomaniac who had been the town nymphomaniac a few decades earlier but now, in her dotage, had switched over to kleptomania.

As I headed for the nurses' station, I bumped into a girl carrying a box of paints that went spilling all over the floor, making a very colorful mess. I apologized profusely and the girl laughed, seemingly pleased that I'd made her spill bright blue paint all over the linoleum floor.

"I'm so sorry, how can I help you?" I'd asked, and she'd looked at me curiously, tilted her head, and then very earnestly said, "Probably in all kinds of ways."

Had I known precisely how many ways she had in mind, I might have simply helped her muck that blue paint off the linoleum and called it a day. Instead, I got her phone number. Right there at the geriatric home where she worked as a nurse's aide.

On the night of our first date, I went to pick Ava up at her basement apartment on Hilda Street. She opened the door, grabbed my arm, and pulled me inside. She wasn't wearing a stitch of clothing. This wasn't commonplace comportment for first dates in Grinderville, where there hadn't been a town nympho since Nellie's notoriety had gone up in a haze of age and kleptomania. Ava stood, absorbing her effect on me for a while before turning to her stereo system and putting on an album of strange folk music. She started dancing around, with her narrow but lovely ass moving beautifully. She had a small patch of light brown pubic hair and her breasts were good, not too big but very clearly there. She started touching herself.

"You stand there and watch," she ordered as she shimmied.

I did as I was told. For a little while. Then I moved close to her, put my hand on her cheek, and stared at her. This seemed to disorient her. I kissed her. Head to toe. She started trembling. Her whole body gasping and coiling. I made certain she was very worked up and then I walked out.

That got her nose open.

Eight months later I married her.

There was a little chapel on Crookshank Road.

My mother was dead and my father was a drunk, but Ava's parents came. They were stiff people who didn't seem to take to me. But that didn't matter.

That night, for our honeymoon, we drove to the ocean and stayed in a rundown seaside motel. Ava was on top of me and underneath me and sometimes behind me. Her body was thin. When we stopped making love long enough to go outside, we walked to the water. One of her now-familiar crazy looks overtook her face and she said, "I always wanted to be a welder."

"A what?" I said.

"A welder. Especially underwater. In the sea. A deep-sea welder."

"Oh yeah?"

"Yeah," she said, gripping my hand and pulling me into the ocean.

A few months after this blessed event, Ava had grown fat. It wasn't what I had expected, but I didn't mind. She kept me interested with her physical and mental transformations. When she was pregnant with Grace she became even more eccentric than usual. She read constantly. Sometimes, in the middle of the night, she would get up and go outside wearing her long white nightgown. She would pace in the backyard as she chain-smoked. Occasionally, her absence in the bed would wake me and I'd look out the window to see a pregnant, smoking apparition.

A few months after Grace was born, Ava got depressed and

stopped eating. For the most part, I was left to take care of our daughter. Ava didn't want Grace sucking on her breasts after the first weeks. I got Grace formula and fed her and changed her.

Ava went on lithium and got fat again. Grace turned one. Then two and three and so forth.

Through all of Grace's and Ava's transformations, I essentially remained the same. Physically at least. Every six months I changed jobs, from carpenter to working in a factory to landscaping to working on a dairy farm. Which is where I got on the first horse I'd been on since I was a little kid. The farmer had a couple of draft horses which his teenaged daughter rode. One day, the daughter asked if I wanted to get up on one of the horses. The moment she asked, I realized that I did want to. She led the horse over to a bale of hay. I stood on this and hoisted myself up onto the big gelding's back. At first, the girl led the horse but, after a while, seeing that I was comfortable up there, she told me how to hold the reins and she let go of the horse's head. The big animal walked ahead slowly. I could feel every nuance of him shooting through my own body and, most remarkably, I felt like I was inside his head, like I could feel his thoughts. It was the most amazing sensation I'd ever had in my life. I stayed up there for quite a long time until finally the girl had to beg me to get down. I guess I knew right then that eventually I'd make a living with horses. I was twenty-four. I knew that it was unheard of to decide on a life of riding at such a late age, but I didn't care. I had something. An unusual level of communication with horses. An ability to feel them.

It took me years to become an apprentice rider. I started off at the unregulated bush tracks, riding quarter horses and Arabians and anything anyone would let me ride. I got laughed at a lot. I was old. I was on the tall side. But I won races, even won them honestly in an environment where every other rider was carrying an illegal buzzer or was up to something that would never fly at a regulated track. I rode mostly on weekends and had various day jobs to pay the rent. But the only time I was truly alive was on a horse's back. I won a lot of shitty little races and eventually I met Henry Meyer, a New York trainer who said he'd help me get an apprentice license in New York. This was the toughest circuit to break into but they said if you cut your teeth in New York you were guaranteed a career.

Soon Ava and Grace and I moved up to Queens. At first Ava hated it. Then her medication was changed and she loved it. Sometimes she'd go off her meds and disappear for days at a time. Henry Meyer's wife, an Englishwoman named Violet, would help me by looking after Grace. Three months ago, it got to the point where I'd really had enough. Ava was sleeping around. She was drinking and taking strange drugs. Most of all, she was breaking my heart again and again.

I still loved her. But I couldn't abide her madness anymore.

And now, I'd met someone else. Someone I could sit with in silence. Someone I could make love to repeatedly. Someone who seemed to understand.

I didn't know what to do with any of these thoughts so I just sat there, listening to Ruby play, wondering what Ava wanted from me. Knowing it was probably just her radar picking up on the fact that I was interested in someone else.

That someone else finally stopped playing piano, turned around on her bench, and looked at me.

"Hey you," she said, as if we were greeting each other after a long absence.

I got up and walked over to her. I pulled her to her feet, held her, and found myself hoping I wouldn't be killed anytime soon.

6.

Innocent Beasts

When my dog Dingo died, I started feeling very lowly. I'd had Dingo for ten years, since my mother's death when I was fourteen. I loved that dog a lot and his absence made everything seem raw and worthless.

I wasn't working much, just a few odd jobs doing carpentry but that was about it. One day, I had some work out at Old Mrs. Simmons's house on Little Egypt Road. Mrs. Simmons was a tiny brittle woman whose mind had gone soft. She often forgot to zip her slacks or button all the buttons of her blouse and her shoes seldom matched. Mrs. Simmons had dozens of chickens and apparently they were a particularly violent breed of poultry because, from what she told me, they were endlessly tearing down their coops. She'd hired me to do some patch-up work and before I was an hour into the job I had chicken shit all over me. By the end of the day, I really stank and I never wanted to see another chicken in my life. I turned down the lemonade Old Mrs. Simmons offered, pocketed the forty bucks she owed me and got in my car.

I was coming around the bend on Little Egypt Road when I saw it. A beautiful fenced-in field and, off in the distance, a dozen or so horses. It's not like I'd never seen a field of horses before. Oklahoma was full of horses. But something about this field seemed magical. I wanted to go in.

I pulled the car up to the gate, got out, opened the gate, and drove on in. The horses were quite a ways off. I drove slowly so as not to alarm them. I reached a grouping of huge gnarled trees and turned the engine off. I just sat there, staring ahead at that bunch of horses. After a few minutes, one of the horses, a big white one, walked over toward my car. I was slightly worried, like maybe I was offending the big beast. I stared out my window. The horse came closer and closer until finally he had his face pressed against the car window. I didn't know how well he could see me, what with his eyes on the side of his head like that, but I could sure see him. As I sat admiring the horse's big white face, he started leaning his massive chest into the car. The horse had to be a thousand pounds and I could feel the car rocking.

I was worried the horse was gonna get mad and really ram the car so I slowly rolled my car window down and tentatively patted his long white nose. This calmed him down some.

Eventually, I opened the car door and the horse backed away, letting me out. I patted him all over his body. He didn't seem to mind. I felt more peaceful than I had since losing Dingo.

PRETTY SOON I found myself going out to the horse pasture every day to spend time with that little gang of half-wild horses. I was working less and less. I wasn't even eating or sleeping much. Just kept going to that pasture. One day, I was out there, sitting by the gnarled trees and watching the horses when this guy came up to me out of nowhere. He was an older guy wearing coveralls and his skin and hair were so yellow he seemed to match the yellow pasture he'd sprung from like some magical creature.

"You got business here, son?" he asked me, walking slowly around me.

"No, sir, just enjoying the horses," I said.

The yellow-looking man grunted.

"I could use you," he said then, after eyeing me from head to toe.

"Oh?" I wasn't sure I liked the sound of this.

"I seen you out here, talking to my horses day in day out. I got twenty more of 'em back about three miles down Little Egypt

Road. You come with me I'll show you what's what with the equine arts."

I didn't know what to think. It was the strangest offer I'd ever gotten.

"Oh yeah?" I said.

"Come on, son, get up off your moneymaker," the old guy said. He was smiling at me, showing pointy teeth. His yellow eyes seemed to twinkle, which was odd because I'd never thought of yellow as the kind of color that could twinkle.

"That's nice of you, sir," I said.

"Don't thank me yet," the guy said, bursting into a laugh that sounded like chain saws on dead trees.

"That there's yours, right?" He motioned at the Chevy.

"Yes, sir."

"You been driving into my pasture for three months. I seen ya," he said, narrowing his eyes. "Let's go. You drive us back over to my barn."

It was a little worrisome to think the guy had been watching me all this time and I wondered how he'd gotten over here in the first place if his barn was miles away. Plus, I'd never heard of any guy having twenty horses down on Little Egypt Road, so it all seemed a little strange. It's not like I had anything better to do than see what would happen though.

We got into the Chevy and he was quiet now as I pulled out of the pasture and back onto the road, going where he told me.

A few miles down, we came to a dirt road with a gate and the guy got out and opened it. I drove in, waited for him to get back in, and then drove ahead.

The road was pitted and muddy and badly in need of work, but flanking it were beautiful pastures full of horses. Eventually, we came to a big red barn. The guy looked proud as we got out of the Chevy. He made a sweeping arm gesture, showing me what was his. The sky was a tender blue as it swept down over the strange man's land.

We went into the barn that reeked of horse sweat and manure

and creosote. It smelled like heaven. There were horses standing in big wooden stalls. Some had their long noses poking out, others had their butts to us and didn't look up from their hay.

"So," the yellow guy said, pausing in front of one of the stalls, "I had a fella quit just yesterday and I need you."

"Yeah?" I said, staring past him at the red horse in the stall nearest us.

"You start off mucking out stalls and we'll take it from there. You can call me Sandman, by the way."

"I'm Ben."

"You got a last name, Ben?"

"Nester," I said.

"I got a horse named Nester," Sandman said.

"Oh yeah?"

"Yup," the guy said.

And that was it. He put me to work. Showed me how to muck the stalls out. Some of them, I had to change all the bedding, take out all the straw, and then put down a layer of lime and fresh straw. It took forever. I did about fifteen stalls and my back started aching but I didn't mind. It was good pain.

Sandman had gone off somewhere and it was just me and the horses and the barn with all those good smells in it. It was a little eerie how there was no one around. I had no idea what Sandman did with all these horses or how many other people he had working for him but I didn't see anyone else all day long.

Once it started getting dark out, Sandman came back and told me I was going to help him bring some of the horses in from outside. I'd never actually had much to do with horses other than hanging out and talking to the ones in the pasture but I wanted to learn. Out in the field, Sandman showed me how to stand at the horse's left side, get the horse to put his nose through the halter, and then slip it over the ears, fasten it, and lead the horse forward. I had trouble with one little horse, a baby, only a year old. I'd get close to him and he'd prick his ears forward and his eyes would get bright but then, the moment I tried slipping the halter on, he'd bolt and throw a little buck and make a squealing sound. Eventually, Sand-man helped me by getting on the other side of the yearling so we had him boxed in, and I finally got a halter on him. As I led him though, he kept trying to take a nip at my arm.

"That one's gonna race," Sandman told me once we were back inside the barn.

"Oh yeah?" I'd put the little guy in his stall and he'd immediately relieved himself all over his clean straw.

"Yup. I got a couple trainers coming by tomorrow have a look at him. Kind of spirit he's got, I bet he makes it. Might even make it to one of the big tracks, win some real money. His mama won a stakes race at Aqueduct in New York once," Sandman said, looking thoughtful.

I didn't really know what he was talking about that day but I learned pretty quickly.

Sandman had two other people working for him. A guy named James who was around forty and hunched over and kind of yellow, too, and a girl, Kathy Kitterman, a small but muscular girl, who was in her early twenties like me. Between those two and Sandman, I had a whole new world of knowledge within a week. I knew all about the different kinds of brushes and leg bandages and liniments. I knew how to muck out a stall and clean out feed tubs and I was beginning to understand about equine nutrition. I started getting a good feeling. I could sense that my mother was looking down from the ether and approving of what I was doing. I thought of my mother a lot on the day when one of Sandman's mares got sold and put on a van headed to Versailles, Kentucky. My mother had been born in Versailles. I'd never been there and I felt like I should go because I know, in her last days, she was missing it badly and I was part of why she never made it back. My mother had been a quiet girl till she hit seventeen and went a little wild. She got pregnant by a guy who took off. Her parents kicked her out and she hitchhiked around for a while and ended up in Oklahoma. Her older brother, Edgar, eventually came and lived with her and helped her out, putting food on the table when she got so pregnant she couldn't waitress anymore. Then she had me. When I was fourteen, she got cancer and started wasting away. As she lay dying, she kept insisting that I had to make sure to get to Versailles one day. I told her I'd do my best. In turn, she hung on as long as she could. The pain from the cancer made her eyes huge and black. When she died, I thought I would die too. I felt so lost. After a few days though, I toughened up. I didn't let anything get inside me. I just moved forward. Until now. With these horses, I finally felt like I'd found something and I was pretty sure my mother would be pleased for me.

ABOUT TEN DAYS into working for Sandman, Kathy got sick and couldn't come in. Sandman said it was time I got on a horse, he needed a bunch ridden and James couldn't do it all and Sandman didn't ride anymore, his bones were too brittle.

They started me off on Bethany, an old chestnut quarter horse mare that Sandman had bought cheap somewhere and hoped to sell as a starter horse to someone just learning to ride. Bethany was big and gentle and lazy and didn't care at all that I didn't know what I was doing up there. No matter what kind of signals I attempted to give her, all she did was walk around slowly, with her head down low. Once in a while, she'd stop and graze a little before eventually deigning to move forward again. I talked to her some while I was up there and she flicked her ears around a little, listening to the sound of my voice, deciding what she thought of me. I guess the verdict was good. She took care of me and made me feel safe. Within a few weeks, I was riding a lot. I fell off every other day and got knocked unconscious once but I didn't mind. When I wasn't riding I was busy mucking out stalls as well as feeding and grooming. I started feeling at ease. A lot of things that had bothered me for years started slipping away. All I cared about were those horses. I thought less and less about my mother. For a long time, I had carried her with me every day. I guess I felt like not having her in my head would be killing her all over again. Now though, with all the horses to think about, my mother went somewhere else.

I'd developed a strong bond with Darwin, the yearling, the one Sandman had been trying to sell off to some racing people. No one had bought him because he was still too wild, and by that age, if a horse was going to race, he needed to know how to get tacked up and handled a lot. And Darwin was a demonseed. Sandman put me in charge of him. I had to get him manageable and then Kathy would start riding him.

I spent hours each day teaching the little guy basics like how to pick his feet up so I could get in there and clean them out—and eventually the farrier could put shoes on him—and pretty soon I got him to take a bit and to stand somewhat still as I put a little saddle on him and tightened the girth.

I started sleeping on some blankets outside Darwin's stall at night. Mostly because I just didn't have any reason to go home. I lived in my uncle Edgar's house even though I'd never felt at home there. Edgar had up and moved a few years after my mother's death, leaving me to fend for myself. He hadn't known what to do with the house so he'd just let me stay in it while he'd gone home to Kentucky. Now, though, Edgar had called the real estate lady in town and had put the house up for sale. There were people tromping through it at the oddest times. I didn't feel safe in there. I had gone and gathered some of my clothes and a sleeping bag and I kept these at Sandman's stable and pretty soon, that was it, I never left.

Sandman knew, I guess, but never chose to address the situation. I availed myself of the hoses in the grooming stall sometimes when I got to stinking. It was fine. There was warm water. And I'd heard how horse shampoo was good for human hair and this proved to be true.

Days turned to weeks turned to months. Kathy was riding Darwin now and we all realized Sandman had been right. The little guy wanted to race. I'd get on Murmur, a big brown gelding that had raced until he was six but now had James working with him trying to turn him into an eventing horse. We'd put Murmur on the makeshift half-mile track Sandman had in one of the fields and he still had the instinct to go. I wasn't by any means an experienced rider and I'd never yet been allowed on a real racetrack but I knew enough to balance and keep out of Murmur's way and let him stretch out. And Darwin learned to run his little heart out with Kathy in the irons, poised with her rear end in the air, letting the little colt pull ahead of Murmur, giving him a taste for winning.

And then the day came when one of the trainers Sandman knew came by to have a look at Darwin. The guy was impressed. Gave Sandman five thousand cash on the spot. I had to load the little guy into the trailer. He behaved perfectly. My heart was breaking.

Somehow, it was worse even than when Dingo had died. I tried to get interested in some of the other horses. I liked a lot of them fine but I didn't have the same kind of bond that I had with the little colt. I was sad but my life at Sandman's was good. I never had to think too much or dwell on anything. At night, I slept in Darwin's empty stall. It was fine.

What sent me over the edge was when I heard about what happened to Bethany, the chestnut mare who'd been the first horse I'd gotten on.

One night, Sandman came and found me in my stall.

"Ben, we got a problem," he said, and I thought he was going to finally address my sleeping in the barn, like maybe he did actually mind it.

"What's that, sir?" I said, because I still called him sir, particularly when I thought I was on the wrong side of him.

"That couple I sold Bethany to? The ones said the woman was gonna take up riding and they needed a nice quiet backyard kind of horse?"

"Yeah?"

"They ain't treating her so good. I happened to be passing by there this morning and I stopped in to check on her. The folks weren't home so I went around back to their little two-stall barn to see what's what. What I found was not good. Bethany was inside there with no light, standing knee-high in filthy, soaked straw and she had sores on her back. Weren't no water in her bucket and when I turned the light on she seemed like she was blinded, like they haven't let her into the light of day. Plus, mare musta lost a couple hundred pounds in the five weeks since she left here. I got sick to my stomach to see it."

I said nothing. I was sick to my stomach too and all I could see was red. A violent horrible bloody red nothing like the rich red of Bethany's chestnut coat. Sandman went on: "I waited till them people got home. Sat there waiting three hours and then when they finally got back, I gave 'em a piece of my mind. And you know what they told me? Told me it weren't none of my business. They done gave me two thousand dollars for that horse and they could do with her as they see fit. I told 'em I was reporting them to the ASPCA and they just laughed in my face, telling me the lady's brother is the sheriff and weren't nobody gonna come around questioning what they did."

Sandman's yellow skin had gone very white and he was clenching his bony fists.

We hitched a trailer up to Sandman's pickup that night just after midnight. When we got close to the people's house, we turned the headlights off and pulled in their driveway, past the house and to the barn. There was a dog but the dog just looked at us and didn't bark.

We got Bethany out of there though she was in such bad shape she had trouble walking up the ramp into the trailer.

We brought her back to our barn, gave her a nice clean stall and some alfalfa cubes and tended to her cuts and wounds for a few hours.

The people came around the next day making threats, saying they knew we'd stolen Bethany. Sandman chased them off his property. But that wasn't good enough.

That night, after Sandman left the barn, I took one of the farm pickup trucks and drove it into town and out to the other side to where the dirtbags lived.

They were pretty careless for people who went around victimizing innocent beasts. Their front door wasn't locked. I walked in the darkened house and took out my little flashlight. I saw some stairs which I assumed would take me up to the bedroom. Sure enough, the first room I looked in, there they were, the happy couple, sleeping like bugs in a rug.

I propped Sandman's shotgun on my shoulder and brought the nose of the thing right up to the guy's temple. Must have been a sound sleeper, he didn't even feel his death sentence resting there against his skin. It sort of made a horrible mess and a fair amount of noise. Woke the woman up but I didn't even let a scream come out of her mouth before I blew her head off too.

On my way out, I checked around to see if they had any other victims. No kids but in the yard I found the dog we'd seen when we'd come for Bethany. He was skinny and his white coat was yellow from dirt and neglect. Dog growled but I talked to him a good while then undid his collar and coaxed him into the truck with me and drove off.

ATTILA JOHNSON

7.

Masked Rider

I popped awake just after four A.M. Ruby and I had been up until close to midnight but nothing could have kept me in bed at this point. I hadn't smelled a horse in a week.

Ruby was asleep, on her side, nightgown bunched at her hips again. I got up quietly and went into the kitchen, passing Stinky on the way. The large cat was on the couch, dozing, his immense belly spilling out from under him. He lifted his head to gaze at me, decided I wasn't going to feed him, and went back to dozing.

Lulu, on the other hand, rubbed against my legs compulsively as I made coffee. I ate a hard-boiled egg that Ruby had cooked the previous night when she'd suddenly decided she had to boil all the eggs in her fridge.

I took a quick shower and dressed then scribbled Ruby a note just as my cell phone chirped. It was Sal calling to tell me he was outside. I went into the hall and locked Ruby's door behind me, taking a brief moment to savor the fact that she'd given me keys.

The neighbor, Ramirez, had his door open.

"Everything all right?" he asked, looking up from his giant mug of coffee. He was wearing a dirty T-shirt and boxer shorts. His thick arms were propped on his yellow kitchen table.

"Fine, thanks, Ramirez. Sal's waiting for me downstairs."

"Good," Ramirez said, nodding then staring back into his coffee mug. The guy, as far as I could tell, never slept at all.

I went down the stairs and out onto Stillwell Avenue. It was still dark out. Here and there, fading stars punctured the sky. The air smelled salty and cold.

Sal had his truck pulled up to the narrow sidewalk in front of Ruby's building. I got in.

"How you doin'?" Sal said. The guy looked wide awake and smelled freshly showered. His shaved head had a healthy pink glow. He had the heat blasting and was in a T-shirt that exposed his heavily tattooed arms.

"I'm good. Thanks for doing this," I said. "It's damned nice of you."

The truth is, I wasn't sure how much good Sal was going to do me if someone was really interested in ending my life. And the more hours that came between me and the incident on the beach the more I'd started wondering if it wasn't just some strange coincidence. A random psychopath that maybe I should have reported to the cops. There was no way to be sure.

Sal drove. The day still hadn't started for most people and the streets were empty. After asking if I minded, Sal put in a Beethoven CD, which he played at an earsplitting volume. Occasionally, he'd shout something at me over the insane roar of the music.

"You know that lady of yours got me into this. This Beethoven shit."

"Oh yeah?" I had to scream for him to hear me. He turned it down a notch.

"I was feeling frazzled when I first met Ruby. The wife was giving me a hard time and my kid didn't seem to like me and my back was going out and I was just a mess. First Ruby tried getting me to do that yoga crap she does," he said indignantly. "Then, when she saw that was going over like a fireball in hell, she got on me to listen to classical. I gotta say, it helps." Sal shook his big bald head and squeezed the steering wheel for emphasis. I nodded, then closed my eyes.

A half hour later, we were pulling into the backside entrance at Belmont. After peering into the vehicle and seeing me, Lazy Susan, the morning-shift security guard, waved us in, not seeming to care one bit that Sal's truck didn't have the proper stickers.

I glanced toward the training track and saw a half-dozen tractors, headlights glowing in the hard darkness as they worked to prepare the surface. I directed Sal to the horsemen's parking lot where he nosed the truck into a spot. We got out and walked toward Henry Meyer's barn.

The backstretch was alive and humming in the cold dawn. Grooms mucking stalls out. Hotwalkers hand walking horses. Radios blaring salsa as if it were high noon in Miami. Sal seemed dazed as he looked around, taking in the activity.

"This your first time on the backside?" I asked him.

"Yeah. Amazing back here," he said, and I smiled to myself, remembering how I felt the first time I'd set foot here, how it seemed like I'd finally found my home.

We came to Henry's barn where Pepe, one of Henry's hotwalkers, was leading a bay filly around the shedrow.

"Attila," Pepe nodded at me.

"Where's Henry?" I asked, stopping to pat the filly on the neck.

"In his office, pulling his hair out."

"Oh yeah? What happened?"

"What happened?" Pepe looked incredulous. "Snow, Attila. Canceled races. Horses high as kites. Henry's got owners crawling down his back trying to figure out what races to put their horses in now."

"Oh," I said. Pepe, who is fiercely protective of Henry and the horses, eyed Sal. Sal stared back at the hotwalker. I didn't offer any explanation for my bodyguard.

I stuck my head in Henry's office. The man looked terrible. The crevices in his face were deeper than usual and the pouches under his large brown eyes were drooping down to his mouth.

"You okay, Henry?"

His head jerked up and he frowned. "Attila, there you are. I was wondering if you'd turn up."

"Oh yeah? You need me?"

"Looks like they're getting the track in shape, I'm gonna send one set of horses out and Layla is sick. I could use you."

Layla Yashpinsky, an exercise rider, was a small muscular woman with an ass of iron and shoulders like a German swimmer. But, for all her apparent physical power, the girl had been out sick ten of the last twenty days. Rumor had it she'd taken up with one of Shug McGaughey's assistant trainers, so maybe she wasn't sick in the traditional sense of the word.

"This is my friend, Sal," I said, indicating my bodyguard. "I'm just taking him around with me for a few days. Hope that's okay. He's interested in buying a horse."

Henry glanced up briefly, grunted a greeting at Sal, and then gave me instructions on what to do with the two horses I was going to work for him.

"Just a very easy gallop with both of them," Henry said, "and if that footing's really bothering them, then use your judgment and just do as much as the horse is comfortable with. I'll be up there in a few minutes to watch."

I nodded at Henry.

Sal and I started heading away from the shedrow, over toward the training track. It was still inky and dark out and a numbing wind was blowing snow everywhere. Sal was hatless, the bare skin of his shaved head exposed to the elements. He pulled his coat collar up closer to his ears.

"You okay? You need a hat?" I asked him.

"I'm fine. My head is always hot," he said, grinning a little.

I was already cold to the bone but it didn't matter to me much. I'd be on a horse soon.

As we came closer to the track, Sal started grumbling about how much he hated the idea of my riding out there, in plain view of anyone.

"It'd have to be a sniper to get at me when I'm on the track, Sal," I tried assuaging him.

"Exactly my point."

"I just don't think that's gonna happen," I said quietly.

"And what, you thought someone was gonna try to take you out on the beach at Coney Island?"

"I'm starting to think that was an unfortunate coincidence."

"Very unfortunate, I'd say."

I just wasn't worried. I was about to get on a horse. This thought was starting to warm me up good when I saw Tony Vallamara walking toward us. It looked like he was staring right at me and I felt my stomach knot up. Tony had been a jockey at some point long before my time. After a few unsuccessful seasons, he switched over to being a jockey's agent. I don't think that went too well either and eventually he turned crooked, orchestrating deals on the dark side of the horse business. His personal organizer was chockful of unscrupulous veterinarians, corrupt bloodstock agents, and down-on-their-luck trainers. Tony had been the first one to approach me about holding a horse back in a race. I had been surprised. That stuff went on all the time at bush tracks but it was the last thing you expected on the New York circuit, which seemed much too carefully monitored and scrutinized for anyone to pull off something as obvious as holding a horse back. At first, I just laughed, thinking it was a sinister joke. But it wasn't. Of course the guy wouldn't dream of approaching any name riders with such a proposal and he probably wouldn't approach *any* riders other than someone as low down as me. At the time, I'd been riding in New York for two months and hadn't had a win. Ava and I were already on the skids with my lack of earning power generating a lot of the turmoil. When Tony approached me about holding back a horse named Razorskin in a little claiming race, it didn't seem like the end of the world. The poor horse stood a raindrop's chance in hell of running better than last anyway. I didn't feel that badly. Took the money and rode the race same as I would have anyway. The horse came in second to last. It wasn't always that easy though. Over the next few months, I took cash for holding horses that did have a chance. There was one horse, a big awkward gelding named Roustabout, that just didn't want to lose. I was doing everything I could. Gave him a horrible start out of the gate, then got him stuck in traffic. But the horse went ten wide, trying to get to the lead. I had to lose my stirrups and even that didn't do it. I waited till we were clear of other horses and fell off. The horse, relieved of his rider, crossed the finish line first by ten lengths and looked proud afterward. I felt sick. And I wasn't the same after that.

When Tony had approached me about fudging my ride on a brave little claiming mare two weeks earlier, I'd refused. Tony had said I'd regret it, but I hadn't taken the threat very seriously. The guy was crooked but I didn't think he was a murderer. Now, I wasn't sure. As Sal and I walked by, the small, ugly man looked at me and sneered. Sal didn't notice. We kept walking.

We reached the rail of the track where the wind was gathering strength, chilling me so much I could feel my toes curling inside my boots. I was so stiff I wasn't sure how I'd be able to ride, but once Sophie, the groom who was handling Jack Valentine, gave me a leg up, all the physical unpleasantness disappeared.

Jack was a sweetheart of a horse. He had trouble staying sound and, even though he was just starting to really get the hang of racing, he probably wouldn't have a long career. Jack was an honest horse though and always gave me as much as he had. This morning that proved to be a lot. I guess that Jack, like all the rest of us, had

had enough with being cooped up. As I asked him to move from a trot to a comfortable canter, he got excited, bucked, squealed, and shook his head, which was pretty uncharacteristic for this horse. He was probably just feeling good though. Like me.

I had a pretty tight hold on Jack's mouth and he was paying attention to me, arching his neck, focusing. I pulled my first pair of goggles down over my eyes then asked him for a slow gallop. The track didn't feel good. It was cold and still partly frozen, quickly turning to mud that was flying up into Jack's eyes and plastering my goggles and vest. But Jack was going nicely. I liked the gelding and he liked me. We were galloping slowly but it still felt like flying.

When we finished, I brought Jack down to a walk along the rail and looked over and saw Henry beaming, the first smile I'd seen out of him since the day Ballistic won us a race.

Sal didn't look nearly so pleased and, when I handed Jack off to Sophie, the big man cornered me.

"I don't like it," he scowled.

"What's that, Sal?"

"You're vulnerable out there."

"I'm always vulnerable out there."

"You know what I mean," Sal frowned.

"Sal, it's okay. I appreciate your looking out for me. But I gotta do my job."

Sal scowled at me a few seconds longer, then shrugged.

And, a short while later, I was wondering if he was onto something.

It was the weirdest thing I'd ever seen happen on the track.

There were about fifteen or so of us out there. I was on a filly named Heroism, a two-year-old who wouldn't start racing for another few months. She was a handful and I couldn't get a good feel for her. Henry had me working her with two older horses. He was so short on help he had Pepe, the hotwalker—who'd only just been licensed—riding a battle-weary gelding named Fierce Fred. Larry, a talented Peruvian kid, was on Whippersnapper, an allowance mare I'd ridden once or twice. The two older horses were going to teach my little filly what's what.

We all three had red-and-blue covers on our crash helmets so it's possible we were indistinguishable. We were hand galloping in tandem, the three horses nose to nose, getting close to full speed when we heard shouting coming from behind us.

Next thing I knew, a horse was trying to wedge in between Larry and me. It all happened very quickly—which was a blessing, I don't think any of us had enough time to panic. As horse and rider shoved between us, bumping both our mounts, Larry tumbled off, over the rail. Somewhere in the blur of what happened next, I got one brief look at the interfering rider and saw he was wearing a *ski mask*.

Both Pepe and I managed to keep our horses calm, which was no small feat since my filly was sky-high to begin with. One of the outriders was galloping ahead, trying to catch up with the horse and rider that had caused the accident and then, to my amazement, the masked rider asked his horse to *jump the rail* and the pair jumped out of the track and over to the far parking lot.

PEPE AND I both pulled our horses up and turned around, trotting back to where Larry had fallen. Another of the outriders had already caught Larry's mare and the old gal seemed none the worse for the wear.

Sal had run onto the track along with a dozen or so others. The paramedics were already bent over Larry but I could see him sitting up, which was a very good sign.

I jumped down off Heroism's back and handed her to an outrider to hold. Sal grabbed me by the shoulders. "Come on, Attila, you're out of here."

"Lay off, Sal," I said, shrugging from his grip and going over to look at Larry. The kid was evidently indestructible. He stood up and seemed more annoyed at being covered in mud than anything else. He looked ready to get back on a horse. Which I wouldn't have minded either. This was serious business though. The clockers and track officials had all come onto the track and were talking with their hands. Soon men and women from the security force were searching all over the backstretch but, incredibly enough, the masked rider and his mount seemed to have vanished completely. And, racing being racing, things went back to business fairly soon. Larry and Pepe and I all had to talk to the head of security and a handful of officials. Pepe and I had both noticed that the perpetrator had been wearing a ski mask but neither of us had gotten too good a look at the horse other than to notice it was a bay and fairly thick, indicating it was an older horse, possibly a stallion.

As soon as he could, Sal took me aside and demanded that I tell Security and whoever else needed to know that I'd been threatened.

"The actual threat came weeks ago, Sal. I really don't think this had to do with me. I didn't feel anything in my gut. It seemed like they were after Larry." This was a blatant lie. I had seen Tony Vallamara just a short time before the incident. I had a strong feeling the whole event had been his doing. But I also felt like, if I kept ignoring it, it would go away. I just couldn't see Tony—or anyone—putting that much effort into destroying me just because I'd refused to hold a horse back. There was something more going on.

"There was no way to tell you and that Larry kid apart from a distance, what with you both having the same color riding hats."

I smiled at his calling it a *riding hat*.

"This ain't funny in my book, friend."

"No, it isn't," I concurred.

"How come when that guy tried to drown you, you were sure it had to do with those threats, but now, now that someone's come close to taking you out *twice,* suddenly you don't think it's got anything to do with you?"

I didn't know how to answer him. I didn't want to think about it. And furthermore, Sal was starting to annoy me.

"Look," I said finally, "I'm done riding for the day anyway. Henry's the only trainer that I ride for that's working any horses this morning. I'll make the rounds and see if any of the others need me to hand walk a few for them. After that, I'm going to the gym, then on back to Ruby's. I'm good. And I don't want to keep you from what you need to be doing all day."

By then, Sal had evidently had it with me. He didn't say another word but I could read the anger and frustration on his face. He shrugged, turned, and walked away.

I breathed a sigh of relief. Sal meant well but I couldn't focus with him around. Not that hand walking a half-dozen horses required much focus. Still, I just wanted to put the entire world out of my mind.

RUBY MURPHY

8.

Velocity

It's not yet seven A.M. when I decide to give up on sleeping. Thinking about Attila out there at the track has made me jittery as hell. I should have gone with him. I might not be able to do much to protect him, but looking at and smelling horses probably would have soothed me. I don't know what possessed me to stay home. Some vague notion of reclaiming my life, I guess.

The apartment is cold and I pull a sweater on over my nightgown. The floor is cold too. I can't find my slippers so I slip my sneakers on instead. As I walk by, I catch my reflection in the closet mirror. My hair has gotten too long and is hanging in nests halfway down my back. My green sweater is dirty and my white nightgown has a coffee stain on it. The sneakers aren't adding much to the look either. Theoretically, it's fine to look like shit in the privacy of my own home, but one day I might forget myself and go out looking like this and it'll be the beginning of the end. After that, I'll talk to myself in public and stop bathing and be two steps shy of the hat factory.

I walk into the kitchen where I brew coffee, feed the cats, and then stare into the refrigerator's innards, trying to will edible food-stuffs to appear there. It's torturous to eat in front of Attila: I always feel like I'm taunting the guy by eating things he has to avoid. And I'm always afraid that the mere suggestion of food will make him feel obliged to vomit up the contents of his stomach. I don't think Attila technically has an eating disorder. Most jockeys have to *flip*, as they call it, in order to maintain their riding weights. At five-foot-five, Attila's on the tall side for a rider and a hundred and five is just not his natural weight. He struggles. Probably a lot more than he lets me know.

There isn't much to look at in my fridge and my keeping the door open has convinced Stinky he's in for a second feeding. I close the fridge door and reach for my box of Honey Nut Cheerios in its hiding place in the cupboard.

I pour myself a bowl and walk into the living room. As I sit spooning Cheerios into my mouth, I notice that the phone machine is blinking. I haven't even glanced at the thing in the last five days. Apparently I missed a call though. I press the Play button and am surprised to hear a message from my mother. This is unusual. My mother likes me but it just doesn't frequently occur to her to call me. It's modest consolation that she calls my sister, Chloe, even less. In Chloe's case though, my mother has a better excuse, since my sister is a nomad and hard to keep track of. My sister is ridiculously intelligent and earned a Ph.D. in applied physics at an absurdly young age. She dabbles in teaching but, after a few months, invari-ably grows restless, quits the job, and moves to a new state. If there's no teaching work to be found, she'll do virtually anything for a short while. Though we've been close at times, after a few weeks of frequent contact with me, Chloe suddenly has enough and doesn't call again for months. Last I heard, she was in northern California working in a zoo, which is perfectly fitting since the strongest thing we Murphy women have in common is a bordering-on-fanatical love of animals. My mother has close to thirty black standard poodles that she breeds and shows for a living. She and her second husband, Richard, live and breathe poodles. They rarely eat or sleep and have not been to the movies in five years.

My mother has left a message simply asking me to call. Something must be the matter. It's still a bit early for most people but not for my mother, who usually rises at five. I dial her number.

"Mom," I say when she answers, breathlessly, on the eighth ring, "it's your older daughter."

"Ruby?" She seems unsure.

"Yes. How are you?"

"Oh fine, I'm grooming right now," she says. I can hear a blow-dryer going in the background.

"You called?" I ask.

"Oh, so I did," she says. I hear a different sound in the background, something like a small airplane engine, revving. Several dogs start barking. My mother hollers at them to shush.

"I was just calling to say hello," my mother says.

I hear myself gasp.

"Everything all right?" she asks in a tone that instructs me to answer affirmatively.

"Oh. Yes. I think so."

"Yes?"

"Yes. Things are fine."

"Job?"

"Good."

"Stinky and Lulu?"

"Very good. Fat. Stinky anyway."

"Still?" My mother sounds incredulous. She only met the cat once about three years ago when she visited me en route to a dog show on Long Island, but she likes to remind me that he's obese. She urged me to try him on a raw diet and I did; however, the pounds did not come flying off.

"I really do think he has a metabolic problem," I tell her.

My mother humpfs in my ear.

"Well then," she says.

"Well," I say. "Everything's okay?" I venture, before losing her for another three months to her strange world of furry black dogs.

"Oh yes. Lilian had six puppies. Two boys and four girls. And we put in a new bathroom," she adds.

"Oh. Wow. That's great," I say. "I painted my bedroom ceiling leafy green."

"Oh," my mother says.

It occurs to me to tell her about Attila, but of course I don't. What would I say? I'm dating an apprentice jockey who may have a hit out on him? My mother might not be surprised but she does love me and she does worry and there's just no need to agitate her. Besides, she has heard of many of my men through the years and no sooner would she memorize their names than they were gone.

"Well, don't let me keep you," I say after a pause.

"Yes, I should get back to it," my mother says, turning the blow-dryer to a louder velocity.

"Bye, Mom, love you," I say.

"You too," she says, hanging up.

I EAT A FEW more bites of Cheerios and then lose interest. I warily eye the piano. I haven't had a lesson in two weeks and I don't have one scheduled. Since Mark Baxter, my gifted but difficult young teacher, does not treat me well unless I show marked progress, I figure I'll let it all slide until the Attila situation is cleared up. Not that I feel particularly confident that things will ever calm down with him. Attila Johnson is a chaotic man. It's part of his appeal.

I get up, put my cereal bowl in the sink, and am about to go take a shower when the phone rings.

"Yes?" I say, half expecting to find that it's my mother, having suddenly remembered that she did in fact call me for a reason. It's just Jane though. My closest girlfriend, whom I've ignored these past weeks.

"You're up?" she says by way of greeting.

"Evidently, yes, how are you?"

"Are you going to work? Where's the jockey?" she says, pronouncing *jockey* like an insult.

"The man has a name. And the Coney Island Museum is only open late in the day in the off-season. Surely you know that by now."

"I forgot. I'm sorry. And how's Hannibal?" Jane says.

"I sincerely hope you called for a reason," I say, trying for my surliest tone, even though if anyone in the world is permitted to insult my lovers and question my taste, it is Jane.

My friend sighs, "I'm sorry, how is *Attila* doing?"

"He's out at the track. Riding. Though all isn't well."

"Oh?"

"Someone tried to hurt him."

"What?"

I relay the story of Attila's near drowning.

"Ever since you first set foot on a racetrack you've been getting into very serious trouble."

"Oh stop. It's purely coincidental."

"That Ariel psycho was not coincidental," Jane says, referring to Ariel DiCello, a disturbed woman who, nine months ago, hired me to follow her boyfriend, a racetracker. It had all happened when I'd made up a little lie about being a private detective. A little lie that had ended up becoming a reality. It got me into a fair heap of trouble too.

"Okay, I admit I took the Ariel thing on voluntarily."

"No one forced you to shack up with a jockey."

"True. But I had no idea he was a jockey in trouble."

"I'm sure you did. On some level." She sighs, "I don't know what's wrong with you this past year. And what happened to Ed? I thought you were crazy about Ed."

"I was crazy about Ed. Am. But he's gone."

"For good?"

"I have no way of knowing that." I rein in my frustration. We've had this conversation several times before.

"How about asking?"

"No. It's one of those things. I have to leave it be."

There's a pause as Jane mulls this over.

"Maybe it's contributing."

"To what?"

"To your cautionless behavior."

"No, it's the yoga."

She snorts. It was at her insistence that I tried and then became addicted to yoga. My daily yoga practice has made me calmer, stronger, and less likely to smoke cigarettes, but it's also made me strangely brave. Mastering mildly dangerous physical tricks like balancing upside down on my forearms while trying to bring my feet to touch the top of my head has made me less afraid of whatever's waiting for me out there in the world. I now try convincing Jane that it's this peculiar yoga-induced braveness that's leading me into trouble. She snorts again.

I successfully change the subject by telling Jane my mother actually called me. Jane is as surprised as I was. She's fascinated by what's left of my family—my father died eleven years ago, and Jane thinks that my mother and sister and I are savages for failing to be close-knit. Jane spends a lot of time with her own mother and was very close to her father until he died. She's mortified that I don't go down to Pennsylvania to visit my mother at least once a week and has succeeded in getting me to call my mother more frequently. She had long claimed this would eventually make my mother call me for no reason. Now it's finally happened. And Jane is triumphant. Eventually though, she brings the conversation back to Attila, asking me what I intend to do.

"I honestly don't know. He won't call the police and *I'm* not going to call them. I just can't do that."

"Please stay away from the racetrack," Jane says.

"That I can't promise. I won't go tomorrow though. I have to go to work."

"Good," she says. She tries getting me to agree to come to a yoga class the following night but I demur.

"I might need to go to sleep early tomorrow night. I've had a draining few weeks with all this shacking up," I tell her.

She snorts yet again.

"Where did you pick up this new habit of snorting?" I ask irritably.

"What snorting?"

"You keep snorting at me."

"I do?" She sounds genuinely baffled. "I'm sorry, I didn't mean to snort. That's disgusting."

We both laugh and then bid each other a good day before hanging up. But I'm not sure what's good about it. In fact, I feel my mood taking a dive. I decide to put on some layers and get out of the house.

There are still enormous banks of snow flanking the streets and few cars are venturing onto Surf Avenue as I cross over and head toward the water.

The boardwalk is deserted and, just ahead, big waves are violently slamming the beach. I sit down on a bench, pull out a cigarette, and light it. I have only smoked one so far today and the nicotine goes right to my head, improving my mood considerably while presumably shortening my life by a few more minutes.

The cold starts seeping into me and I get up and walk. I walk all the way to Brighton Beach, burying my hands in my pockets and mentally running through images of the last few days. Attila. My friend Big Sal. Suddenly, Ed Burke intrudes. I find myself wondering what he's up to in Florida. Wondering if he's met a girl down there. I find the thought disturbing and I go back to thinking about Attila. Not that this is particularly soothing. I don't know what I feel for him, but I certainly don't want anything bad happening to him and somehow I doubt that Big Sal's ministrations will do him much good. I start feeling panicked and I quicken my pace as I head home.

I get back into my apartment, remove my coat, and look at the answering machine. Six messages have come in over the last hour and that can't possibly be good.

BIG SAL

9.

Women's Studies

I got in the truck and peeled out of the parking lot. Didn't make it real far though. I should have realized they'd jack up security after what happened on the track. But I wasn't thinking. I was pissed off. The lady security guard who had waved Attila and me through earlier was so uptight now that she had a damned *weapon* drawn.

"Sir, could you step out of the vehicle, please," she said.

She was a chubby little thing, her green uniform clinging to her for dear life. Her flat brown eyes looked like a snake's.

"Yes, ma'am," I said, getting out of the truck.

She fired off a series of questions about why didn't I have the proper stickers for my vehicle and what was I doing there. I explained how she'd waved me and Attila in just a couple hours earlier, but she wasn't buying it. She made radio contact with other security people and pretty soon there was a big to-do and they had to summon Henry Meyer to vouch for me.

At first, the trainer looked at me blankly. Then recognition dawned.

"Oh, Attila's friend. Right. What were you doing with him anyway?"

"Just hanging around," I said, wanting very much to tell him the truth, but not doing it. "Attila was showing me what's what. I'm thinking of getting into a syndicate, buy into a horse or two."

"Huh," Henry grunted, like this was one of the worst ideas he'd heard all day. "Yeah," he said, turning to the three security officers now collected there, "he's one of my riders' friends. It's okay."

The chubby brunette officer looked resentful. This was probably as close as she'd ever come to having a reason to shoot someone and I'd rained on her parade. My kind of girl.

I got back in the truck and drove off through the bowels of Queens and home to my other kind of girl. My wife. She was actually home. And, I have to say, she nearly gave me a heart attack.

"Baby, where you been all morning?" she purred, surprising the hell out of me for even noticing I hadn't been around—and compounding that surprise by seeming glad to see me.

She was wearing her spandex workout pants and a little tank top distended by her glorious tits. I guess I stared at her with my jaw hanging open.

"What's the matter, Sal?"

"Nothing's the matter," I said.

And then, she started fumbling with my pants, right there in the living room.

"Where's Jake?" I said, not wanting to emotionally scar the kid with the vision of his mom blowing his dad in the living room.

"Play date. All afternoon, baby." She'd undone my belt and pulled my jeans over my ass and I already had a hard-on that could have drilled a hole in the ceiling.

And then my wife blew me. I came in about thirty seconds.

"Hair-trigger response," she said, touching me with pride. "How long I gotta wait?" she asked, pulling her spandex leggings down just below her large pale ass.

"Apparently not very long," I said, entering her first with my fingers, then with my quickly rejuvenated hard-on.

"I want another baby," she said then, bucking her hips into me.

This was something of a shock. A few months earlier, she hadn't wanted me inside her. Now she *really* wanted me inside her. Women. Go figure. Another fucking kid though? Jake was my life and that seemed like enough. Plus, erratic as Karen was, I was pretty sure she wasn't gonna stick with me that much longer. Then it would be *two* kids growing up with jerk parents taking out their bitterness on them.

"You went off the pill?" I said, just like that, as we stood unceremoniously fucking in the living room.

"Yes," she said with a thrust of her hips.

"No way, Karen," I said, abruptly pulling out of her, causing her to whine like a dying lawn mower, "not the way you're erratic. I don't want *two* kids growing up with divorced parents."

Usually I didn't speak my mind with her quite this frankly. I had in the very beginning. When I'd met her, she'd been starting over after being a high-priced call girl supporting her coke habit. The first time she walked into my home group of AA, every guy in the room pretty much instantly wanted her. And I instantly wanted to kill those guys. I felt possessive of Karen before I'd even talked to her. And, to try and do things right with her, I'd been completely honest about everything. But a lot had changed in eight years.

She wheeled around, face red with anger, her workout pants still down around her hips, exposing her bush.

"What the hell are you talking about, Sal?"

"Don't take it like that, baby," I said. "Come on, I'll get a condom."

This infuriated her even more. She pulled her pants back up and stormed upstairs, leaving me there in the living room, with my dick literally hanging out. Maybe my diplomacy skills left a little to be desired.

I didn't know what to do. So I pulled my pants back up, got my keys, and went out.

I got in the truck, started the engine and the Beethoven. Ruby was on me to expand my repertoire and listen to some Bach and maybe Shostakovich but I hadn't gotten there yet. I liked Tchaikovsky, but when I'd told this to Ruby, she had scowled and, the next time I'd seen her, she'd given me five new CDs. Bach, Handel, some moody Russians, and some guy named Schoenberg. An opera no less. I wasn't ready for that. Or was I? Right then I needed some serious mood alteration. I riffled through the glove box until I found the Schoenberg disc. I stared at it for a minute. *Moses und Aron* it was called. Ruby had told me how Mr. Schoenberg had only used one *A* in Aron because otherwise the title would have had thirteen letters and he didn't want to bring bad luck on his opera. I took Beethoven out and put in Mr. Schoenberg. Full volume even though I had no idea what I was in for. The music came. A low rumble of male voices. It was pretty strange sounding but not bad strange. I put the truck into drive and pulled ahead.

For about ten minutes I succeeded in not thinking. Not about Karen, not about Ruby's damn jockey. I just drove and listened to that crazy, dark music. Then I found I'd pulled up outside of Johnny's candy store on Havemeyer Street.

I turned Mr. Schoenberg down. Very gently so as not to offend. I'd gotten that way with classical music. If I had to stop it before listening to the whole thing, I turned it down in tiny increments so as not to shock myself or offend the spirit of the dead guy who'd composed it. I suppose a coupla the CDs Ruby had told me to buy were by guys who were actually still alive. But Mr. Schoenberg had died fifty something years ago.

I stared at the bright yellow-and-red entrance to Johnny's. The place had been in the Del Tredici family since the turn of the century. At one point though, Johnny's dad had gone under and rented it to some Dominicans who turned it into a bodega, painting it that red and yellow that is apparently in the bylaws of some Bodega Decoration Code. Eventually, Johnny had gotten on his feet enough financially to take the place back over and restore it to a candy store—bookie in the back—but he'd never gotten around to painting it and it was now a crumbling yellow and red. He'd put up a green awning that said JOHNNY'S CANDY and someone, maybe his kid Nicky, had pointed out that the shop was now flying Rastafarian colors. But it's not like any Jamaican guys were mistaking it for a social club. Everyone within a twenty-block radius knew non-Italians weren't gonna get a warm reception there. Unless they were dropping a few thousand on a long shot at Aqueduct.

I got out of the truck and went inside. Johnny's daughter Nan was sitting there, smoking and reading *People* magazine. On the counters around her were big old-fashioned glass containers full of colorful candies. The candy aspect of the store didn't do booming business considering that the neighborhood, which had been predominantly Spanish for a few decades, was now infested with white hipsters who mostly steered clear of candy—coming in only occasionally to soak in the quaint factor.

Nan's cigarette was propped between her lips and a good two inches of ash threatened to fall on her huge belly. Girl was eight months pregnant. I'd once made the mistake of mentioning to Karen that Nan was knocked up and smoking and Karen had stormed in there and given Nan a piece of her mind—along with photos she'd downloaded off the Internet depicting birth defects in kids whose mothers had smoked. As a result, I'd been persona non grata at Johnny's for a couple of months and Karen had been permanently banned from the place.

"Hey, girl," I nodded at Nan. She looked up from her magazine and scowled. She was a cute kid actually, a petite brunette with blue eyes. She'd just turned twenty and was apparently already starting on her mama's path of popping out a kid every other year. This was her second—the first, Mimi, currently asleep in a stroller behind the counter, had come out just fine, no birth defects in spite of the smoking.

"Pop's in the back, Sal," Nan said, going back to her magazine. She was still scowling—now with something to really scowl about considering her ash had fallen onto her stretchy pink top.

I went to the side of the counter and through the little door, down the hall and to the back room. Johnny was on the phone, as was his son, Nicky. A third guy whose name I couldn't remember, some kind of cousin, was staring at the TV that was broadcasting the OTB channel. Normally, this time of day, the channel would have been broadcasting Aqueduct, but with the Big A being closed, they had some Gulfstream Park races showing.

"Howya doin', Sal?" the cousin said.

"Good. What's up?" I said.

"Nothing at Aqueduct today. Fuckin' snow."

"Ehh, watch your mouth, Fulvio," Johnny said, having just hung up from taking a bet. Johnny was Catholic. We all were, but Johnny's Catholicism adhered to a peculiar moral code that said being a bookie and hitting the sauce were okay but no cursing or birth control. "Sal, howya doin'?" he asked me.

"Good," I nodded.

"Where ya been?" he asked, though he knew damned well his daughter hadn't let me set foot in the place for three months.

"Busy," I said, playing his little game.

"You remember Fulvio, right?" Johnny wanted to know.

I nodded again. No wonder I hadn't remembered the guy's name. What the hell kind of name was Fulvio? I knew the kid had been born in Naples. His folks had come over when he was little so I didn't think he even spoke Italian anymore but he had a seriously Italian name.

The phone rang and Johnny got it.

Nicky had hung up from his call now.

"Hey, Sal, howya doin'?"

I was getting a little sick of telling them how I was doing, but unless someone else came in the room I wouldn't have to answer the question again after this.

"Good, Nicky, how's by you?"

"Took a bath on the second at Gulfstream."

"Sorry about that."

"Yeah," the kid shrugged.

Nicky was a good-looking kid. One thing you could say for Johnny and his missus, at least six of their eleven kids were good-looking.

"Who's Velasquez riding at Gulfstream today?" I asked, figuring since I'd somehow ended up here, I must have had a bet on my mind.

"He's on a maiden filly in the next race. I can give you twenty to one on her."

"Yeah? Who's the filly?"

"First-time starter. Dunno. But she's by Hennesy," he said, uttering the sire's name with reverence.

"Yeah, that and two dollars will get her on the subway."

"Yeah, could be," Nicky said. "Two hundred large at Keeneland yearling sale though, and she's got John Ward training her."

"Uh," I grunted. I liked the trainer's record and Velasquez, the jockey, was a monster. I didn't put a whole lot of stock in yearlings costing too much though. Didn't mean they could run. I was the kind of guy who rooted for underdog, inexpensive horses. I'd almost had to kill myself when Funny Cide had lost the Belmont Stakes. Like everyone, I'd been hoping for him to stick it to those regally bred million-dollar colts one more time. It hadn't been his day though and a blue-blooded horse won.

"You want it or not?" Nicky said, getting a little impatient with me.

"Sure. Twenty to win," I said.

A few minutes later, I watched Velasquez shoot the filly out to the front of the pack and stay there until two lengths from the finish line when a 35–1 filly caught her.

I felt a little depressed but not too bad and, since I wasn't sure why I'd come here in the first place, I decided it might be time to get on with my day.

"I guess I'm gonna get going," I said to Johnny.

"Oh yeah?" he said. "You need a drink, Sal?"

"No thanks, Johnny," I said, feeling a little aggravated since, after ten years in AA—I had actually told Johnny about it—he still offered me drinks every chance he got.

"You got any more bets to place?" he said.

"I dunno. What's on at Aqueduct tomorrow? I hear they're opening up again."

"Yeah. Ain't much to like. My uncle Davide got one of his in a race," Johnny shrugged. Johnny was loyal to his uncle and this loyalty extended to his touting the uncle's racehorses. Uncle Davide is, from what I gather, pretty high up in what's left of the mob in these parts, but the guy does not have an eye for horses at all. I've never seen anyone pick out bum-luck horses with more consistency than Davide. I don't think he's ever had a horse run in the money, never mind win a race.

"Yeah? How's Davide doing?" I asked.

"Oh, he's fine," Johnny shrugged. "There's a decent allowance colt in the fourth tomorrow," he added, brightening, "Oat Bran Blues. Good horse. But he's got that apprentice Attila Johnson in the irons and I heard something about the kid holding his mounts back for a little extra payday. Probably why he'll go off at twenty to one or so."

Bingo. This is why I was here.

"Yeah, I heard that apprentice ain't crooked anymore."

"Oh yeah?" Johnny suddenly looked more interested in me than he'd been in a number of decades.

"Yeah. I know someone who knows him."

"And what, the kid *admitted* he was fudging?"

"He ain't a kid actually. I think the guy's in his thirties or something," I said, choosing not to answer the question as it might involve me in a way I didn't care to be involved.

Johnny looked at me blankly. I got up to leave, wondering if he was gonna press the issue.

"Come on, Sal, tell me what you heard."

"I just heard he wants to win," I said, and then I went out, nodding at Nan, who was smoking another one by now.

I got in the truck. Put Mr. Schoenberg back on. Thought about Karen. Wondered what might befall me if I went home. I couldn't figure it out. I put the music up a few more notches. Decided I might actually like opera.

10.

The Blind Eye

Eventually, the chaos over the masked rider passed and I went ahead and walked a half-dozen horses for trainers I knew— including Arnie Gaines, the trainer Ruby had walked hots for nine months back. I stopped by Henry Meyer's barn again to talk to him about how he wanted me riding Oat Bran Blues, the big floppy-eared bay I was riding in the fourth race the next day.

I stuck my head in his office and saw Henry's wife, Violet, sitting in Henry's chair, her feet up on the desk. She was frowning in concentration as she studied tomorrow's *Form.*

"Ms. Kravitz," I greeted the lady.

In spite of having married into one of the most misogynistic professions going, Violet Kravitz held on tight to her maiden name and the appellation of Ms.—even though, back when Ava and I were still attempting something, Ava had proudly come in one day waving a *New York Times* essay by a saucy young woman who was dead set against Ms. and insisted on being called Miss.

"Attila," Violet said, looking at me over the top of her spectacles. "What exactly happened on the track this morning?"

My stomach knotted. I wondered if she'd heard rumors about me and suspected this morning's mayhem had had something to do with me. I hoped not. I respected and was fond of both Henry and Violet and would never do anything to interfere with one of their horses.

"Damnedest thing I ever saw," I said.

"You keep out of harm's way, all right, young man?" Violet's blue eyes had grown wide. She was so guileless. It made me feel soiled in contrast.

I nodded.

"You're going to do right by Muley tomorrow, yes?" Violet asked.

Oat Bran Blues was known as Muley around the barn. His right ear was stunted and flopped to one side like a mule's—a result of having explored a bees' nest as a foal. He'd been stung mercilessly and the ear had given up on growing. At seventeen hands, Muley was a big horse, but the tiny flopping ear gave him a clownish appearance that he always seemed to be compensating for by being spooky and difficult under tack.

"I'll try to keep out of Muley's way, ma'am," I told Violet.

She laughed at this. Women love the way I always defer to the horse, though it isn't something I do to curry favor. Early on in my career I'd been taught well by an old claimer named Justa Bob. Nothing fazed Justa Bob. He was just a racehorse. Just a claimer. But wise. All I had to do was lightly hold his mouth in my hands as he methodically took care of business. He would stand quietly in the gate, break perfectly, then settle in a few horses wide, calculating exactly how much effort was required to pick off the horses in front of him. He would switch leads without being asked, giving himself an extra gear and, with less than a furlong to go, he'd bring himself up to the leading horse's shoulder. Two strides shy of the wire, he would surge just enough to get his nose in front. The plain, brown gelding showed me how races were won.

They weren't all like that though. You had your first-time starters and your crazies who were wound so tightly they'd become uncoordinated and fall on their faces if you didn't tell them how to put one hoof in front of the other. The ones I loved best though let me know what they wanted and I gladly obliged.

"Don't ma'am me, Attila, I don't want to feel like I'm eighty please."

"Sorry, Violet." I grinned at her, feeling a wave of fondness for this eccentric and gentle woman.

She then went on to show me, with much disgust, the *Racing Form* handicappers' notes on Oat Bran Blues. The comments weren't favorable. About the horse or his rider. It angered me.

"Don't look like that, dear," Violet said. "I wouldn't let Henry continue to put you on our horses if I didn't believe in you."

I felt myself flushing.

"Did you need Henry for something?" Violet asked. "He's at the racing secretary's office, probably back in a half hour."

"Just wanted to go over any special instructions for Muley's race."

"You know Muley. He means well but he's spooky. We'll have a shadow roll on him this time, ought to help. Just keep him out of traffic and let him do his thing."

I thought back to the first time I'd seen a shadow roll. Someone had had to explain its function. How you put it on the noseband of the bridle and its fuzzy bulk prevents the horse from seeing shadows on his own nose—which might frighten him.

I nodded at Violet, then told her I was going to go have a little chat with Muley.

"Good." Violet smiled, pleased.

I walked down the aisle, stopping to greet Ballistic, running a hand down his white blaze. The horse doesn't have the best barn manners though; he pinned his ears and showed me his teeth.

"Yeah yeah," I told him, "you're the boss."

I went down to Muley's stall and let myself in. He was truffling at his empty hay net but he put his ears forward and lifted his head to look at me. "Hey you," I greeted the horse as I went to stand next to him. He bumped his nose against my forehead and nuzzled at my hair.

"Easy, it ain't hay," I told him. He obligingly kept his teeth behind his lips.

I spent about ten minutes with the big gelding, feeling the way I always do around a horse I like. Like I'm a kid. Untouched by the world and all my self-made problems. Nothing to cloud me, just the warm inquisitive presence of the horse. A lot of jocks don't spend much time hanging out with horses. To them, horses are vehicles for income and stimulation. Sure, they feel them on some level—they wouldn't be good riders if they didn't—but they're not prone to hanging around the barn much. To me, that's the gold. Horses are intensely social creatures. They're often frustrated at humans' failure to understand them, but if you just put in that extra something, scratch that special spot behind their withers, pay attention to what they're telling you, they let you into their world.

After socializing with Muley for a while, I headed home to change into jogging clothes. I walked the two miles to where I rent a basement from an insane Irish family. I hadn't been there in a while and Mrs. O'Rourke, the matron of the family, was hanging out on the glassed-in porch like she'd been waiting for me all week.

"Where you been, Johnson?" she demanded—not that I was tardy with rent or had perpetrated any tenant crimes. The woman was just nosy. She wanted to know about my life, hoping its hardships would make her own shine in contrast.

"I met a lady," I said, jutting my chin out a little, trying to indicate that this was no mere girl, but a lady, a class act, a woman worth bragging about.

Mrs. O'Rourke's eyes seemed to bulge more than usual. "You're not legally separated from that nice wife of yours." She curled her lip in disdain.

"She's not so nice. And no, I'm not legally separated, but that's just a matter of a very short time. Have a nice day." I turned and marched down the three steps to the basement.

I flicked on the overhead fluorescent, illuminating my little dungeon. The floor was strewn with muddy clothes and boots. In the corner was a twin bed with flower-patterned sheets, next to this a small pressed-wood dresser. Above it hung a Powerpuff Girls mirror, bequeathed to me by my daughter. There was one window and a tiny toilet and shower stall behind a curtain in the back. When I'd rented the place, I'd been so anxious to get away from Ava it had looked like heaven. Now, after the dilapidated glory of Ruby's place, it didn't seem like much. But I wasn't planning to spend a lot of time here.

I went right to the scale to see how much weight I had to get rid of for tomorrow's races. I actually kept my eyes closed then finally braved looking down. One-thirteen. I had to lose seven pounds by tomorrow.

I bundled myself in half a dozen layers of sweat suits and long johns and was sweating profusely before I'd even stepped outside to start on a quick eight miles.

As I broke into a jog, my body protested. After all the inactivity of last week, I'd made the body ride three horses and now this. Under normal circumstances it'd be nothing, but there was nothing normal about anything anymore.

I ran. Through the entrails of Queens. Past row houses and warehouses, marshland and shacks. I considered hauling myself all the way over to the Queens/Brooklyn borderline to check out the Hole, a place Ruby had told me about. She and a racehorse she'd been trying to protect had once been held captive there, in the Hole, a little cul de sac near some projects where members of the Federation of Black Cowboys had erected stables. Ruby's telling me about it was the first I'd heard of the Cowboys or this Hole of theirs and I was curious. Apparently, a fair number of retired racehorses are saved from grim fates and end up at the Hole where members of the Federation work with them patiently, calming them down and teaching them until they become mellow round-bellied horses even a child could ride.

Considering that my knees were about to buckle, my many layers of clothing were soaked, and I had already run four miles, I decided to visit the Hole another day. I headed home.

Mrs. O'Rourke was thankfully not at her post on the glass porch and I didn't have to contend with her scrutiny. I went down into my cave, peeled off my wet clothes and got into the shower. The water was rushing around me when I thought I heard something. I poked my head out and heard pounding at my door. I suddenly felt cold under the shower's hot water. The knock was either Mrs. O'Rourke wanting to give me grief or somebody far more nefarious wishing to do me harm. No one knew I lived here.

I didn't answer the door. I finished showering, dried off, and then peered out the filthy Venetian blinds. I didn't see anyone standing there.

I turned my cell phone on. Seventeen messages. I checked the call log. Fifteen from Ava. One from Ruby and one from Sal. I skipped through all the Ava messages since the only thing that mattered was if something had happened to Grace and, had that been the case, Ava would have left word with Henry Meyer or John Troxler, the trainers she knew I spent the most time with. I listened to Ruby's message—she'd heard I'd ditched Sal and was calling to check up on me. She was at work at the Coney Island Museum and I was welcome to come hang out with her there. Sal had left a grouchy message offering his services again. Services that I considered more seriously in light of the knock at the door. I decided to at least call him. He picked up before it even rang.

"You all right?" he barked into the phone. I could hear a loud string section swelling behind him. Didn't sound like Beethoven though.

"Fine thanks, Sal. Sorry if I was rude earlier. I just needed to do my thing at the track."

"Good thing that didn't involve gettin' capped."

"Yeah," I laughed halfheartedly, "how you doin', Sal?"

"Good," he said, though it didn't sound like that was entirely true.

I told him I was going to get on the subway and make my way over to Ruby's.

"I don't like it," he said. "I'm coming to get you."

"By the time you make it out here, I could be at Ruby's already."

"As a matter of fact, I'm in Queens right now."

"You are? What are you doing?"

"Driving. Little problem with the wife."

"Oh," I said. I knew how *that* one went. I gave Sal directions to my basement.

"I'll see you in ten minutes," he said as a chorus of voices rose in the background.

I stared into the Powerpuff Girls mirror and considered myself. I had enormous purplish circles under my eyes and new lines etched into the sides of my mouth. I turned away from the mirror, packed some clothes into an overnight bag, and finished getting dressed. I then found myself drawn back to the mirror. I'm not a vain guy. I know I'm decent looking and women give me the once-over. But I've never spent a lot of time looking at myself and it was startling to see what was there. The man staring back at me was frazzled and his decently put together features were getting lost under a map of new wrinkles. The eyes looked haunted. Or maybe *hunted* would be more accurate.

Before I had time to get too macabre dwelling on my unsavory personal appearance, I heard a horn honking outside. I peered through the blinds and saw Sal's truck glowing red against the gray day.

As I hopped into the truck, I saw Mrs. O'Rourke come tromping onto her porch to see what the honking was about. The matron tolerated honking about as well as marital separation. I think she shouted something at me but Sal's window was down and the music was blisteringly loud. It was some sort of opera and it drowned out whatever recriminations were issuing from Mrs. O'Rourke.

I got into the truck and settled into the passenger seat.

"Thanks, Sal," I shouted over the music.

"No problem," he shouted back.

He drove.

We made it to Surf Avenue in no time at all. The Cyclone roller coaster stood steely gray against the matching sky. Sal found a parking spot right in front of the museum entrance. He checked in his rearview mirror, presumably scanning for hit men. He craned his thick neck and looked all around the vehicle.

"I'll come up with you for a while," he told me.

We climbed the dark narrow stairs leading to the museum. The place smelled musty and a little salty. The paint was peeling like sunburned skin off the ancient walls of the hall.

The sight of Ruby gave me an electrical charge. She was an ember in the museum's dimness. She was wearing her red fake fur coat thrown over her shoulders and her hair was spilling down wildly. As she stood up to throw her arms around me, I noticed that her lower half was gorgeously packed into a tight-fitting black skirt.

I held on to her until we both started to feel self-conscious. It was only then that I noticed another woman sitting there on a stool behind the dark little counter.

"This is Jane, my best friend," Ruby said, making me think of a little kid the way she said *best friend*.

"Jane, this is Attila."

Jane offered a smile. She wasn't your femme fatale type by any stretch and she was too slender and elegantly boned to be called handsome. Her black curls were cropped close to her head and she wore no makeup. Ruby had referred to her as a natural beauty and I concurred.

Sal and Jane knew each other but there didn't seem to be any great love going on there. As I gave Ruby details of what had happened on the track this morning—Sal of course had immediately called in a report to Ruby—Jane and Sal seemed to pointedly ignore each other. Just as I was wondering if I should tell Sal and Ruby about the mysterious knock on my door, a strange-looking man came up the stairs hauling two big laundry bags.

He frowned at the lot of us.

"Hi, Bob," Ruby said nonchalantly. "Attila, this is my boss, Bob," she said.

Bob shook my hand. He looked like a diabolical clown. He was bald on top and wore the rest of his hair long. He was sporting pink-tinted eyeglasses, bright green pants, and an orange sweatshirt.

"Anybody come in?" he asked Ruby.

Ruby had told me that the Coney Island Museum wasn't

exactly a thriving emporium. During winter, sometimes only three or four people came in all day and usually just to use the bathroom—for which Ruby charged them a dollar. Ruby brought in her laptop and whiled away the hours working on her notes for the book she and Bob were thinking of writing about the history of Coney Island. The only existing histories were dated and one of them was out of print. And both Bob and Ruby were passionate about their seedy home's history.

"Two German guys from Berlin," she told Bob now. "We did all right," she said, opening the cash drawer and showing him a little stack of twenties, "they bought three copies of *Sodom by the Sea* and a shitload of mugs and T-shirts."

"Nice," Bob beamed at her, revealing a row of irregular but white teeth.

"I'm going to throw my wash in," he said, picking his bags back up and heading to the front of the place. I knew he lived somewhere in the building. He'd bought the beautiful old structure fifteen years earlier for a song. He'd offered Ruby one of the empty floors, but the walls were full of holes and there was no way to sufficiently heat it, so she'd elected to stay in her own apartment.

Ruby and Jane had launched into some sort of discussion about yoga. I knew from overhearing some of Ruby's phone conversations with her friend that these two could go on for hours about intrigue and personnel shifts in the world of New York City's yoga centers. A world that, for all its promise of physical flexibility and spiritual equilibrium, was evidently as cutthroat and fraught with drama as horse racing.

Sal was getting restless. I had a feeling he wanted to tell Ruby his troubles, but not with the rest of us present. Eventually, he announced that he was going to go visit a friend over in Sea Gate, the strange gated community south of Coney.

"I'll keep my phone turned on if you need me," he told us.

Ruby and I both nodded at him. The big guy was hesitating though. His face clouded over and he shifted his weight from one leg to the other. Then he reached in his back pocket and pulled out his wallet.

"I'd feel better if you two went and stayed in a motel for a while till this crap blows over. I can give you some money."

Ruby and I protested both the motel and the money, but Sal insisted.

Eventually, Jane piped in. "It might be prudent," she said.

We all stared at her.

"Yeah?" Ruby squinted. "What about my cats?"

"Take them," Jane said.

"Yeah?" Ruby seemed to be warming to the idea.

She looked at me. I shrugged.

"Okay, Sal," she said, "we'll do it. Put your money away though. We're fine."

Sal grudgingly put his wallet back in his pocket. He contemplated us for a few moments longer then grunted his good-byes and walked heavily down the stairs.

"I think he's got a problem with his wife," I told Ruby after we heard the door close behind him.

"Yeah," she sighed and tilted her head, "he usually does. He's desperately in love with her. He's always telling me he never should have married someone he was that much in love with. Which is ridiculous."

Ruby frowned now, clearly miffed with this notion. I tended to side with Sal on the matter though I didn't volunteer this opinion. I'd been desperately in love with Ava and it had led to fifteen years of torture. I was crazy for Ruby now, but it was different. A little saner. Thinking about her didn't make my heart stammer with doubt.

Jane announced it was time for her to head back to Manhattan. She rose from her stool, stretched her arms out, then unceremoniously bent at the waist, put her palms on the floor next to her feet and wiggled her butt.

"Stop that!" Ruby exclaimed. Jane ignored her.

"She's always stretching in public," Ruby said, turning to me. "It's embarrassing and disgusting."

I didn't think it was either of these things, but I was a little surprised when, continuing the display, Jane suddenly propped her foot against the wall, at the same height as her head, then leaned forward, draping her torso along the extended leg. Ruby protested a bit more and finally Jane, her muscular kinks evidently dispensed with, began putting on her many layers of sweaters, coats, and scarves. She wrapped the final scarf, a brown thing with pink polka dots, around her head, draping it under her chin. She looked like a demented Russian farm girl.

After extracting a promise that Ruby and I would in fact go stay in a motel, Jane bid us farewell and descended the creaky stairs. At last, I was alone with my girl.

I folded her into my arms, nestling my face into her dark hair that smelled of cigarette smoke and salt.

"Wanna go to a motel, baby?" I said into her ear.

"Yes," she said in a soft voice.

"What about that place in Sheepshead Bay? You know, that weird little motel we passed by the other night?"

I felt her body stiffen.

"No," she said, pulling away from me

"Why, it's a dive?"

"No," she said again.

"What's the matter?" I looked down into her gray eyes. They'd turned black. Something I'd said had touched a nerve.

"What is it?" I asked, worried now.

"Nothing, just some history I have with that place. I don't want to go there."

"What do you mean, *history*? What, you stayed there with some other guy?" I was joking but she winced and I saw it was true.

"Oh," I said, feeling like a balloon someone had stabbed a fork into.

"We'll go somewhere else," I said quickly. "Don't worry."

She still seemed frozen though and I hated it. Hated that she had memories of another man. Memories that still meant too much to be spoken of. She'd mentioned an FBI guy she'd met when she'd saved that racehorse nine months earlier. She'd told me she'd had something going with the guy but she never mentioned how it ended or why. I'd tried to turn a blind eye to the whole thing. After all, I was technically still married and my unbalanced wife was calling me fifteen times a day. But the way Ruby had winced indicated that there was still a live wire there someplace. Hopefully, I could diffuse it soon.

I scooped her back into my arms and held her until I felt the stiffness leave her body.

RUBY MURPHY

11.

Counting Horses

Someday I may actually have to break down and learn how to drive. It's getting frustrating to have to take car services every time I need to get somewhere beyond biking distance. It's just that cars seem like bad magic to me. I don't entirely understand how they work and it strikes me as nothing short of miraculous that people aren't constantly careening into one another. I have trouble even being a passenger. I keep imagining trucks colliding with whatever car I'm in, sending me flailing, severing limbs, cracking my skull open. If I were actually driving the damned contraption, I would probably go into cardiac arrest. I realize it's profoundly un-American of me not to drive. But I never felt profoundly American to begin with. I'm from Brooklyn.

"The car service is coming in twenty minutes," Attila calls out from the living room.

"Okay," I say, but nothing is okay right now. At first, the idea of going to a motel seemed adventurous in spite of the fact that we're doing it to safeguard Attila from harm. Then, when Attila mentioned the motel in Sheepshead Bay that happens to be the place where Ed and I first slept together, it rattled me. I tried to get over it. I'm not, after all, doing anything wrong. I just don't need or want reasons to think about Ed.

I start throwing clothes in a weekend bag, then trap the cats in the bedroom as I go into the hallway closet to get the carriers out. Cats are not travel enthusiasts and the sight of their carriers usually sends them darting under the furniture.

"You okay?" Attila asks. He's sitting on the couch, looking at me.

"Yeah. Cats hate travel." I try attributing what must be my obvious low mood to worry over the cats.

Attila's not really buying it. "You don't have to do this, Ruby. You can leave town and forget you ever met me," he tells me, opening his vivid eyes wide.

"I doubt that very much," I say, putting the carriers down and walking over to him. He reaches up, takes my left hand, and softly kisses it. "Good," he says.

We look at each other for a long moment and I feel him reaching a place in me, a savage place filled with crippling lust and tenderness.

"I've got to finish organizing stuff," I say after a few moments of thick silence.

Attila nods.

I move into the kitchen where I pack up cans of Pet Guard and two catnip mice. I also bring my tiny portable coffeemaker. It's dangerous for me to leave home without it.

A few minutes later, I've loaded the reluctant cats into their carriers and Attila hoists Stinky while I take Lulu and my overnight bag.

THE WOODLAND MOTEL falls about twenty stars short of five. In fact, it's barely a half step up from a hooker hotel. It's a long tan vinyl-sided building gazing out over an ill-paved parking lot that butts up against the edge of bustling Linden Boulevard. Some of the room numbers are peeling off the doors and the two cars in the parking lot have seen better decades. East New York isn't known for its swank accommodations but the one thing this dump has to recommend it is that it's about halfway between Coney Island and the racetrack.

Attila pays the driver, then unloads the cats as I walk into the office to check in. There's a large woman sitting behind a bullet-proof window. She's avidly reading *TV Guide* and doesn't bother to look up when I walk in.

"Hi," I say loudly, wondering if she can hear me behind the partition.

She frowns, knotting a pair of highly unnatural-looking black eyebrows before finally looking up. Her eyes are tiny and dark.

She lifts her multiple chins at me which I take to mean "what do you want?"

"I called earlier, Ruby Murphy?"

She sneers slightly, asks for payment and, after I've given her my forty-nine bucks, hands me a key.

"Thank you." I smile at her. She frowns again and goes back to the *TV Guide*.

Attila is waiting outside, obviously lost in thought. He's staring down at his ungloved hands, picking at one of his cuticles. He doesn't seem to register that I'm here until I'm two inches in front of him.

"Where do we go?" he asks, looking up abruptly.

"Room eight," I tell him, taking Lulu's carrier.

Room eight is decorated in a disturbing brown. The pressed-wood dresser is brown. The thin bedspread is brown and the dirty wall-to-wall carpeting may have once been tan but is now brown.

As Attila comments on what a very brown room this is, my entire life suddenly flashes in front of my eyes. I begin wondering exactly how all my highs and lows and in betweens have brought me here. I can't say I ever had a vast plan. I never sat down and mapped out where I wanted it all to go. If I've ever had any calling in life it was probably to run away with a small traveling circus. But by the time I was old enough to do such a thing, circuses were few and far between. So I drifted. Then settled at Coney Island and took up piano. I get a lot out of both my home and my instrument, but sometimes I wish I'd made a plan. Problem is, I don't have an obsession the way Attila does. I want a horse pretty badly and sometimes I think I should go work at the track and get my fill of horses, but I don't know enough to be anything more than a hotwalker and that, I know from experience, is a pretty difficult and incredibly low-paying job. So here I am. In a brown room with an intensely appealing but disturbed jockey with a price tag on his head.

"Are you feeling low? Is this too depressing?" Attila is looking at me intently.

"It's fine," I lie. "Let me just get the cats settled."

I reach down and open Stinky's and Lulu's carriers. Their eyes are huge as they emerge. Lulu immediately darts under the bed while Stinky glances around, looks disgusted, and lets out a demanding meow. I get a dish from my bag and fill it with water from the bathroom sink. All the while, Attila sits on the bed, staring ahead.

I go over and put my hands on his shoulders. He looks impossibly sad. I can't say I feel particularly cheerful myself. "I think I need a nap," I tell him.

"It's not that late."

"I know. I'm tired though."

He frowns slightly. The truth is I just need to shut the world out and I suppose Attila knows this. I grab my toothbrush and face cream from my bag and go into the bathroom. At least the bathroom isn't brown. I stay in there awhile. I brush my teeth even though I haven't eaten anything in a long time and I'm starting to feel starved. When I was growing up, both my mother and father were obsessed with fat. They never carried an extra ounce of fat and lived in fear of doing so. Unlike Attila, they didn't have professions that demanded fatless bodies. They just didn't like fat. As a result, both my sister, Chloe, and I had phases of veering toward anorexia. We'd freak out if we saw anything resembling fat on ourselves. We were always hungry and avoided bread, sweets, and pasta like the plague. Then one day I realized I just wasn't fat and I ate again. I have some meat on my ass but it belongs there. Chloe remains underweight.

I stand at the sink staring at myself. My face looks a little hollow and my eyes seem huge. I look frightened and hungry. I suppose I am both.

I come back out of the bathroom and find Attila lying on the bed reading *The Thief's Journal* by Jean Genet. He picked it off my shelf one day and immediately became engrossed. The guy can read. In my time, I've associated with some distinct nonreaders but Attila's not one of them. He rips through books about three times as quickly as I do. I lie down next to him.

"I'm going to nap now," I inform him.

He looks up from his book and leans over to kiss me lightly. I kiss him back, then curl onto my side and close my eyes. I'm so weary I feel like I'm encased in cement. Stinky jumps up on the bed and comes to lie near my chest. I bury my nose in the fur of his neck and start counting horses, hoping to lull myself to sleep.

12.

Savage in the Heart

I was in Clove's stall, squatting down near the mare's hind end, feeling for heat in her legs. She'd worked her five furlongs in a thudding minute and six seconds and had galloped out lethargically. This wasn't normal. Even for an old claiming mare like her. I ran my hands down her cannon bone, then cupped her fetlock, expecting to feel a little filling or at least some heat. Nothing. I went over each leg. They were all fine.

Throughout my little inspection, Clove kept craning her neck to look at me. She seemed politely bewildered, happy for the attention but not sure why it was being lavished upon her.

"Why'd you work so dull, huh?" I asked the mare as I stood up and patted her neck.

Her ears shot forward and her eyes tried to tell me something but I couldn't for the life of me guess what. I started scratching her cheek. Her eyes drooped shut.

"What's the matter with Clove?" I heard a voice say. I turned around to find Lucinda, the exercise rider I'd hired to work my three horses for the duration of the Gulfstream meet, or until I finished up this particular investigation for the Bureau—whichever came first. As far as Lucinda knew, I was just some horse-loving guy who'd had an early midlife crisis and gotten a notion to train racehorses—and wasn't really up to snuff just yet—which made Lucinda and me a good match. She'd been an A list exercise rider on the New York circuit but a serious accident had taken her nerve. She'd stopped riding and had gone home to North Carolina. But, like any true horse person, Lucinda had gotten to missing the brutal hours, excruciating physical regime, and low pay of racetrack life. She'd come down to Gulfstream and some of the lesser trainers gave her a few horses to work each morning. She rode well. Had nice, quiet hands. Everyone said she wasn't the same rider she'd been a year earlier, but I hadn't known her then and she seemed to ride my horses just fine. I wasn't blaming her for Clove's dull work this morning.

"Oh, hi," I said, smiling at the girl. "I can't find anything wrong with her. Guess she was just feeling lazy. What did she feel like to you?"

"Hard to say," Lucinda shrugged. "She wasn't rank or anything. Seemed like she was into working. Just didn't have much in the tank. You really gonna race her?" Lucinda tilted her head and squinted at me.

"Yeah, I've got to," I said simply.

"You broke?" she asked.

"Just about," I said. I was running my operation with money the Bureau had shelled out but it was a point of honor: I wanted to make money, not lose it.

"Then drop her down to ten thousand," Lucinda said. "Either she'll get claimed or at least maybe earn a little purse money."

"Nah, I like her. I have hopes for her."

Lucinda rolled her eyes at me but smiled a little, which was nice. She was a tense girl. Intelligent, even pretty, but tense, as if endlessly on the verge of snapping. I'd almost never seen her smile, so I was pleased to have provided amusement—even if it was at the expense of my mare.

"You have hope based on what?" Lucinda said. "The fact that she can outrun some goats?"

I'd told Lucinda how I'd found Clove: living in a tiny paddock on a goat farm outside Wellington, Florida. At that point I had just arrived in Florida, had claimed one horse, Karma Police, out of a race at Calder Racecourse and was hunting around for two more. On the afternoon in question, I'd been heading to Riggs Farm, a small breeding and layup operation where there were a few older racehorses for sale. I was hoping to pick out two. I was driving to the farm slowly, taking back roads. I hadn't been down here long and was surprised at how rural and lush the area was. It was one of those days when the world, and particularly this little patch of Florida, looked lovely. The sky was cloudless, the temperature hovering just above seventy. I passed a wide flat pasture filled with goats. I'd never seen so many goats in one place and I slowed the car down even more. Which is how I noticed the sign. A handwritten sign duct taped to a railroad tie at the end of the goat farm's driveway: "Racehorse for Sale." Generally, you didn't go looking for racehorses at goat farms but what the hell. I pulled into the farm's driveway. There was a series of sheds and, off to the side, a small yellow ranch-style house.

I parked the car and got out. No one came to greet me so I walked toward one of the sheds. Suddenly, a woman with a pitchfork materialized from I'm not sure where.

"You Sonny Boy?" she asked. She was holding the pitchfork like a weapon.

"No, ma'am," I said. "My name's Sam Riverman. I noticed your sign about that horse for sale."

"Huh?" She dug her fingers into the pitchfork as if it were my flesh.

"You have a sign saying you've got a racehorse for sale."

"Racehorse?" she said.

"Yes, ma'am," I said, motioning to the road where the sign was.

"Oh that. That's Katrina's sign."

I waited for an explanation but none seemed forthcoming. Thankfully, a young woman emerged from the house and walked toward us. She was a sturdy, no-nonsense kind of woman walking quickly on short powerful legs.

"Can I help you?" she asked.

"I was inquiring about the horse for sale," I said.

"What about her?" The woman frowned at me. She wasn't a

great beauty to start with and the frown didn't help. Her thick eye-brows pulled together making her face look like thunder. I was starting to regret having come here at all, but I had a feeling if I tried to back out now the first woman would get inventive with the pitchfork.

"I'm looking to buy some horses. Saw your sign."

"Well, Clove is a bay mare. Eight years old. Fifty-two starts, five wins, and I can't remember how many seconds and thirds."

It didn't sound like I'd stumbled onto Seabiscuit, but it did seem like the mare might be in my price range. I asked to have a look at her and was somewhat begrudgingly led behind the sheds where I saw a heartbreaking sight.

The mare was standing in a paddock so small she barely had room to turn around. There were flies all over her and she was underweight. She didn't look up when we approached.

"That's her," the younger woman said. "My uncle Jimmy was running her at Tampa Bay Downs. He died and left her to me. I don't have any purpose for a racehorse," the woman said.

She opened the gate to the paddock and motioned for me to walk in. The mare finally looked up and that's all it took. She had the saddest eyes I'd ever seen. I knew that even if she was dead lame I had to buy her and get her out of there. I negotiated a price with Katrina as the first woman stood by, still clutching that pitchfork. Goats roamed, occasionally stopping to stare and bleat a little. I made arrangements to pick Clove up once I'd borrowed a horse trailer. I promised myself I would do this by the next day, so as not to leave that poor horse living in those conditions.

Clove definitely wasn't the best investment in the world, but she proved to be a lot more horse than I'd expected. She was completely out of shape and malnourished but she was sound. I took her to a cheap conditioning farm and left her there for a few weeks to get her ready to start seriously working. I went to visit her every day and was gratified to see her coming to life. After just a few visits she started recognizing me and would nicker when I approached her stall. Her eyes livened up as she put on weight and her coat started shining. When I finally brought her over to Gulfstream, she actually looked like a racehorse, had some muscle on her and had electricity in her body. I liked my other two horses just fine, but Clove was my favorite. And now, Lucinda was laughing at my mare—or at my blind faith in her. I suppose I couldn't really blame the girl.

"That was a slow time for her?" Lucinda asked, referring to Clove's dull workout, even though she knew damn well those fractions were terrible.

"A minute six would be slow for a carriage horse, no?"

Lucinda laughed, showing her small teeth. She was an attractive girl and she seemed to like me, maybe even be interested in me. I was stuck on someone else though. Ruby. I'd been a little stupid and, when the Bureau had sent me from New York down here to Florida, I hadn't initiated an official "relationship talk" with Ruby. We'd been seeing each other for a few months but I was deathly afraid of trying to pin her down. She'd always struck me as being savage in the heart. Untamable. I knew she liked me, probably even loved me, but I hadn't wanted to force her into any pronouncements she wasn't ready to make. And now, I could hear in our increasingly strained phone calls that there was another guy. And I was stuck down here under endless blue skies. And so was Lucinda. We chatted on about Clove and about my other two horses. We discussed the fancy French turf horse Bobby Frankel was running in a Grade 1 stakes later that day and I could tell from the dreamy look Lucinda got that she wished she'd get to work a horse like that. Or maybe she was getting dreamy over Frankel. Women loved that guy. He wasn't young or flashy but he was smart and funny and seemed to be the only wildly successful trainer who wasn't a soulless conservative creep. And what's more, he was good to his horses. Even though I was mistrustful of most trainers, I'd always had a good feeling about Frankel and evidently Lucinda had too.

I was enjoying my chat with her but I needed to get some Bureau work done. I didn't want to be abrupt with Lucinda though.

"Well," I said, leaving it at that.

She had her hands tucked into the front pockets of her jeans and she brought them out now. She started picking at one of her cuticles, frowning as she stared down at it.

After an awkward few seconds she looked up at me.

"What are you doing later?" she asked.

There it was.

"Well," I said carefully, "I think I have to do some work at home."

She looked embarrassed.

"Okay," she shrugged, then abruptly turned and walked away.

"I'll see you tomorrow morning? You're gonna ride Karma?"

"Yeah," she called out, without turning back.

I watched her walk away. She was narrow but muscular and moved with a slight stiffness that I guessed was a result of her accident. I noticed a groom from the next shedrow staring after her.

I felt badly for putting her off, but the truth was I did actually have work to do. The Bureau had sent me here to look into a sponging epidemic. Sponging was a particularly evil trick involving slipping tiny sponges up racehorses' nostrils before races. Basically impossible to detect unless you had the veterinarian dig up there. It's not like it had a fatal impact on the horses, just impeded their breathing enough to make them run lackluster. Could demoralize the hell out of a poor horse. And, of course, cause some pretty big upsets in the outcome of a race. It pissed me off—as did anything involving people doing shitty things to horses. I wanted to get to the bottom of it for the sake of the horses and the fairness of the game. The Bureau itself was wearing thin on me though. The horse-related assignments were great, but the rest of the Bureau business I could live without. For the most part, it was just boring as hell. And now it had pulled me away from a girl I'd wanted to try going the distance with. I'd had to pack up, put on a new identity as one Sam Riverman, former Xerox salesman, and come down here, to Florida.

I decided to give each of my horses a quick grooming. I rubbed Clove some more and then did the other two, Karma Police and

Mike's Mohawk. None of them were particularly noteworthy speci-
mens of the thoroughbred breed—although I liked all three of
them just fine. They were close to bottom of the barrel claimers but
they were all three sweet, well-intended horses. Which was good
since I was not only training them but cleaning their stalls, feeding,
watering, and grooming them as well as walking them off after their
workouts. The Bureau had dropped enough money for me to have a
few horses but not enough to hire any help, apart from riders.

I finished grooming Mike and put him away. I was planning to
spend the next hour or so attempting to get chummy with Roderick, head groom for Giovanni Corso, one of the trainers who, I was
pretty sure, was up to no good. Roderick, a huge redheaded fellow,
was slow. Developmentally challenged. Whatever the correct lingo
was. I didn't think he was actually in on any of his employers' shady
activities but I thought I might be able to learn something if I could
befriend him.

Before heading over to Corso's shedrow, I stepped into the tiny
office I shared with two other trainers. Those two had both already
headed home for the day since, unlike me, they could afford to pay
someone to feed their string at night.

I walked into the sour, windowless office and turned on the
overhead fluorescent. I glanced into the little mirror hanging above
the desk. One of the other trainers, Gerald, was a real lady-killer
and spent a lot more time checking his hair and sunglasses than he
did training his horses. The mirror was his. And I can't say I liked
what it showed me. I'd had to change my appearance for the assignment and this had meant growing facial hair. It made me feel dirty
all the time and I don't think it did wonders for my looks. I looked
like some kind of fucking hippie.

I sat down in the straight-backed chair and stared at the phone
for a few minutes. Eventually, I picked it up and dialed. On the
fourth ring, Ruby's machine came on, telling me she couldn't get to
the phone but to please leave good messages. I wanted to hang up
but didn't.

"Ruby, it's Ed. Just saying hi. Call my cell when you have a chance."

I hung up.

The overhead fluorescent was throbbing like a migraine. I locked the office and made my way toward Corso's barn. A radio was blaring light jazz. The music rendered all the more vapid by the volume. An old man limped along next to a chestnut horse. Though the old guy had a stud chain running under the horse's lip, the chestnut was pulling the man, leading him to specific patches of grass that the horse would then nibble at lightly before taking offense, picking his head up, and pulling the old guy a few feet farther to a different patch of grass. The man seemed fine with letting the horse pull him around. Probably relieved at not having to decide where to go anymore.

I found Roderick in front of Corso's shedrow, hanging bandages out to dry. I watched him carefully pull all the wrinkles out of the wet bandages then make sure they were all hanging evenly. He stood back to examine his handiwork.

"Roderick," I accosted him, "how's it going?"

He turned to look at me. He was frowning and didn't seem to remember that we'd met in the cafeteria a few days earlier.

"I'm Sam. Sam Riverman? Met you in the cafeteria a few days ago? I got a little string of claimers?"

"Oh yeah," Roderick said, less than enthusiastically.

"How ya doin'?"

"Workin'," he stated, letting his eyes skate over the whole barn area. It was impeccably clean. Sterile. No music. No cats or goats. All the dirt was raked.

"You want to get a drink later?" I asked him.

Now the guy really frowned and I realized I'd fucked up. He probably thought I was coming on to him. There are all kinds on the backstretch, including guys who'd hit on a slow-witted meatsock like Roderick. I should have been more careful. I guess I was losing my touch.

I tried to backpedal. "I don't know too many folks around here," I said, motioning around me. "I just got into all this. I'm hoping one day I can hire a little help. Word has it you're the best."

"Yeah," he said, cocking his big red head, like maybe the flattery had actually had an effect. "I got my hands full as it is and you couldn't afford me anyway." He laughed hard at this.

"Okay," I shrugged, knowing it was time to back off. "I'll see you around, huh?" I turned away from the big lug. And came face-to-face with Lucinda. She was all cleaned up now, wearing dark blue jeans and a vivid blood orange T-shirt. Her long hair was loose.

Roderick suddenly came to life.

"Hi, Rod," Lucinda smiled at him. I hadn't realized the two of them knew each other.

"Lucinda," he choked out.

"Sam?" She looked at me. "I thought you had work to do." Her eyes got smaller.

"I got an hour to kill before feeding," I said.

"Oh." She looked down at her feet.

"Let's have a drink," I offered, looking from Lucinda to Roderick. Lucinda agreed. Roderick did too. Which might not have been what Lucinda had in mind but it was fine by me.

We made our way over toward the track. The announcer was just calling the seventh race and we all listened as Birthday Suit and Alacrity battled neck and neck. Birthday Suit got a length on his nearest opponent and crossed the finish line first.

"I'd like to work that one," Lucinda mumbled, more to herself than us, but Roderick heard.

"He's one of Will Lott's. Probably ain't gonna happen. Lott's got Asha Yashpinsky. Puts her on all his big shots," Roderick said, looking at Lucinda earnestly.

"Oh, I know it ain't gonna happen, Rod. I can dream though, can't I?"

I listened to them going back and forth. Hoping maybe Roderick would say something useful but not really expecting it.

We went into the clubhouse, heading for the second-floor bar. It wasn't crowded. Most of the people hanging around were serious handicappers or low-end owners. A few heads turned when we walked in. I knew Lucinda came here fairly often to mingle with owners, trying to scrape her way back to working good horses. I didn't think she was sleeping with anyone to attain this goal. She wasn't really the type. Probably just talked to them a little, turning her big eyes on and making sure they got a good look at her ass when she walked away.

We took stools at the bar and we all ordered shots of Jack from Battle Annie, the brassy blonde who'd been tending bar at race-tracks since Secretariat's time. Battle Annie would be remembered long after most trainers, riders, and horses.

I put the shot glass to my lips, letting it rest there a fraction of a second, anticipating the warmth to come. I hadn't even realized I'd felt badly until the shot hit and my mood improved. Lucinda drank hers and pink bloomed on her white cheeks. She looked pretty. Ruby crossed my mind. I ordered another shot. The eighth race was about to go off and we watched the post parade on the monitor. Roderick and Lucinda discussed one of the entries. A filly facing the boys. I ordered a third shot.

A man with a red face sat down next to Lucinda. He was over-weight and looked rich. An owner. He was wearing a pink shirt that clashed with his skin. I could tell from Lucinda's body language that she knew who the man was and had willed him to sit there. As the owner started talking to Lucinda, Rod and I sat in silence, half lis-tening to Lucinda who was spending a few moments letting the owner think he was getting somewhere with her before steering the subject to his horses.

Eventually, Roderick announced that he had to get back to his shedrow. I said I ought to go feed my string too. Lucinda's owner had taken off. It was unclear if she'd accomplished anything with him.

"Want some help?" Lucinda asked me. Roderick's big face went a little slack. She hadn't offered him her help.

"It doesn't take long to feed three horses," I told her.

"I don't mind," she insisted.

We all three headed back to the barn area. Lucinda and I bid Roderick farewell in front of Corso's barn then made our way over to my spot in silence. The same old guy with a limp was still grazing that same chestnut not far from my barn. Lucinda greeted him. He smiled at her.

"Who's that?" I asked her.

"Old Bill," she said. "Hotwalker. Used to be an owner. His business went under and his wife left him. He showed up on the backside one morning going from barn to barn till he found someone who would hire him to walk hots. He was sixty-five then and this was a while back. Guy doesn't have any sense about horses. He's been stepped on and pinned against more walls than anyone I know, but he's never let a horse get hurt or get away from him."

I nodded in silent appreciation of Old Bill.

All three of my horses had their heads poking over their stall guards as they stared at me intently, ears forward, all of them too well mannered to bite at the air or kick the sides of their stalls.

"You got yourself three very polite horses," Lucinda remarked.

"Yup. Figured if I'm gonna struggle along trying to keep claimers sound and feeling good, I might as well get some with nice manners."

She laughed. She was sweet.

I gave the horses their dinner as Lucinda refilled their hay nets.

"I guess that's it," I said. "I'm gonna go home and do some paperwork."

Lucinda stared at me with those strange blue eyes of hers. It made me nervous.

"I'll see you tomorrow," I said. She nodded but didn't move. "Okay?"

"Sure," she said. She looked sad.

I turned and walked very quickly to the lot where I had my Honda parked. The shots of whiskey had already worn off and left a headache in their wake.

As soon as I got inside the car, I turned my cell phone on, hoping to find a message from Ruby. There wasn't one. The boss had called wanting a progress report. My cousin Erica had left a bubbly message asking me to call. Erica still lived in the old neighborhood on Long Island and periodically felt it her duty to call and bring me up to speed on the incredibly tedious neighborhood gossip, hoping this would make me divulge fascinating facts about cases I was working on. The girl couldn't get it through her head that what I did for a living was basically incredibly fucking tedious.

I got back to the unattractive complex where I rented a small apartment. Because this is Florida, even a low-rent complex like mine has a swimming pool, and this particular pool is not known to attract any great beauties. Willow Clark, the sun-ravaged matron who spends 90 percent of her life lingering by the pool in a string bikini that does nothing to hold back her tides of flesh, was in her spot and, as I came by, lifted extravagant sunglasses and eyed me.

"Hi, Sammy," she said, giving a little wave.

"Mrs. Clark," I said, shoving the key in my lock and retreating into my apartment.

Cat came and rubbed her tiger-striped body against my legs. I picked her up, scratched under her chin, and pulled my cell phone out of my pocket to see if a message from Ruby had miraculously appeared. It had not.

I opened a can of food for Cat and poured myself a finger of whiskey. I drank it down quickly, trying to kill the headache. I made a few notes on my pad about Roderick even though I really hadn't learned anything interesting. Eventually, I put a PJ Harvey CD on my portable machine. I can't say it made me feel much better but at least it didn't hurt.

13.

Darwin's Hiccup

I'd left Oklahoma three days after I'd taken care of business with the dirtbags that had abused Sandman's chestnut mare. It had been a big to-do in the town. The lady hadn't been lying when she'd told Sandman that her brother was the sheriff. And the sheriff didn't take lightly to someone blowing his sister's head off. They immediately launched a big investigation. Apparently though, the dirtbags hadn't told the sheriff about me and Sandman coming to take the mare back from them. The cops only paid Sandman a quick visit asking if he knew what had happened to the horse he'd sold those people. Sandman told them the lady lost interest and just gave the horse back. I guess that kind of thing happened often enough and Sandman was a trusted member of the community and so that was that.

As soon as the cops left, Sandman told me to split town and never show my face again. He never came out and said he knew I did those people in, but of course he did know. It was his shotgun that had done it and Sandman must have noticed it missing. I'd carefully wiped it down and taken it apart and put most of it in Dirt Stick Pond and the rest in Miller's Pond.

I packed my few items of clothing. I put Crow, the dog I'd rescued from the dirtbags, into the Chevy and we drove off.

I drove east.

I was not too far from Baltimore when I ran out of money. I got a job in a box factory. At night, I slept in the car with Crow. They wouldn't let me bring Crow in to work though so I didn't last that long there. I made my way to Laurel Park Racetrack and, after making a nuisance of myself awhile, finally found a lady trainer named Nancy Cooley who gave me a job walking horses off after their morning exercise. I moved into one of the dorms with eight other grooms and hotwalkers. Crow had to sleep outside but I built him a little shed and put my old sweater in it for bedding. Crow was happy. He'd put on some weight and his white coat was shiny and healthy. He'd been timid for a few weeks after I'd first gotten him but already he was coming out of his shell and people liked him. Things were okay for both of us.

Several months passed. Then a year.

I got promoted to groom and Nancy even had me rubbing a nice little stakes filly named Glassy Jane. She was a pretty chestnut filly, very calm and affectionate and basically a joy to look after. I still thought about Darwin though.

Finally, one day about a year and a half after I'd left Oklahoma, I found what I was looking for scouring the results charts in the *Daily Racing Form*. A three-year-old colt named Darwin's Hiccup had run second in a maiden race up at Aqueduct, in New York. My horse had just been named Darwin. None of this Hiccup business. But maybe there'd already been a racehorse named Darwin and the Jockey Club made them come up with another name. I dunno. They'd registered the little guy as Darwin's Hiccup. It was definitely him though. Listed his dam as Bubbledance and she was the one Sandman had told me about. The mare that had won a stakes race in New York.

The trainer for Darwin's Hiccup was a guy named Robert Cardinal. Right away, I started asking folks around Laurel what they knew about the guy. At first no one had heard of him, but then it turned out that my very own boss had actually been his assistant for a few months a long time ago.

"He's a good-hearted guy but he's had some shitty luck lately," Nancy Cooley told me in that no-nonsense way she had. "How'd you hear about him, Ben? He bringing a string down to Laurel? You gonna turn your back on me and go work for Cardinal?" She was teasing me I guess. She was a nice woman. Always paid me on time and never poked into my business.

"No, nothing like that, Miss Cooley, just he's training a colt I'm interested in."

"You're interested in a colt? What, to buy? You been holding out on me, Nester? You some trust fund kid slumming on the backstretch?"

She was laughing. Her blue eyes were sparkling and her choppy hair was sticking up more than usual, like it was laughing too. She was making me nervous though. I didn't want to tell her the story about Darwin and me since it would lead back to Sandman and Oklahoma and, potentially, my having killed those people.

"No," I said, "I've just been trying to pick out horses to follow and that's one that I decided to follow. I'm just trying to learn."

She grinned at me. Then patted me on the arm and bustled on down the shedrow.

I found the phone number for Aqueduct and called up asking for Robert Cardinal's barn. A mean-sounding woman told me he was stabled at Belmont. I called there and actually got Robert Cardinal on the phone. When I offered my services as a hotwalker, he gruffly told me he had all the hotwalkers he needed. I wasn't gonna let that set me back though.

The next day, I went into Nancy's office. She was hunched over a condition book, trying to find the right race for a problematic two-year-old she'd just been given to train. Her hair was drooping a little and she looked tired.

"Miss Cooley?" I said, because she hadn't looked up even though she must have sensed me standing there.

"Oh, Ben, hello," she said.

"I'm sorry but I've got to give my notice. I'm gonna go up to New York. To Belmont," I said, feeling sort of frightened but excited too.

"Oh? You got an offer up there?"

"Nah. Just always wanted to see New York."

Nancy Cooley frowned a little.

"It's a little tougher up there, Ben, you know. You're a good worker and I'd recommend you to anyone who asked but you might have a hard time getting hired."

"I know," I said, "but I'm gonna take my chances. I appreciate all you've done for me. I don't want you to think I don't. And I feel bad about leaving Glassy Jane."

"She'll miss you. I will too," Nancy Cooley said.

I felt a little embarrassed. I hadn't known she cared either way. Sure, I was good with the horses but so were plenty of people.

"That's nice of you to say, Miss Cooley."

She looked at me for a few moments then asked when I wanted to leave. I told her as soon as she could spare me. She shrugged and told me to give her a few days.

They were a long few days. But, on the fourth day, she told me I could go. She'd gotten Mary, a young girl just out of high school, to take over the horses I was rubbing. I packed up my clothes and waited till no one was around. I'd never said good-bye to anyone other than my mother and I didn't feel like starting. Even with the horses. Even Glassy Jane. She'd be fine and somewhere in her she'd know I was thinking about her. Crow and I walked to the parking lot where I had the Chevy parked and got in and started heading north.

As I got farther and farther up the New Jersey Turnpike things got uglier. Meadows and fields gave way to factories and swamps. There was more traffic than I'd ever seen in my life and the sky was filled with stinking smoke. Crow didn't seem to like it. He'd curled up in a tight ball and had long stopped looking out the window.

Eventually, we were in a line of traffic waiting to go through the Lincoln Tunnel and I could see the skyline. It looked like nothing I'd ever seen, even though I had seen it in pictures.

Once we were in the city, I didn't really know what to do. There was traffic and noise everywhere and people kept getting in the way of the car. Crow was sitting up again now, looking out, and he seemed as baffled as me.

We ended up sleeping in the car, in an outdoor lot. You weren't supposed to sleep in your car but I paid the guy an extra ten bucks and he let me stay there. I didn't sleep much though. Woke up before dawn with my teeth feeling mossy and my stomach rumbling. I locked Crow in and went around trying to find a working pay phone. I needed to call Belmont to get directions. Originally, I'd thought I'd wander around Manhattan a little but now that I was here, I just wanted to get out to the track. Only I didn't know where it was.

All the phones I tried were broken. Some of them had no dial tone, others didn't even have a phone, just a silver cable with wires dangling like veins from a severed neck. I finally found a working phone inside a tiny grocery store. I dialed the number I had for Belmont but there wasn't any answer. I tried three or four times and I could feel the guy at the counter staring holes in my back. I turned around and looked at him. He was a round, dark-skinned man drinking a beer even though it was barely past dawn.

"You know the address of Belmont Racetrack?" I asked him.

He looked at me like I was insane and told me to get out of his store.

The sun had come now, streaking the sky violent pink against the cold gray of the city. I went into a bagel store and bought bagels for Crow and me. Cream cheese on his, jelly on mine.

I went back to the car and the dog and I ate in silence, staring out at the weird world beyond the car windows. A pack of dark-skinned kids wandered into the parking lot and started looking at the cars. They were mostly boys but there was one girl who seemed like the leader. She was wearing a red down vest and skin-tight red pants that barely contained her body. She had a black slinky ponytail down to her ass and huge gold hoop earrings that danced when she walked. She shimmered toward my Chevy. I could see her skinny eyebrows knitting together, wondering what I was doing sitting in my car in a parking lot like that. She came to stand right in front of the car and leaned her forearms on the hood and grinned at me. Crow was growling low in his throat. The girl and I stared at each other like that and then she came around to my door and motioned for me to roll down the window.

"Whatchudoin' in there?" she said, jumbling her words together so fast it took me a minute to figure out what she'd said.

"I was sleeping. Now I just ate. Me and the dog," I said, motioning at Crow.

Crow had stopped his low growl and was just staring at her.

"Whereyoufrom?" she said with the words all mashed together.

"Oklahoma," I said and then wanted to kick myself because I'd decided I was never going to tell anyone where I was from lest it lead me to trouble.

"Gethefuckouttahere," the girl said.

She turned around, facing the half-dozen boys she had with her. "My man here's from *Oklahomahhh*," she said in a mocking drawl.

None of the boys said anything. They were restless, jiggling change in their pockets, punching numbers into their cell phones.

"Come on, Denise," one of them said.

"Suck my dick, Razor," she said.

It occurred to me that these kids might have firearms tucked under their puffy down jackets. Crow didn't look like much but he was fifty pounds of solid muscle and, the one time someone had tried to kick my ass at Laurel, Crow had jumped the guy and actually gone for his jugular. The moment I'd told Crow to stop, he'd stopped but he'd done damage. The guy had to go to the hospital to get stitches. After that, no one fucked with me.

Now, I figured if any of these kids made a wrong move, Crow would be on them.

"You know the address of Belmont Racetrack?" I asked the girl.

She squinted at me. "What?"

"The track, Belmont."

She looked puzzled.

"You came all the way from *Oklahomahhh* just to go to Belmont?"

"Yeah," I said.

"Shiiit," she whistled through her teeth.

"Kareem," she said, turning to one of the boys, "where's Belmont at?"

"Long Island," the kid said.

"Where on Long Island, motherfucker?" the girl asked impatiently.

"Out at the end of Queens. You gotta take a train at Penn Station I think."

"My man here ain't on no train, he got himself a vehicle," she spat. "Come over here, tell him how to get to Belmont."

"I dunno how you get there by car, Denise."

Denise was losing patience with her troops.

"Any of you motherfuckers know how to get to Belmont by car?" she said.

They all shrugged. One of them piped up saying he could ask his uncle. Denise pulled a cell phone from her pocket and handed it to the kid. The kid dialed. Pretty soon he was talking. Denise impatiently took the phone from him.

"I want you to tell my friend how to drive from Delancey Street to Belmont," she said into the phone before handing it to me.

I put it to my ear and listened to another fast-talking voice telling me a lot of incomprehensible shit. I pretended I understood it all so that maybe Denise and her friends would leave me be.

I handed the phone back to her.

"You got it?" she asked.

I nodded.

"All right then. You have a nice day, mister. God bless."

With that, she gestured at her crew and they all walked away.

By the end of that day, after getting lost a few dozen times, I finally made it to Belmont. The security people wouldn't let me in the backstretch though and I was too tired to think fast. I parked the car in a little lot behind a beauty salon and hunkered down for another night in the vehicle. My body was sore from sleeping in the car but now I didn't even care anymore. Darwin was in a stall somewhere on that vast backstretch and I would see him soon. I got in the backseat. Crow took the front.

I really needed to brush my teeth.

ATTILA JOHNSON

14.

In the Hole

When something bothers Ruby, she sleeps. Which is what she's doing now. It's barely eight P.M., and no sooner did we check in to our hideout at this somewhat sinister motel than she released her cats from their carriers, unceremoniously peeled off all her clothes, got under the covers, and passed out.

For almost an hour now she's been sleeping soundly between the cheap yellow sheets. And I've just been sitting at the edge of the bed, trying to read but staring into space. Maybe I'm thinking some things through. Maybe not. Sometimes it's difficult to know what's happening inside yourself.

Ruby's big cat, Stinky, is lying right near my girl's head, apparently unruffled by the new environment, but Lulu has been cowering under the bed since we first got here and I suddenly feel terrible about this. I get down on all fours and crawl under the bed, trying to coax the little cat out. Right at that moment, my phone vibrates in my pocket, startling me and causing me to bang my head on the bedsprings.

I curse, crawl back out from under the bed, and go into the bathroom, closing the door before looking at the phone. I don't recognize the number but I sense that it's Ava calling again. I put the phone back in my pocket and stare at myself in the bathroom mirror. The circles under my eyes are getting bigger and my crew cut is growing out, making me look like an exhausted rooster.

I come back out of the bathroom and find that Ruby has come to life and is sitting up, smoking in bed.

"You're smoking," I say.

"I am," she agrees. She keeps claiming she's down to two cigarettes a day—but I've already seen her put away half a pack today.

"You're going to come with me tomorrow?" Though she'd said she was planning to come to the track, with this apparent mood of hers hanging like a curse over the evening, I'm not sure of anything now.

She narrows her eyes, takes a pull on her cigarette, and then nods.

"Something wrong?" I venture, sitting down at the edge of the bed.

"Why?"

"You don't seem like yourself."

This statement evidently amuses her. She smiles, then reaches for me, pulling my head to her chest and cradling me as if I were a child. This gesture gives me a pang as it makes me wonder how my own child is doing. I wish I could just call Ava and find out, but any information she might yield about our daughter's well-being would be prefaced by an insane litany that I'm not willing to deal with.

"You don't seem like yourself either, Attila," Ruby says into my hair.

"I'm myself," I assure her, and then one thing leads to another, and, proving to each other that we are indeed ourselves, we start rolling around on the bed, dislodging Stinky and making the ancient bedsprings creak.

Once Ruby and I have climaxed and all is apparently well in our little corner of the world, we lie back with our heads resting on one pillow. I feel my eyes closing and, next thing I know, I'm being shaken awake.

"What?" I say groggily.

"You were screaming," Ruby says, bunching up her forehead.

"I was?"

"About a horse. You kept saying, 'Get the horse up, get the horse up.'"

"Oh," I say.

"What were you dreaming?" she queries. But I don't want to tell her. I was dreaming about an accident. An ugly one involving a great many broken bones. *My* broken bones.

"Don't worry," I tell Ruby.

She looks like she's ready to issue some sort of lecture but thankfully the cats start clamoring for food, blessedly distracting her from whatever was at the tip of her tongue.

Still naked, Ruby goes to forage through her duffle bag, producing two cans of Pet Guard which, she loves to tell me, is one of the few brands of commercial pet food one should ever feed one's cats. Not that I have any cats. Ava is allergic and my parents weren't animal people. How exactly they came to spawn someone like me—who feels sympatico with each and every living creature—I'll never know.

Ruby opens the cans, dumping the contents onto two paper plates. As the animals crouch and attack their meal, Ruby stands watching them. She has one hand propped on her soft, white hip and her hair is falling over her breasts. She looks like she's nursing a thought that I will never be privy to. I'd very much like to coax it from her but I don't think I'm in a position to press issues of secrecy considering that my wife is leaving me dozens of messages a day.

"I want to go to the Hole," Ruby suddenly announces.

"Oh?" I say. "Now?"

She nods.

"It's cold," I say simply, knowing she's as weary of the cold as I am.

"I know," she shrugs.

"That's why you wanted to stay at this frightening motel? To go to the Hole?" I ask.

"No, not at all," she frowns, "just it's one of the only motels I know that's sort of halfway between Coney and Belmont. I told you that. But since we're here, I wouldn't mind going to the Hole."

She looks determined and it's probably in my best interest to humor her. A few minutes later, we've both bundled up and are ready to head out. Ruby seems hesitant about leaving the cats though, like someone is going to break into this horrible little motel room to steal two aging felines.

"They're great cats," I tell her, "but I promise you, no one else considers them priceless."

This actually makes her laugh and I feel a weight lift off me.

The wind whips our faces as we cross Linden Boulevard and walk downhill onto an ill-paved little road. The glow of a half moon throws light over our surroundings. Disused truck trailers are stacked two high all along the road. Tall metal fences surround small barren yards. It's not exactly a bucolic setting. As we walk closer to one of the fences, I see that some of the truck trailers have been made into stalls. Hearing our footsteps, several horses poke their heads out over their half doors.

"I can't believe there are horses here."

"It's kind of beautiful, huh?" Ruby says.

I nod, though I'm not sure I agree.

"Hey," Ruby says, "I think Coleman's here." She indicates a light that is emanating from a stable about a hundred yards ahead of us.

We walk over and are greeted by two surly-looking pitbulls. Ruby starts talking sweetly to the dogs but this doesn't seem to soothe them much until an older black guy emerges from the ramshackle stable.

"Shush up, Honey," he calls to one of the dogs. "Who's that?" he says, squinting into the darkness.

"It's me, Coleman. Ruby Murphy."

"Ruby? Where the hell you been?" The man fumbles with the gate's lock, his big knobby fingers working slowly at the padlock.

He pulls the gate open and squints at Ruby, like he's still not sure it's her. His brown eyes are slightly milky and it's not until

Ruby is standing a few inches in front of him that his whole face lights up. He puts his arms around her in a loose hug and looks at me over her shoulder.

"Who's this you running around with?"

Ruby makes introductions but the cowboy seems wary of me.

"He's a jockey," Ruby tells Coleman.

This appears to elevate me slightly in the cowboy's esteem.

"Oh yeah?" He cocks an eyebrow at me.

I put my face into a pleasant expression.

"What kind of name is Attila for a white man?"

I smile and shrug though in truth I'd like to slug him. This is probably the hundredth time someone has asked me that question. Although the only other Attila I know of is Attila the Hun, who was, as far as anyone knows, a Mongol, Attila Johnson evidently sounds like a black man's name. People of all colors have asked me about it and the fact is, I long ago demanded an explanation of my name from the responsible parties—my parents—to little avail. My father would grunt and my late mother would get defensive. It is one of our family mysteries. No one knows what possessed my parents. They weren't hippies, intellectuals, or anything other than working-class white Southerners. My brother's name is Wayne and my sister is Susan. I was their last child but, since I have only two siblings, it's hard to imagine they'd already exhausted the list of conventional names. At one point I considered changing it, but eventually, I came to embrace it. Besides, by all accounts, the original Attila was an excellent horseman.

Coleman invites us inside his tiny barn. Horses poke their heads out in the aisle and appraise us with varying degrees of interest. As Ruby and Coleman talk, I visit with some of the horses and just zone out, not thinking of anything at all.

I snap out of my reverie when I realize that Ruby has led an Appaloosa out of its stall and appears to be tacking the horse up.

"What are you doing?" I ask my girl.

"That girl needs to get on a horse," Coleman intervenes irritably, like I have personally been keeping Ruby away from horses.

"You're gonna ride now?" I ask, looking from my watch to Ruby. "It's almost ten P.M."

"Lucky doesn't care," Ruby states.

I gather that Lucky is the horse and that I have no say in any of this.

I feel a sudden and complete sense of powerlessness. The one thing I felt certain of during this erratic week was the developing bond between Ruby and me. Now it seems like that's tenuous too.

I stand to the side, watching her tighten the girth on the saddle. He's no great beauty this Lucky. His head is a big square thing stuck haphazardly at the end of a thin neck. His body is small and not particularly developed, but the horse is well groomed and there's a healthy shine to his flecked-with-rust white coat. As Ruby leads him outside, I notice that Lucky's croup, the engine at the back end of him, looks good, like the horse could really generate some power if he needed to.

I follow girl and horse to a small riding paddock behind Coleman's barn. Coleman drapes his arms over the top rail of the paddock and I take a seat on a barrel nearby. To my right, I can see the towers of the nearest housing projects, looming there in the shadows just half a mile away. Behind us the traffic on Linden Boulevard is grinding down to a dull roar, its furor slowing as night advances. All in all, it's a damn strange place to be riding a horse. But Ruby is riding all right. She's completely transformed. Her face is smoothed of all the worry and her body seems to have melted into the horse's. Her legs are dangling, feet out of the big western saddle's stirrups, as she and Lucky slowly walk the periphery of the paddock. I can see she's getting him used to her, letting him know she'll do her best to be light with her hands and keep her body in alignment with his.

I've never seen Ruby on a horse and it does something to me. Over the years, working at the track, I've seen a lot of attractive women on horses but for some reason it didn't affect me the way this is affecting me. I can actually feel the undiluted joy flowing out of the girl. And Lucky is responding. Though at first he was holding his head up high, protecting himself from these unknown hands and the way they might pull on his mouth, already he's trusting her a little, dropping his head, beginning to use the muscles in his back.

She asks him for a trot and this seems to frighten him. He throws his head then goes into a fast choppy trot. Ruby brings him back to a walk and talks to him. The girl doesn't know much about riding but she can read horses. She asks him to stop and start a few times, does a few figure eights with him, then asks for a trot again. This time there's improvement. The little horse transitions into a smoother, slower trot that Ruby sits comfortably and I start gaining more insight into what attracts me to Ruby. Horses. She intuits them just as I do. And that's rare.

I pull my collar up around my ears. I forgot to bring a hat and it can't be more than thirty degrees out. I sink into my jacket, looking for warmth as I listen to the soft rhythm of Lucky's hooves striking the hard dirt of the paddock. For a few moments, I feel good, like all will be well in my world once more.

This feeling dissipates. Though Ruby's mood is improved after her nocturnal equestrian experience and we snuggle up close to one another in the bed, when my alarm clock goes off at four-thirty the next morning, Ruby is fractious.

At first, I attribute this to her not being a morning person. I find myself hoping that she'll come around once she's got some coffee in her. I try to be quiet and keep out of her way as she feeds the cats and drips coffee in the portable machine she's brought. I wait until she's ingested two cups of the stuff before I finally look her in the eyes. She's clouded though, unreadable.

"You don't have to come with me," I remind her as she begins to get dressed.

She looks up at me. "I know. I want to come."

I kiss the back of her neck as she puts on a pair of red mittens. She's unresponsive.

She's arranged for Big Sal to take us to the track and, as soon as we step out the motel room door, we see him there, in his glaring red truck. He has the window rolled down and some very gloomy-sounding opera is wafting from the truck's stereo.

"Morning, kids," he greets us, evidently pumped up on coffee and music.

Ruby gets in first, mumbles a hello and asks to stop at the nearest coffee shop for more fuel. I wedge myself between Ruby and the truck door and proceed to leave Big Sal and Ruby to their own conversational devices as I start going into *the zone*, beginning to get my mind clear and focused for riding.

As soon as we get to the backside, I start to feel a good deal lighter. Ruby is still acting strangely and Big Sal saw fit to keep blaring the morbid opera all the way out here, but in a few minutes I'll be on a horse. Not much else matters.

A HALF HOUR later I'm on Jack Valentine, working under lights since it's still well before dawn. The air is cold but crisp, cleaner than usual. Henry has told me to just give Jack a very gentle mile jog but the moment I pick up the reins, I can feel that the horse wants more. He takes the bit, letting me know he wants to go.

"No, fella, not today. Footing's still bad," I talk to him softly. He flicks his left ear back to better hear me but the right ear is keening forward, telling me he doesn't care about footing. I have to work hard to keep him steady and slow and my arms start to ache from the effort. Jack in turn is confused. He's basically a gentle horse— takes pride in his work and in pleasing the humans around him— but he's a racehorse, a thoroughbred, a descendant of Seattle Slew. He wants to run.

Around us, other horses are working at full speed and Jack wants to follow. I hold him. A gray colt blisters by, pinning his ears, saying something that only Jack understands. Jack seems offended. He pins his own ears and pulls on me. I talk to him. Cajole with my hands. He throws his head, bolts for a second, then feels guilty about this behavior and lets up a little, arches his neck, and puts in a few yards of soft, measured cantering. When we've finished, I can tell he still wants more.

"Sorry, buddy, not today. Soon though," I croon in his ear as I steer him over to where Ruby is standing at the rail. I'd actually forgotten about her for a few minutes. Forgotten to worry over her mood and the fact that she must be freezing as she stands there in the blackness of morning.

"He's gorgeous," Ruby says softly as she looks Jack over.

"He's a nice horse too," I tell her. She cracks a smile as she rubs the brown gelding's nose and coos over his expressive eyes. Jack seems to be cooing over her too. He needs to be walked off but Sophie, his groom, has a hard time pulling him away from Ruby. He's ruffling Ruby's hair, already trying to groom her though he's only known her two minutes.

Violet Kravitz is standing nearby. She appreciates anyone who appreciates Jack Valentine—who is the only horse she and Henry actually own—so she's quite warm to Ruby when I make introductions. The two women glow at each other and, a few moments later, as Big Sal and I head over to John Troxler's barn, Violet takes Ruby's arm and the two walk off, heads together, like they've known each other for years.

I stare after them for a second.

"I guess those two hit it off, huh?" Sal says.

I nod and bury my hands in my pockets as we approach John Troxler's shedrow.

Troxler is in a stall, removing a bay colt's night wraps.

"Hi, John," I call in. He glances up at me. Doesn't look like he's slept in days. His kind face is puffy and deathly pale.

"I'd like you on that Kissin' Kris filly," he tells me.

I nod. A tall order. The filly is only two and everything frightens her. I've only been on her once and I just couldn't find a way in. Every movement of my body seemed to shoot down into hers like an electrical shock.

"Laura's got her almost ready," John says.

I go to the filly's stall and look in. Laura, John's assistant, has the filly ready to go, but she is standing with her, talking to her in a soothing voice that doesn't seem to be helping much. The filly looks at me and her eyes seem to widen in fright, like she knows something terrible is coming. I put myself into a calm, almost dead state of mind, trying to make it impossible for her to find a trace of anxiety in me.

As Laura leads the filly out of the stall, she looks around and snorts. She catches sight of a tarp that she clearly thinks is some sort of filly-killing monster and she spooks, skittering to the left and nearly getting away from Laura who, the whole time, keeps talking to the filly in a soft voice.

It doesn't get much better on the track. Laura gives me a leg up and the moment the filly feels my weight on her back, she starts trembling. I take a very light hold of her mouth and ask her to walk forward. She takes a few steps to the side, then spins and crow hops. I struggle to stay in the saddle and, when she comes to a standstill for a moment, I close my eyes and reach for the filly's fragile mind. *It's fine,* I tell her, *I will not let anything hurt you.* She seems to take this information under consideration and finally walks forward in a straight line. When I ask for a trot, she puts her head in the air and flicks her ears back and forth, scanning for warning signs. I continue sending her protective thoughts and eventually she puts her head down. We transition to a canter and then a gallop and the filly drops lower to the ground. She finally becomes focused, interested in learning how to be a racehorse. Ahead, dawn is beginning to stain the edge of the sky.

15.

Symptoms

Within five minutes of meeting me, Violet Kravitz grabbed my elbow, steered me away from the rail of the track, and brought me to her shedrow. Right now, she's installed me in a remarkably uncomfortable chair in the barn office and she's furiously digging through the desk drawers, searching for I'm not sure what. With her tiny spectacles, long graying hair, and layers of flowing clothing, she looks more like the poster woman for some genteel English soap than a racetracker. But horse people are born of contradictions.

"I'm sorry, Ruby," she says after a few moments of diabolical foraging. "There's something I must find at once."

I don't know what it is she so fiercely needs to find, and she's not volunteering this information so I try to get comfortable and just soak in the soothing sounds of the stable area.

After a few moments, Violet finally locates some tattered Thoro-Graph sheets and becomes engrossed in reading over some statistics.

"I'm just trying to figure out what Jack Valentine will face in this race on Friday," Violet says when she looks up and sees me watching her.

Eventually, she sets the sheets down, wipes a strand of hair from her eyes, and levels a firm blue gaze at me. "So," she says. "You are involved with Attila."

I'm taken aback. Though at least she didn't call him *the jockey*.

"Yes," I say, suddenly wondering if Violet is a close friend of Attila's ex.

"His taste is improving," she states, smiling. "I was never a fan of the wife."

"What's she like?" I ask, maybe too eagerly.

"Oh . . . difficult . . ." Violet lets out.

"Oh."

"But so is he. You realize that?"

"Sure."

"No, obviously you have no idea."

"What do you mean?"

"You've dated racetrackers before?"

"Sort of," I say, figuring Ed Burke counts since, although he's technically an FBI guy, he was—and still is—posing as a race-tracker.

"'Sort of.' Well, dear girl, you realize that a life of horses is not something you choose. It chooses you. It *demands* you."

"Yes," I say, nodding, "I do know that."

Violet smiles faintly. "I never expected to be here, doing this." She motions around us at the dour little room. " I grew up in a very rural part of England. There were horses everywhere and I liked them immensely. But it certainly didn't occur to me that they'd one day be my life's work. In fact, I never knew what my life's work was. I married my first husband at a young age, and for a few years I was a housewife. But the husband was an idiot and I left." Violet shrugs, looks at me over the tops of her glasses, sees that that I'm interested, and continues.

"I worked as a secretary in an accounting firm in London for a number of years, then took up with a magician, of all things. He was American. Not a terribly successful magician. But he did earn his living from magic. I worked as his assistant. We traveled around the United States, attempting to enchant people. It was a strange life. One night, we were driving through a thunderstorm in Missouri when there was a terrible accident. He was killed and I had my skull crushed." Violet pauses and absentmindedly rubs her face.

"I was saved, obviously, but my face had to be reconstructed," she says, pushing her hair aside to reveal a large dent at the top of her forehead.

"I was in hospital for several months. I came to terms with losing Theo, my magician, but I had no idea what to do with myself. I was lost. I took a job as a secretary in Kansas City but it was a hateful job and I wasn't terribly fond of the city either. Eventually, I met a man many years my senior. He was terribly rich and not unattractive. He invited me to spend a month with him in Saratoga Springs, where he went each summer to follow the racing meet. I was thirty-seven by the time I first set foot on a racetrack but, no sooner had we watched one race than I realized that I belonged in this place. My liaison with the older man didn't last, but when New York racing moved back to Belmont for the fall meet, so did I. I took a job in the office at Belmont and soon afterward met Henry. I had never truly been in love before so it was dizzying." Violet is smiling now and looks impossibly young and happy.

"We married after a brief courtship. I was delighted to tie my fortunes to those of a man who had horses in his blood. But it hasn't been easy. We have very little money and it is often heartbreaking work. Both Henry and I love our horses very much but that alone does not make them stay sound and win races." Violet sighs.

"All of this to say—be wary of horse people, dear girl." She beams at me. "Particularly riders. They're a strange breed."

I figure I'm an equally strange breed and am about to tell Violet this when she beats me to it.

"I realize you're not a conventional girl. I issue these warnings because I suspect you, too, will turn into a horse person."

"Oh," I say, feeling flattered, "I don't have money to buy a horse and I'm a bit too much of a princess to start as a hotwalker and work my way up."

"Be that as it may, I predict you'll end up spending a great deal of time with horses," she says. She then narrows her eyes and sniffs at the air.

"Are you a smoker?"

I feel like she's asked if I'm a hooker.

"I'm trying to quit," I say.

"But you have cigarettes on you?" Her eyes light up.

"Yeah, a few, why?"

"May I have one?"

"Sure," I say, surprised. "You don't look like someone who smokes."

"Oh I don't. Not really. Henry lost his mother to emphysema so I only smoke very occasionally and never in front of my husband. I'd be immensely grateful if you'd loan me a cigarette though."

"Sure," I say, fishing for the pack in my jacket pocket.

"Oh not here." Violet looks terrified. "We'll take a walk. But first, I will introduce you to our string." Violet pushes her chair back and stands up. "Come then."

She takes a dark purple shawl down from a coatrack. She covers her head with this and opens the office door. Soon, Violet is introducing me to the fourteen horses under her and Henry's care. When we have patted many necks and glanced at many pairs of straight, well-made legs, she brings me to Jack Valentine's stall for a formal introduction.

We reach his stall just as the gelding is being led back in. The groom, a small, muscular white woman who's only wearing a long-sleeved T-shirt in spite of the severe cold, eyes me warily. Violet introduces me as her dear friend. The groom warms a little and reluctantly steps out of the stall, leaving Violet and me to ogle the dark brown gelding.

"He's a big one," Violet says proudly, as if she'd made him herself.

"What a face," I say, scratching the horse's muzzle as I admire his well-made head and expressive eyes. Jack starts gently truffling at my hair again.

"Aha," Violet says, noticing the gelding's tender gesture, "you've been approved of."

I smile at the lady.

"Well then, shall we take that walk we discussed?" she says in a stage whisper.

"Yes, of course."

We walk away from the shedrow. Violet scans around, presumably looking for spies who might report her smoking.

"Shall I give you one now?" I ask.

"No no, dear girl, no. I have a spot."

She leads us to one of the shabbier-looking barns. There are half a dozen horses stabled here but it's a low-rent outfit. The aisle isn't raked and there are no color-coordinated trunks and stall guards. We walk to the right of this barn and here, at last, Violet stops and extends her hand like a greedy child.

I give her a cigarette and light one myself. I watch her inhale deeply and slowly.

"Ah, it's awful but so delicious," she sighs, exhaling. "And now, dear girl, all about you."

"All about me what?"

"I have told you my life story and now I must have yours."

I am suddenly reminded of a scene in high school, when I met my first best friend, Bliss. She was a tall handsome redhead who seldom showed up for school, but somehow passed all her classes. She didn't seem to have time for her mere mortal classmates and I'd always been afraid of her until one day we encountered each other in the girls' bathroom. She asked if I had a cigarette and I gave her one. We smoked, talked, and promptly became inseparable.

I give Violet a brief biographical sketch, telling her that my life was similar to hers in that I was restless and didn't know what to do with myself. I tell her about nearly drinking myself to death before age thirty but then finally sobering up, landing at Coney Island, and calling it home. I tell her a little bit about last spring, when I worked as a hotwalker and, through a series of unlikely events, got to the bottom of a racehorse killing scam and was able to save a young colt I'd grown fond of.

"So it's true!" Violet exclaims. "You *are* a horse person."

"Oh I've always loved horses, yes. I've always felt like I could get inside their heads and feel them. I'm convinced it's the only reason I do well when I actually put money on a race. If I can see the horse in the flesh beforehand, I can usually guess how it's feeling and bet accordingly."

"You're in trouble, dear girl," Violet laughs. "Those are the symptoms."

We finish our cigarettes and I watch Violet frantically searching her pockets for a stick of gum to hide her smoker's breath. At last she finds the gum, pops it in her mouth, then asks me to sniff her hair.

"You don't stink," I assure her. "I probably ought to head back to the track and watch Attila ride," I add. I feel so at ease with Violet that I'm tempted to tell her that someone is trying to kill Attila. But I keep my mouth shut.

Violet and I agree to meet up for a sandwich later on and I head toward the track. I start to feel anxious again, worried about Attila's situation and not knowing quite what to do about it. One minute I feel like the unpleasant events of the last few days have all just been a coincidence, the next minute I feel certain someone is about to kill the man I'm sleeping with and that if I don't tell the police soon, I will, in a sense, be responsible if something bad befalls him.

I reach the rail of the training track and gaze out at the working horses and riders. I close my eyes to better hear the sound of their hooves pounding the dirt of the big sandy track. For a moment, I'm at peace again.

16.

She Run Good

I rolled over and almost had a heart attack when I made contact with another body. I was about to reach for my weapon when I realized the body belonged to Lucinda and that I had invited her to be here.

I sat up and looked over at the girl. She was lying on her side, turned toward me but sleeping at the far edge of the bed. She had one hand tucked under her cheek. Somehow, she looked weak in spite of her muscular body's obvious strength.

After taking a nap yesterday evening, I'd awakened feeling panicked. I'd put on clean clothes and had taken a quick walk to clear my head and think things through. The Bureau. My horses. Ruby. When I got back to the apartment I tried calling Ruby again. No luck. My facial hair was itching and I was lonely.

I called Lucinda. She sounded a little aloof but did accept my invitation to go out for a late dinner. We had wine with our meal. Whiskey after. I offered to drive her back to her place. We got into my car. She gave me a soft sad look, then tentatively reached over and brushed her lips against mine. I put my hand on hers. Her skin was rough. She kissed me again. Harder this time. I took her home with me.

She stood perfectly still as I removed her clothes. I tried to be tender. She was nervous. It was awkward and vaguely painful. And now, here she was. Sleeping at the far edge of the bed, as if afraid of intruding, even in sleep. She was naked and the sheet had come off the bed.

I went into the kitchen and put a can out for Cat. I watched her devouring the little brown squares of meat, then proceeded into the bathroom to throw water on my face. I looked in the mirror, watching droplets trickle from my beard. I realized that until now I had never slept with a woman while sporting facial hair.

When I emerged from the bathroom, Lucinda was sitting up. She had pulled the sheet all the way up to her chin. Her hair was matted, her eyes were puffy, and she looked frightened.

"Good morning," I said.

"What time is it?" she asked abruptly.

"Quarter to four," I said, motioning at the bedside clock.

Lucinda jumped out of bed. I got a good look at her back and the dark pink scar that was violent evidence of her accident. It was thick and ran the length of her spine. I felt my stomach knot up.

"You're looking at my scar," she said.

"Sorry," I said.

She gave me a dirty look, then went into the bathroom. I heard her running water in the sink.

I went into the kitchen and shuffled around. I made coffee, poached some eggs, and toasted four pieces of bread before Lucinda appeared. She looked considerably happier than she had upon waking. She smiled and looked around the kitchen. Cat had finished her cubes of meat, but was lingering near the bowl, licking her paws.

"I made breakfast," I told Lucinda.

"Can't eat now," she said.

"You can't? You have to ride though, you need energy."

"Nope. Slows me down," she said, shooting a dirty look at the toast.

"I'll watch you eat," she said, sitting down in one of the kitchen chairs.

I felt uncomfortable choking down my eggs as her eyes bored holes in me. She said nothing as she sipped black coffee. I tried bringing up a few topics. Who she was riding for this morning, Will

Lott's new turf mare, like that. Anything I said or asked was met with monosyllabic grunts. She evidently felt as awkward as I did. This was a relief, really.

Twenty or so minutes later we left my apartment together. She said she had some riding clothes in a tack room at the track and didn't need to go home.

I parked the car then walked Lucinda to Don Beach's barn, which was on the way to mine. The sun wasn't thinking about coming up yet but the backside was alive and thrumming. The radios were going. Horses were whinnying. Buckets were rattling.

"I'll see you a little later?" I said as we lingered there at the edge of Don Beach's shedrow.

"Yeah," she shrugged, not seeming to relish the idea.

"Everything okay?" I asked. I could feel eyes on us. One of Don Beach's grooms was staring. Within a half hour the backside would be talking about how the attractive exercise rider who'd had an accident and lost her nerve was sleeping with some claimer trainer with a beard.

"Sure, everything is fine," Lucinda said then turned her back to me.

I wasn't at all sure she'd turn up at nine to work my horses. Clove was racing and I was only going to walk her that morning but the other two needed work. I chastised myself for everything as I headed to my barn to feed.

My horses looked worried. Humberto, the groom who feeds for both the trainers I share the barn with, was already there, dispensing grain to everyone but my three. I greeted the stocky Peruvian man. He favored me with a grunt. He seemed to get along with the horses just fine but he didn't have any charm to waste on people.

MY HORSES WERE relieved when I dumped breakfast into their feed tubs. They'd all changed hands so many times before they'd doubtless had some very shitty handlers and missed more than a few meals. It made me a little sick to think about.

I stood in Clove's stall while she ate, watching to make sure she was cleaning up every last bit of her light breakfast. I didn't need to worry. She inhaled the stuff then rattled her tub with her nose, letting me know she wasn't pleased about the tiny portion.

"You're racing today, girl," I told her, patting her neck. She truffled at my sweatshirt pockets, looking for the treats I normally kept there.

"Sorry, girl. Not today."

I started taking off the wraps I'd had on her overnight. Her legs felt good. Cool, firm.

"How do you feel?" I asked her. For an answer, she put her nose back into her empty feed tub. I took this as a good sign.

I WENT ABOUT my business, mucking the stalls and grooming. Humberto had a salsa station going. It was giving me a headache but I didn't want to start anything by asking him to turn it down. My efforts to block the music out led me to worrying over Ruby. Why she hadn't called back. How I would sound to her when we did talk. If she would read my voice, my pauses, and know that I'd slept with someone else and that it had only made me miss her worse.

The morning stretched out under a bed of clouds that was turning the day humid. It was getting close to nine. The plan had been for Lucinda to work my two horses right after the track renovation break, so they'd have the best footing possible. My horses needed all the help they could get. But nine had come and gone and I was about to give up when Lucinda appeared. Her hair was pinned up and her chaps were covered in mud. She looked good though. Like she'd absorbed a nice portion of the speed and power of the horses she had worked.

"Hey," I greeted her, trying for a relaxed tone, like I'd never had any doubt she'd show.

"Ready?" was all she asked.

Though she obviously didn't have much to say to me, she communicated with Mike's Mohawk well enough. I sat in the grandstand with binoculars, looking on as the woman I'd slept with worked my horse. I'd told her to give him a slow two-mile gallop. His back had been bothering him and I didn't want to push him until he was a hundred percent. The horse wanted more though. Bobby Frankel's star four-year-old, the one that had won the Derby the previous spring, was breezing under much scrutiny from the press and half the backside. The big dark colt came up to Mike's flank, and my gelding fought Lucinda. Mike's Mohawk didn't know or care that he was a six-year-old Ohio-bred claimer. He didn't want the other horse getting by him. Lucinda battled with Mike for a few moments and finally got him to settle and focus and let the other horse blow on by.

Lucinda and I laughed about it later, after we'd worked Karma and put both him and Mike away.

"Nobody told Mike he's a claimer, huh?" Lucinda said, grinning.

"That's my horse," I said. I asked her if she wanted to get some lunch but she declined. I was relieved. Maybe last night would blow over like a mediocre dream.

BY EARLY AFTERNOON, there was nothing to do but wait around for Clove's race. The race was a seventeen-thousand-dollar claiming event for fillies and mares four years old and up. At age eight, Clove was definitely *up*. I'd fussed over the mare a lot already, there wasn't anything more to do for her and I really should have tended to some Bureau business but I just couldn't. I tried calling Ruby again. The machine came on requesting that I leave good messages. I hung up and dialed her cell phone. The girl hates phones but back a few months ago, when I was still in New York and could never track her down, I bought her a cell phone. Not that she ever turns it on. I was expecting to get the voice mail and I almost hung up when she answered.

"Yes?" she said. She must have known it was me, caller ID would show my number. But maybe by now she'd forgotten my number.

"Ruby, it's Ed."

"Hi," she said. It was hard to read her tone. I could hear familiar background noise.

"Are you at the track?" I asked, feeling a bit indignant that she'd be at a racetrack without me.

"I am," she conceded. "Are you?"

"Yeah, of course, where else?"

"You don't sound happy about it."

"I miss you, girl," I said, surprising myself by getting right to the point.

"You do?"

"That surprises you?"

"Oh—" She fell silent. I waited. She didn't add anything to that "oh."

"What are you doing at the track?"

"Watching some races. With Violet Kravitz."

"Who is Violet Kravitz?"

"Married to Henry Meyer, the trainer? Had Spyglass, that nice sprinter last year?"

"Oh. Right. How'd you meet her?"

"Long story," she said.

There was another pause.

"I miss you too," she said then.

My mood improved considerably.

"Yeah?" I said.

At which point Lucinda appeared out of nowhere. I think I winced at the sight of her.

"Look," I said to Ruby, "I got a horse running this afternoon, I'd better get her ready. You gonna be around in the next few days? Can I talk to you a little more?"

"Oh," she said, a weird tone in her voice, "there's intrigue actually. I'm not really around. But sort of."

"What?"

"I'll tell you about it. Soon."

"Oh," I said, feeling deflated.

Lucinda was looking at me. Her eyes were so dark they were impossible to read.

"I'll talk to you soon?" I said into the phone.

"Yeah. Soon," Ruby said.

And that was it.

I hit the Off switch and put my phone back in my pocket. I looked at Lucinda.

"I didn't get any lunch yet. Was wondering if you still wanted to eat," Lucinda said, her voice catching a little.

What with fussing over Clove and worrying about Ruby, I hadn't eaten either. I figured going to the cafeteria with Lucinda might put me in the path of Roderick or one of the others I was trying to establish contact with.

I found myself enjoying Lucinda as I watched her shoveling food into herself. When she'd refused breakfast this morning I'd suspected some sort of eating disorder, but, unless she was planning to trot off to the toilet and vomit, the girl apparently believed in feeding her healthy appetite. She was putting it away and, seeing the look of surprise on my face, motioned at her food, and said, "I don't store it, I burn it."

I could feel eyes on us as we ate. Obviously word had in fact spread about Lucinda and me. No one knew me from a hole in the wall but Lucinda had been a top exercise rider. Her accident—and her coming back from it—was the stuff of minor legends. People knew who she was and they wanted to know her business. All the more if it involved a low-rent trainer who couldn't possibly advance her stalled career.

As we left the cafeteria, Roderick accosted us. He was warm now. Evidently, my friendship with Lucinda had earned me points.

"I was thinking," he said, "you get so you need some help with your string, maybe I could give you a couple hours here and there."

"Oh yeah?" I said, trying to look pleased. "That'd be great, Rod, thanks. Course, I'm not there yet. Can barely pay myself. But it's nice of you."

Roderick grinned, though more at Lucinda than at me.

"I gotta go get my mare ready, she's racing," I told Roderick.

"Okay," he shrugged, looked at Lucinda from under his eyelids then turned and walked off.

Lucinda seemed oblivious to the fact that the slow-witted groom wanted to follow her off the edge of the earth. She also didn't seem to have anything to do with herself. I asked if she wanted to come help me get Clove ready.

"Sure," she said.

She was hard to read. Not that I wanted that badly to read her, just that I felt like I owed it an attempt considering our two bodies had pressed up close to each other.

FORTY MINUTES LATER, Lucinda stood at my side as I gave the jockey I'd hired, Sylvere Osbourn, a leg up onto Clove and led the pair around the walking ring.

"What you want me to do with her, boss?" Sylvere asked in a condescending tone.

Sylvere had been a very successful apprentice in his native Panama before coming up to the States to seek his fortune. He wasn't a bad rider but he refused to play politics and gave trainers and owners his undiluted and unsolicited opinion on just about everything. He'd have been better off having never learned English. There were plenty of riders who spoke not a word of it and thus couldn't get themselves into hot water mouthing off. It was all the same to me though, the guy could ride and he was the best I could afford.

"She likes to come from behind so keep her in back of the pack awhile but don't wait too long to make a move," I told Sylvere. I'd gotten hold of tapes of three of Clove's past races and had studied her preferences. I was hoping my conveying these to Sylvere wouldn't go in one ear and out the other.

"She's usually got enough in the tank to come wide though and she likes that better than waiting in traffic," I added.

Sylvere nodded but I wasn't exactly confident that he was going to follow my instructions. Of course, the way Clove had worked in a minute six, I didn't have any great expectations. I watched him steer Clove onto the track and meet up with the pony horse. Clove looked pretty lively, like she was excited about racing.

I went to one of the betting windows and put fifty bucks on her to win. It was a stupid thing to do but I had to do it. To her credit, Lucinda didn't bet my mare. Even though doing so might have curried favor with me.

"You don't think she's gonna do it, huh?" I asked Lucinda as we walked over toward the rail.

"She might," the girl said diplomatically.

The horses were at the gate now. Clove loaded in peaceably and stood well as she waited for the bell. A moment later, the gates sprung open and the twelve fillies and mares bounded forward. I checked the tote board. Clove had gone off at 40–1. Second longest shot on the board.

To my astonishment, Sylvere seemed to be following my instructions. He was letting Clove settle at the back of the pack. A small chestnut filly had set the pace and it looked fast. At the quarter mile the announcer called the time: twenty-two and change. Which was suicidal for a route race for claimers and, ultimately, would benefit Clove's running style. I felt a quiver of hope. Which shrank at the three-quarters pole when Clove was dead last, close to fifteen lengths off the leader. I looked away, pained. Suddenly though, Lucinda grabbed my arm.

"Look," she said, motioning wildly at the track, "she's coming on."

Sure enough, my bay mare was on the move. Like a damned bullet. Using herself so beautifully it looked like the other horses were standing still. She effortlessly passed horse after horse, and, with less than a furlong to go, she caught the pacesetter and pulled ahead, widening the margin to two lengths under the wire.

I felt my heart hammering my chest.

"She won! She won!" Lucinda was saying, in case I hadn't noticed.

This was my first win as a trainer. At 40–1 no less. And I'd bet fifty bucks on her. Not bad for a day's work.

Lucinda was still at my side as I walked out onto the track and grabbed Clove's bridle. Sylvere looked extremely pleased with himself.

"How you like me now, boss?" he said, grinning down at me.

I reached up and shook Sylvere's hand then led Clove into the winner's circle. Her eyes were huge and she was blowing pretty hard but her ears were forward; she was proud of herself. It was all I could do not to kiss the horse as I stood there, trying to keep her still for the photographer.

Once the photographer finished, Sylvere leapt down off Clove and, accepting a few handshakes from well-wishers, made his way to the jocks room to change his silks.

Lucinda was still glued to me as I led Clove back to the barn to walk her off and bathe her. I made a big fuss over the mare and she was clearly pleased with herself. She actually seemed to be holding her head a little higher and she had a new brightness in her eyes.

And then, as afternoon loosened and turned to evening, after I'd groomed and wrapped and lavished attention upon Clove and finally put her up for the night, I found myself with a great deal of nervous energy. I didn't want the electricity to end. Lucinda was still there. Raking the aisle in front of my horses' stalls.

I was torn. I didn't think I could please this girl even if my heart had been fully in it. And it wasn't. All the same, I felt like she'd had something to do with the beautiful hue of the day and I felt like I owed her something. I asked her to come home with me. She accepted. Not showing any feelings about it. Just saying, "Okay."

17.

The Comfort of Strangers

When I finally laid eyes on the little guy, my heart started beating so fast I thought it might come drumming out of my chest. Darwin was three now but to look at him, I'd have guessed four. He was rippled with muscle and built solid from the tip of his nose to the end of his tail. What had been just flecks of gray in his coat had taken over now. He was a rich, dappled gray. He looked like a racehorse even though he'd only run one race so far. He was fussing at his groom, giving the guy just enough of a hard time to let him know who was really in charge. I felt so proud of the colt.

By now I'd been lurking around Belmont for a few days and had finally gotten a job grooming for a trainer named Carla Friedman. She was a tiny chain-smoking gal running a small string of claimers and low-level allowance horses. Of course, I'd asked Robert Cardinal, the guy training Darwin, for a job. But he wasn't particularly friendly and said he didn't need anyone right now. I'd then looked for trainers with barns close to Robert Cardinal's. Which is how I'd found Carla. Even though I still didn't know much about racing, I could tell that Carla was unorthodox in her training methods. She couldn't afford to hire exercise riders so she galloped her own horses, in a *western saddle*. I'd watched her galloping a few that morning and it was the craziest sight you'd ever see. All those riders out there with their butts pointed in the air as they galloped and then here comes Carla, riding cowboy-style in that huge saddle, going full steam. She was the laughingstock of the backside but I knew from looking in the *Racing Form* that she actually won races sometimes, which, she'd told me right off, she attributed more to her knowing massage therapy than anything. She had been a masseuse—a people masseuse—who loved horses, and one day she just woke up with a bug up her ass and went and worked at the track. No one she worked for would let her massage their horses because they thought she was weird, but she worked as a groom and then as an assistant for a few trainers and eventually took out a training license. Apparently she'd rubbed some goodness into her horses because none of them were much to look at. Didn't move well and had obscure pedigrees. But Carla massaged the hell out of those horses and, in gratitude, they sometimes won races.

Darwin, I knew just by gazing at him right then, was going to win some races too.

I carefully studied his groom, making sure the guy was respectful of the young colt. I started involuntarily making that noise in my throat, the little chirping noise I used to make to Darwin, and though I was standing more than a hundred feet from him, I swear, the little guy heard. His ears suddenly shot forward and he abruptly turned his head in my direction, nearly pulling his groom's arm out of the socket. I started slowly walking over toward the colt. I was being real conscious about how I was walking and I was thinking over what I was gonna say to the groom.

"Nice-looking colt," I ended up saying. I was fighting with myself, holding back from throwing my arms around Darwin's neck and burying my face in that dappled coat of his.

The groom looked me up and down, like he thought I was going to *attack* him or the colt. After a few long, awkward moments, he nodded a little. He was a young guy, probably barely in his twenties. He was the right height to be a jockey but too stocky. Had sort of rock-musician long black hair and a nose piercing even though he was Spanish and in my travels I'd noticed Spanish guys were a lot less inclined to pierce things.

I don't know quite how I did it, but I got the guy—his name was Petey—talking to me, warming to me a little. I guess when I set my mind to something, I can be pretty determined, and I *needed* for Petey to like me, *needed* to have access to Darwin.

"Yeah, the boss he got hope for this one," Petey was saying now, scratching between Darwin's ears—which I found slightly offensive because Darwin had always been fussy about his ears and I was upset that he was letting this pierced guy touch them.

"Yeah?" I said, trying to swallow my discomfort about that tender gesture between my horse and a stranger.

"Yeah, we're running him next week, I guess. Be his second start but he's barely three. February colt."

Of course I knew this as well as anything. That Darwin had been born on February 13. But I just nodded and looked mildly interested.

Eventually, when I'd gotten a decent eyeful of Darwin and felt I'd cemented the beginnings of a friendship with this Petey person, I had to head back over to Carla's barn and tend to things before everyone on the backside started getting suspicious about my lurking around Robert Cardinal's barn.

I found my boss in the horrible little room that serves as her office. Carla had company in the form of a thin blond woman who offered a smile full of teeth.

"Ben, this is my friend Ava," Carla said, waving her cigarette in the blonde's direction.

"How do you do?" I said, nodding at the woman.

For some reason, Ava giggled before telling me she was doing just fine.

I sort of got a lesbian vibe off the two women. I'd had a feeling my boss was batting for the other team and, while Ava didn't look particularly dykey, it seemed to me there was something between those two that certain folks would call unnatural.

Then, as if to prove me wrong on this theory, Ava invited me home that night, though not in a lewd manner. When she heard me and my dog were sleeping in my car, she insisted I come use her couch.

I guess I was pretty uptight about it. I don't like strangers, and fair-haired women make me nervous. My mother was dark-haired. The girl I'd dated in junior high had been dark-haired. I didn't trust blondes. But I did desperately need a warm shower and a good night's sleep, which I hadn't had in eons—and I didn't suppose Crow would mind sleeping in a house for a night either.

Ava lived in a narrow frame house with a patch of concrete in front. We entered through the living room, where there was a child sitting on a couch, watching TV.

"Ben, this is my daughter, Grace," Ava said.

The kid didn't look up, but that didn't bother Crow. He immediately jumped on the couch and started licking her face like she was his long lost mistress. Between Darwin letting that groom touch his ears and Crow instantly attaching himself to the kid, this was a day for disloyal animals.

"Where's Janet?" Ava asked the child.

Grace shrugged. Ava opened her mouth wide and hollered, *"Janet,"* causing a tiny curly-headed woman to materialize.

The curly-headed woman scowled at Grace then quickly explained to Ava that she'd forbidden Grace from watching TV till her homework was done but the kid had ignored her.

"I don't know what to do with her, Miss Ava," said Janet. She was a fortyish white woman with a Southern accent. She had beady eyes and I immediately mistrusted her.

As Ava and Janet discussed various household issues and the kid watched TV and my dog remained planted at the kid's side, I stood there daydreaming about how good Darwin had looked.

"You look so uncomfortable, Ben," Ava said, startling me. "Come, let me give you a tour of the house."

Apparently, while I'd been daydreaming, Ava had told curly-headed Janet that she could leave, because the little woman was fussing with her handbag and putting her coat on. No sooner had she walked out the door than Ava took my hand and guided me down the hall. I was very ill at ease and wanted to just take back my hand, get my dog and go. But I didn't. Ava showed me her bedroom and then Grace's room. The latter didn't look like a little kid's room at all. It was kind of austere. The only toys were some neatly arranged plastic horses.

I tried to make appreciative noises about the house even though I'd never understood why people expected other people to be interested in their houses. And this one was no beauty. It had a sad, claustrophobic feeling. As Ava showed me the small, depressing kitchen she seemed to feel the need to explain herself to me.

"I invited you here because you seem like a nice man and I hate to think of you sleeping in your car. I hope you don't think it strange. People tell me I'm too friendly," she said, laughing. "Must be that innate Southern hospitality."

"Oh," I said.

"I'm from North Carolina, you know."

"Is that right?" I said dumbly.

She laughed again.

"I never had the accent. Guess I wanted out of North Carolina the second I stepped out of my mama's womb and I must have vowed never to speak like a Southerner," she said as she led us out of the kitchen and back into the living room. "Funny though, the older I get, the more I miss the South. Maybe that's why I hired Janet as a nanny. I can't say I actually like the woman but something about her Southernness instills trust in me."

I nodded even though I was only half listening. As I looked around the living room, I noticed some win photos from Aqueduct hanging on the wall. I guess Ava saw me looking.

"My husband," she said.

It had crossed my mind to be worried that maybe Ava was interested in me so I was relieved to hear about the husband.

"He's a rider," she added. "We're separated though."

I looked toward the little girl, who was still sitting on the couch with my dog lying worshipfully at her side. Grace seemed oblivious to the mention of her father though. She was absentmindedly patting my dog's head.

"Looks like someone made a new friend," Ava said, but neither Crow nor Grace glanced up.

I guess I got a little more comfortable as the strange evening progressed. Ava eventually started pulling out containers of leftover Chinese food from the fridge and reheated their contents for dinner. It wasn't particularly good but I was grateful for the free food. As we ate, Ava chatted idly about bad weather, my boss Carla, and mortgage rates, as if she'd known me all her life. The kid didn't have much to say at all and to be honest, didn't seem particularly bonded to her mother, though she sure as hell bonded with my dog. When, an hour later, Ava started harping on Grace to get ready for bed, to my horror, the kid took Crow with her. Ava didn't even think to ask me if it was all right, so I just had to stand there, trying to look nonchalant as my dog's toenails clicked against the wood floor as he followed the little girl to her room.

A few minutes later, Ava handed me a blanket and a pillow.

"You'll be all right?" she asked, indicating the couch.

I nodded.

"Good night then," she said. There was sadness in her smile though I couldn't imagine I had anything to do with it.

I lay there for quite a while listening to the sounds of Ava getting ready for bed. She ran water in the bathroom and traveled several times between the bathroom and the bedroom. At last, I heard her bedroom door close. I hoped to hear Crow's toenails on the floor but I didn't. I lay staring into the darkness until I was sure that both Ava and Grace were asleep. I got up, walked softly down the hall to Grace's room, opened the door and looked in at my dog. He was curled on the little girl's bed, happy as could be. I went back to my couch, thought of Darwin, and eventually fell asleep.

18.

Ten Kinds of Trouble

It's a blisteringly cold morning here on the Belmont rail and I'm feeling useless as I try keeping an eye on Attila. Any number of deadly things could happen to him on the track and I wouldn't be able to intervene. All the same, short of getting on a horse and riding next to him, this is the best I can do.

I borrowed my wife's tiny binoculars that she bought when she went on a short-lived opera kick, which at the time I couldn't understand at all but now, thanks to Mr. Schoenberg, I have empathy for. I put the binoculars to my eyes and focus on Attila, who, between his bright orange safety vest and the fact that he's on the lone gray horse on the track, isn't hard to pick out.

I keep my eyes glued to man and horse for a few seconds then peruse the rest of the track. It's business as usual though, a bunch of horses and riders, all of them looking like they belong there. I put my binoculars down for a minute and fish for a piece of gum in my jacket. I don't even like gum but lately I've been wanting to smoke so I guess gum is better than putting the old poisons back in the old lungs. I'm just starting to get morbid, thinking of my wife's crazy hormonal desire for me to knock her up, when an excited Attila is suddenly right in front of me.

"You see him go?" he yells down at me from atop the gray horse.

"Looked good," I say even though my attention was lagging, and in fact I missed the action, which is bad. I'm not much use to the guy if I can't even keep my eyes on him when he's on the track.

"Where'd Ruby go?" I ask Attila, wanting to cover my embarrassment at what a lousy bodyguard I am.

"Still off with Violet, I guess," he says, dismounting.

"With who?"

"Violet, wife of Harry."

"Oh," I say. "Whatya gonna do now?"

"Eat," he says happily, giving me a big smile. He hands the gray horse off to a girl with a ponytail.

I watched Attila "eat" the other day. Five cornflakes and half a protein bar. Which I assume he vomited up shortly after putting it down.

"I'll join you," I tell the jockey.

I follow Attila toward the backside cafeteria. We walk over to the counter where a brassy redhead—who sort of reminds me of an aged version of my wife—greets Attila.

"Where've you been, Johnson?" she says, offering a coy smile. "I've been waiting."

"Hiya, Dora," he nods to her, "can I get a poached egg?"

"Anything you want, baby," Dora purrs. "How you like your chances on Oat Bran Blues this afternoon?" she asks, resting her fists on her formidable hips.

"You know," Attila shrugs, "we got a chance."

"You got a chance? You gotta give me more than that, baby, I work hard for my paycheck." She keeps one fist on her hips while waving at the surroundings with the other.

"Then for you, I'll win it," Attila says. Dora grins at him.

Attila and I find a table and sit down. I watch him contemplate his poached egg and container of skimmed milk.

"You sure you're not hungry?" he asks me.

"Nah, I'm good." I lie because the fact is I'm starving but I feel uncomfortable about eating in front of this guy who subsists on air.

Attila stares at me for a moment then finally takes his spoon to the poached egg. He consumes the thing in two bites then takes a swig of milk.

"How you gonna stay alive on that kind of diet?" I ask him.

"I'm used to it," he shrugs. "You got a cigarette?"

"Cigarette? No. I haven't smoked in close to a year."

"Me either," he says.

"And what, you're gonna start back now?"

"Just wanted a drag," he says. At which I find myself launching into a lecture on the nature of addiction. How one drag will lead to one cigarette will lead to two will lead to two hundred. After a while, I catch myself and shut myself up. Attila is looking at me with wonder.

"Thanks, Sal," he says eventually, "I'm not gonna take it back up. Just a little nervous about this race today."

"Oh yeah? How come?"

"Wanna win it," he shrugs.

I'm getting the feeling there's more to the story here, that Attila is nervous about something other than the race. He's not forthcoming though and truth is I'm finding it hard to talk to the guy at all and am relieved when we leave the cafeteria and head over toward Henry Meyer's barn to look for Ruby.

The temperature seems to have dropped and the wind's gotten wilder, throwing straw and trash around. Everyone on the backside is moving quickly, ducking from the wind. Attila and I walk in silence and I feel myself sighing with relief when we get to the barn and find Ruby there, standing outside one of the horses' stalls, nuzzling with the beast like it's a damn kitten.

"There you are." Ruby turns to grin at us.

"I'm gonna take a nap in Henry's office," Attila tells her. "Wanna join me?"

I suddenly get embarrassed because there's something deeply sexual in that question and I look away, pretending to be fascinated by the horse Ruby was snuggling with. Actually, he's sort of a sweet-looking horse, has his ears pointed forward in a friendly way and has very gentle-looking eyes. I start to pet the horse and have become somewhat absorbed in this when I realize Ruby's talking to me.

"Huh?" I say.

"I was saying we've got to go over to Aqueduct in about a half hour. Henry and Violet already shipped Muley over a while ago. You want to give us a ride?"

"Oh, sure, yeah, I was planning on it," I tell her.

"Thanks," she says. "You like him, huh?" she asks.

"Like who?"

"Jack Valentine."

"Who the hell is that?"

"The horse, Sal, the one you're petting."

"Oh, him, yeah, seems like a nice horse."

I can see that Ruby is smitten with this horse. That's the thing with her, she's so goddamned enthusiastic. Makes you want to fall in love with her just to get a little bit of that enthusiasm coming your way.

I leave Ruby and Attila to their business in Henry Meyer's office and I head back to the cafeteria because the truth is, I'm starved.

This time, I notice a lot of people looking me over. Like I don't belong here in their little world. I don't suppose I *do* belong, but I'm hungry as hell. I go over to the counter, to the redheaded woman who was fawning over Attila. I order a burger but the woman's less chatty now that I'm alone. I think a lot of women figure that since I'm a big guy, I've got big appetites. In everything. And particularly in women. Females either come on to me like crazy or just ignore me completely. The redhead seems to be falling in the latter category. If she'd talked to me, I might have tried to sound her out, get a feeling for what kind of gossip is circulating about the jockey. But, like I said, she's not paying me no never mind.

I get a burger, a Coke, and a coffee and I'm just getting ready to bite into the burger when a young woman catches my eye. She has a broad, freckled face and a wild mane of blond hair. She's not overtly beautiful but something about her gets my attention. I assume she's some sort of rider since she's wearing horsey boots and has a smudge of dirt on her face. I study her high round ass as she selects a box of cornflakes and a juice, pays for these, then goes to sit at a table directly across from mine. I keep an eye on her as I down my burger and Coke. I watch her inhale her food in a few seconds flat, after which she sits looking forlorn, like she's deliberating about a second box of cornflakes but probably has to keep her weight down for riding. I have an urge to talk to her but I shouldn't. My wife may be a nutjob and maybe we're close to over, but still.

I am completely taken aback when, as I walk by the girl's table, she parts her lips slightly, smiles, and says, "Hi."

I guess I probably do a double take because her smile starts turning into an outright laugh.

"Hi," I say back.

"I've never seen you before," the girl states.

"Uh . . ." I stutter.

"Who you work for?"

"I don't," I say, gathering myself. "I mean, I don't work at the track."

"Oh?" She lifts her little blondish red eyebrows and I swear to God, I've never seen anyone look so cute lifting their eyebrows.

"I'm spending the day with a friend, he's a rider," I explain.

This warrants another "Oh?" and another hike of the eyebrows.

"Maybe I'll see you around," I say abruptly. I then hustle my ass out of there before I land in ten kinds of trouble.

I walk back to Henry Meyer's barn as quickly as possible. I keep my head down for fear the girl will somehow materialize in front of me. I finally slow down as I reach Henry's shedrow. As I look ahead to the barn aisle, I get a little confused. There's a person upside down. It takes me a minute to realize it's just Ruby, doing some of that yoga she does. Though why on earth she'd do a headstand on a patch of cold dirt in thirty-five degree weather, I'm not sure. The jockey is standing nearby, watching, and Jack Valentine, the horse, has his head hanging out over his stall guard, looking with interest at this instance of human folly.

"Hi, Sal," Ruby calls out.

"You're gonna get your head dirty," I say.

"No no, I've got a little rub rag down there," she tells me and now I notice that she's put some sort of fabric there under her head.

"May I ask why the hell you're standing on your head?"

"I was getting a headache," she says.

"Oh."

"We should get going," she adds as she starts slowly lowering her legs.

"Yeah," I say, "I know."

Ruby is facing up again now. She gets to her feet and swats at her hair a little.

"Feel better?" the jockey asks her.

"Yeah, I think I do," Ruby smiles.

I ask Attila if he noticed anything suspicious while I was gone and of course he claims he hasn't, but I don't trust the guy to be honest. Jockeys, from what I can tell, are more reconciled to the idea of death than the rest of the population, and Attila more than most. He just doesn't appear worried about having a price tag on his head. Me, I'd fly to fucking Tahiti and live in a hut the rest of my life rather than walk around as a target. But to each his own.

We make our way over to my truck and get in. Attila is quiet and I can sense he's preparing himself for riding. Ruby is quiet too. I drive.

I've never known why New York racing moves to Aqueduct for winter. There's not much of a stable area there and most trainers keep their horses at Belmont and ship them over on race day. Belmont is much more beautiful than Aqueduct, so I just don't get it. I decide to ask Attila about it.

He doesn't seem to hear me though and Ruby answers.

"It's 'cause Aqueduct has that all-weather inner track. It's got a special surface so they can run even when it's really cold. Plus, the paddock viewing area is indoors and race fans can stay warm."

"Oh," I say, and, since Ruby doesn't seem to be in a chatty mood and I don't want to break Attila's focus by putting on the Schoenberg, I start daydreaming about the exercise rider from the cafeteria. I keep seeing her in the back of my mind. Smiling. Lips parted. It's quite a vision.

We reach Aqueduct and soon we're all huddled around the stall where Henry's got Oat Bran Blues. I half listen to Henry giving

Attila his riding instructions for the race and, about twenty minutes later, I walk with Attila over to the jockeys' room.

We don't have much to say to each other and are walking in silence when I notice the exercise rider from the cafeteria right smack in front of us.

"Hi, Layla," Attila calls to her.

"Hey, Johnson," she says, nodding to him then turning to me and grinning.

Attila makes a quick introduction and Layla and I exchange a long look before Attila and I start walking again.

"Who's that?" I ask him, trying not to sound particularly interested.

"Layla Yashpinsky. Exercise rider. Nice girl. Got a sister that's the hottest exercise rider going."

"Oh yeah?"

"Yeah. Layla rides some for Henry and Violet now and then and she ponies a little too," Attila says.

"What's 'ponies'?"

"You know, the pony riders who escort the racehorses to the starting gate. She's some sort of a substitute pony rider I think."

"Oh," I say.

We've reached the jockeys' room now and, since I'm not allowed in, I leave Attila to his own devices and wander off to buy a program. I think about the exercise rider as I open the program and glance from it to the tote board. Attila's mount is one of the longest shots on the board. But I like long shots.

19.

Hush

Ruby hasn't seen me ride a race since that day, lifetimes ago—but really only three weeks ago—when we met here at Aqueduct. I'm still convinced I won that race because of her. Because of the way she stared so intently at old Ballistic. Because of her red coat and the notion I had before even speaking to her that her toenails would be painted bright red. And today I want to ride well. For her and for myself, to put myself at peace after the madness of these last few days.

Normally I might try talking to some of the other guys in the jocks room but today I just nod at everybody and keep focused. I sit down in a corner and work on some of the yogic breathing techniques Ruby's taught me, pulling air deep into my lungs and distributing it throughout my body. I sit with my spine straight and my eyes closed and after twenty or so minutes like this, I am very calm. By the time I walk out into the paddock, I feel good. I'm visualizing the track and what I've got to do to give Muley a good trip and a real shot at winning.

It's a cold day but it's bright and cloudless and, in spite of this being just another allowance race, there are a lot of owners in the paddock, several with their kids in tow. Sons dressed in conservative blue blazers. Little girls in shiny shoes.

I feel cheerful, almost optimistic as I go to stand in the center of the walking ring, next to Ruby and Violet, who are talking with a tall blond woman.

"Attila, this is Jessica Dunn, Oat Bran Blues's owner," Violet introduces me to the woman.

"A pleasure," Jessica Dunn says, extending a hand to shake. Her grip is firm and her smile is genuine. She's an elegant, kind-seeming woman who, Violet has told me, is a successful painter who one day got it into her head to buy a racehorse. Muley is the first horse she's owned and this will be his first start under her ownership.

"He's a fine horse," I tell her.

"I'm very fond of him," she smiles, and brushes a strand of long hair from her eyes.

I kiss Ruby for luck then walk over to Muley, who Henry and Sophie, the groom, have led from his saddling stall.

"Do your best," is all Henry says as he gives me a leg up.

I feel Muley quiver a little under me. The horse has a sensitive back and it takes him a minute to absorb the weight of a rider. I stare at his ears and talk to him softly, letting him do what he's got to do to get ready.

As Sophie leads us onto the track and over to Juan and his pony horse, I feel Ruby at the rail, watching me. Ava used to turn up now and then to cheer me on if she was having a good day. But I can't remember the last time Ava had a good day or even spoke to me coherently. And, to be honest, I don't want to be thinking about Ava right now.

Muley loads into the gate without fussing but then spooks when the assistant starter climbs up into the stall. The colt rears and I almost get pitched off. I've barely got my feet back in the stirrups when the bell goes off and the gates open. Muley takes an awkward step and nearly falls to his knees. For a moment, I imagine the worst but the colt gamely recovers and lurches ahead. He's a big colt but capable of using himself well and he's got some speed. He accelerates powerfully and in a few strides has caught up to the last horse in the pack. I keep a hold on him because, surging as he is, he's threatening to clip heels with the horse in front of him. I feel him fighting me. I click off the seconds in my head and calculate that the frontrunners are setting an honest pace and if I plan to really try to win this, I've got to catch up. Soon.

I steer Muley three horses wide to the outside of the pack and then let him loose a little. He passes two horses. We're coming around the turn now and I try to keep him as close to the rail as possible without bumping into a gray colt running to our left.

"Careful, junior," the gray's jock, Richard Migliore, calls out to me.

I ignore him. Bad enough he's calling me "junior" when I'm only five or six years younger than him, but I'm not even that close to his damn horse. I feel myself getting angry. Muley picks up on this and, probably thinking I'm mad at him, surges ahead again. By now we're almost around the bend so I let my horse go. He passes one more colt. I ask him to switch leads, which he graciously does at once, catching up with the two frontrunners now. Luis Chavez is on the favorite, a little chestnut named Saint Maybe who has his nose in front of a long-shot bay. I see Chavez look over his shoulder, watching me and Muley coming up to Saint Maybe's hind end. I hear Chavez chirp to his horse but nothing doing, Muley's on a rampage and we go flying by the chestnut, fighting the bay for the lead. As the bay's jock hisses at me to forget about it, our horses eye each other and Muley sticks his nose in front. The other colt fights right back. We're about three jumps from the wire and there's nothing between the two colts. I show Muley the whip and this pisses him off so much he surges one last time, getting a nostril in front of the other colt at the wire.

We've won.

I stand up in the irons and ask Muley to pull up but he's still angry about my showing him the whip. He's the kind of horse that knows his job and resents being reminded of it. Now he wants to teach me a lesson. I let him run another furlong before getting tough with him, pulling on him until at last he slows down. I turn him around and start slowly cantering back to the winner's circle.

As Muley winds down to a trot, I let myself look over toward the rail and sure enough, there's Ruby, grinning like an idiot. I smile at her as I pull Muley up in front of his groom and let her lead us into the winner's circle.

Henry and Violet are beside themselves telling me what a nice job I've done. Jessica Dunn is beaming at me. Chances are, everyone she knows told her never to expect to do more than lose money on owning a horse, so to win with her very first horse is probably beyond beautiful for her. Jessica reaches up, takes hold of my hand, and squeezes it. I squeeze back, glad to win one for a lady who seems like someone I'd actually like to be friends with. I scan around and see Ruby, standing next to Violet now. Both women are beaming like I've just won the Derby.

Muley shakes his head a little, wanting me off his back now that his work is done. I wait for the photographer to capture the happy occasion before hopping down. I tell Ruby I'll see her a little later then I head back into the jocks room to change silks since I've actually got a ride in the next race too.

"Nice work, junior," Richard Migliore says as I pass him in the hall.

"Thanks," I say, still not thrilled with the *junior* business but well beyond caring at this point.

I start wondering if maybe I can pull off another win. I've never won two races in one day, never mind two races back-to-back. I feel confident though, like anything is possible.

But a daily double is evidently not in the stars for me today. Two jumps out of the starting gate, I realize that my mount, Appellation, a seven-year-old claiming mare, is sore. She was a little stiff warming up but it seemed like the kind of stiffness that would pass. It hasn't. The old girl just isn't running well. I've only been on her once before and she wasn't the smoothest of rides then, but this is more than awkwardness. The mare is unsound. I start cursing out Nick Blackman, the hack who calls himself a trainer and entered poor Appellation in this race. I'm not sure how Blackman held the mare together long enough for the track vet not to notice the old girl was off. Maybe Blackman's paying the vet off. Who knows. But I should have been wary. I knew Blackman's reputation.

My good friend Richard Migliore happens to have his filly right next to mine.

"Pull her up, junior, she's gonna break down," he shouts.

He's right. I ask the mare to slow down and I pull her up.

A few minutes later, I ride Appellation off the track and hand her off to her groom and Nick Blackman curses me out. I curse him right back until Appellation's owner, an old man with a bad attitude, comes over. At this point, Blackman turns his back to me and starts drumming up excuses for the benefit of the old man who, of course, wouldn't notice if his mare was missing an entire leg.

I'm not sure how I brought myself to ride for Blackman at all. But at least I didn't let the mare break down on the track.

I skulk off, not caring what Blackman or the old fuck thinks of me.

I go back to the jocks room where I avoid eye contact with the others and change back into my street clothes. As I emerge, hoping to put the whole episode out of my mind, what is fast becoming a bad afternoon gets worse.

"Johnson," a voice says behind me.

I turn around and come face-to-face with a man I've never seen before. He's well over six feet and his upper body is massive. He has rust-colored hair and a flat nose smattered with brown freckles. He doesn't look like an easygoing guy.

"Yes?" I raise my eyebrows at him.

"A word about race five tomorrow."

I don't like the sound of this. He's using the same tone of voice that Tony Vallamara used when he'd come ask me to hold a horse back. And tomorrow's fifth race happens to be the one I'm riding Jack Valentine in. Even if I was up for fudging a race, this wouldn't be one I'd fuck up.

I look at the guy, waiting for the foul words to come out of his mouth.

"You're gonna have a little incident," the guy says.

"I am?"

"Yes. You are. I'll make it worth your while."

"I'm sorry, I'd prefer not to have any incidents," I say calmly.

"Is that so?" the guy says.

"Who are you?" I ask.

"My name's Fred," the guy says, not mentioning anything about Tony Vallamara or who it is that's interested in my holding back Jack Valentine. And it sure isn't Henry or Violet. They'd personally maim me if they thought I gave Jack anything less than my best. I start wondering if this Fred character is a cop of some kind.

"I just don't do that kind of thing," I say.

"Well that ain't what I heard," Fred says.

"You heard wrong," I tell him, turning my back and walking off.

"I'd think twice on this one, Johnson," the guy threatens. I ignore him and keep going.

I'M FEELING very low by the time Sal drives Ruby and me back to our little hole-in-the-wall motel on Linden Boulevard. Night is coming on like a curse and my mood is getting dark in spite of Ruby and Sal being so pleased over my win. Of course I haven't mentioned the episode with that creep asking me to hold back Jack Valentine. I need to think it through before telling anyone about it.

As we pull into the parking lot of the Woodland Motel, Ruby and Sal are babbling on about something to do with classical music. I hop out of the truck, listening to Sal issue a warning that we're not to stray from our motel room without him. I feel a tightness in my head and chest and I sense I'm going to blow my top. At Sal. At this motel in a strange wasteland of a neighborhood and even at Ruby, for having a friend insane enough to appoint himself my bodyguard. And then, just as I'm about to say something unpleasant, a black man on a white horse appears out of nowhere. Even though I know we're not far from the Hole, seeing a cowboy come riding off Linden Boulevard is so incongruous that I am enchanted.

Of course it turns out that Ruby knows the cowboy.

"Hey Neil," she says, smiling and going over to pat Neil's horse.

Sal's standing there, by his red truck, seeming to hesitate, like maybe the black cowboy and his horse are here to snuff my lights out. My mood sours some more.

"We're good, Sal," Ruby says, feeling Sal hesitating over there. "Neil is a friend of mine."

She makes introductions all around and I excuse myself, telling Ruby I'm going in to shower. I leave her to her little festival of weirdos even though in truth, Neil's horse looked like a fine old horse and I wouldn't have minded getting on him as a lark.

I let myself into the room, turn on the lights, and am almost tripped by Stinky, who launches himself at my legs. I curse out loud and I swear, the cat actually frowns at me. I feel instant guilt. I consider yelling out to Ruby to get in here and feed her cats but then I decide I'll try to change the tone of the evening a little and actually do something nice. I take two cans of cat food from the bag where Ruby's got her cat stuff. Stinky starts meowing and Lulu actually deigns to come out from under the bed. I put the unappealing gray meat into the cats' bowls and then stand back, watching them attack the food.

I go into the bathroom and start the water running in the tub even though the tub looks a bit dirty and I'd probably do better to shower. I've stripped down to my boxers and am about to close the bathroom door when Ruby finally comes in from the parking lot.

"What's the matter with you?" she asks.

"What? What did I do?"

"You're in a horrible mood."

"I am?" I ask innocently—though of course it's true.

"Was it something I said?" She furrows her brow.

I shrug.

"What's that mean? Was it?"

"I fed your cats," I say.

"I see that. Thanks. But what's the matter?"

"Nothing." I look away because I feel like I'm going to start crying.

I can't remember the last time I cried. Even when things were going terribly wrong with Ava and I knew Grace was affected by it, I didn't cry. Or the first time I held a horse back in a race for a few lousy bucks. I didn't cry. And maybe I should have. Because it's all catching up to me now. And I don't know how to tell her. This woman with violent red toenails. I don't know quite how I've ended up here with her or how to tell her what's wrong. So I just tell her I'm sorry and then close the bathroom door.

RUBY MURPHY

20.

The Sadness of Humans

Attila pulls the bathroom door shut gently, as if trying to soften the harshness of his refusal to talk to me. I stare down at Stinky as he inhales his food, oblivious to the sadness of humans. Lulu, who picked at her food and then walked away disdainfully, jumps up onto the bed next to me and bumps her head against my arm. I absentmindedly pet her and look around at the horrible brown hotel room with its soiled curtains and furniture, all of it evenly synthetic and appearing to have sprung from the thigh of some malevolent Zeus. As I let my fingers make little ridges in the soft fur of the cat's head, I suddenly realize I have to get out of here. Immediately. Though I feel like my being near Attila will keep him safe, I know that's not true. My presence isn't doing either one of us any good. I feel like he's shut the door on me in more ways than one and I need to go home and clear my head.

I shove clothing into my overnight bag and pack all the cat products into a shopping bag. I take the Yellow Pages from the nightstand and thumb through until I find a local car service. I call and order a car.

I'm ushering Stinky into his carrying case when my paramour emerges from the bathroom wrapped in a towel that was probably once white but is now a depressing gray.

"What are you doing?" Attila asks, looking at me with violently bright eyes.

"Going home."

"Just like that? Why?"

"I'm not doing you any good here and I really want to go home." I stand up and carry Stinky's case to the door.

"Ruby!" Attila shouts behind me as if I were fifty feet away.

"Attila." I turn around. "I have to go home. I need rest. I'm sorry." I add, softening, "We'll talk tomorrow."

"We will?"

"Unless you don't want to."

"I want to," he says.

He picks up Lulu's carrying case and the bag of cat products and brings these out, like he's suddenly resigned to my desertion and trying to hurry the process along.

I see the car service pull up in front of the motel office. I shout, trying to get the driver's attention. When this fails to work, Attila, clad only in his towel, sprints out into the parking lot, over to where the cabbie is parked. It's thirty degrees out and parts of the parking lot are frozen over but Attila doesn't seem fazed at all and I suddenly feel I've made a mistake. How could I lose patience with someone who'd sprint into a frozen parking lot in a towel just to save me from walking a few extra steps?

I'm dumbstruck. By Attila, by the fact that I'm so moved by the gesture.

As the cabbie turns around and pulls up in front of the room, Attila returns and stands in front of the open door, jumping up and down to warm himself.

I load cats and bags into the backseat. The cabbie frowns. "You bring animals?" he asks in an accent of indeterminate provenance.

"Cats. Nice cats. I'll tip you well."

He growls. I notice great tufts of white hair sprouting from his ears.

Attila has stopped jumping up and down and is just hugging himself for warmth. His eyes have turned a cold dark blue.

"'Bye," I say, ineffectually, "I'll talk to you tomorrow."

"Yeah," he responds.

I turn and get into the car. I give the driver my destination. He grunts and pulls ahead. I look back at Attila, who is still standing in the doorway, hugging himself.

IT TAKES A Herculean effort to haul both cats' cases and my bags up the stairs to my apartment. Ramirez has his door open.

"Ramirez," I nod, looking in at him. He's sitting at his kitchen table, staring down into an empty soup bowl. He has a yellow plastic flyswatter sitting by his right hand.

"Flying cockroaches?" I ask as I set the cats' cases down and pull my keys from my pocket.

"No," my neighbor says humorlessly, "just flies. I hate flies."

I can see he's not in the mood for conversation and I mentally chastise him for leaving his front door open when he's in a foul humor. I'm also slightly miffed that he doesn't seem to give a rat's ass about where I've been or why I took the cats there.

"Have a good night," I say, opening my door.

He grunts.

I turn back to look at him, feeling badly that he's so depressed. "Elsie will be back soon," I tell him, even though I have no way of knowing this.

"I sure as hell hope so," he says sadly.

I go into my place, release the cats from their cases, and walk into the kitchen to fill their water bowls. My apartment is a mess. There are clumps of cat fur all over the rugs, CD cases on the floor, and dirty dishes in the sink. I water the cats then go into the living room and sit on the couch. I hold my head in my hands and think. I stare at the phone for a moment then walk over to the piles of CDs. I tentatively pull out a recording of Schoenberg piano pieces played by Glenn Gould. Then opt for Townes Van Zandt instead. I'm about to hit the Play button when the phone rings. I stare hopefully at the caller ID, wanting Attila's cell phone number to appear there. But the little screen reads: *Hildebrandt, Jane A.*

I pick it up.

"Jane."

"Ruby?" She sounds surprised. "I tried your cell phone and it was turned off. I thought I'd just leave you a message at home. I didn't expect to find you there. What are you up to? Don't tell me you've got the jockey with you, attracting trouble."

"No."

"No?"

"No, I left him at the motel."

"Oh. Why?"

"He was being difficult."

"Ruby," she says sternly, "I thought you were going to stop being fickle with men."

"I was. I am. I'm not being fickle. He won't talk to me and I'm not doing him any good. You don't like him anyway."

"I haven't formed an opinion about him. I've barely even met the man."

"Well, I'm not being fickle. He puts me in danger and furthermore I think he still covets his wife."

"He's married?" she gasps.

"Technically yes."

I tell her what I know about Attila's marital status and about all other developments, including the accident on the track.

Jane is upset.

"Ruby, why are you doing this?"

"I'm doing what I need to do. Don't yell."

"I'm not yelling."

"Can we change the subject?"

"I'd prefer not to."

"Let's talk about Liz," I insist.

"What about her?" Jane asks. Liz, who I met last spring at Belmont when she was working as a groom, has become a good friend. Not long after I met her, she stopped working at Belmont and took a less taxing job at a riding school in Jamaica Bay. We've stayed in touch though and sometimes go to the races together. I was with Liz the day Attila came to find me in the grandstand and introduce himself. In fact, she's the only one who didn't disapprove of my dating him. She's long coveted jockey Shaun Bridgmohan—though she refuses to actually ever try to meet him since she's idealized him to a degree that borders on spiritual. Liz insists that watching Shaun ride is a nearly mystical experience for her. But she doesn't want to meet him and I think my dating Attila has given her some sort of vicarious jockey thrill.

One night a few months ago, I invited Jane and Liz and her young daughter, Georgeann, to dinner. Strangely enough, Jane and Liz recognized one another. They'd apparently met in college some fifteen years earlier. The two never really got to know each other in those days but, after being unexpectedly thrown together again, they've grown close and now seem to spend more time together than I spend with either one of them.

"Where is Liz?" I ask Jane. "I've tried to call her a few times and I've left messages but I haven't heard back from her."

"Oh, she went to Florida for a week," Jane says.

"Florida?"

"Yeah. I think she recently broke up with a guy and you know how she gets."

"No, how does she get?" I ask. I hadn't even known Liz to date anyone since breaking up with Georgeann's father.

"She likes to travel after a breakup—whereas you just take up with the nearest jockey."

"I'm not sure why you're being so spiteful today."

"I'm sorry," Jane sighs. "I'm just worried."

"I'm worried too," I admit. "I don't really know what the right thing to do is."

Jane offers a few suggestions, such as calling the police or the FBI or, specifically, Ed Burke of the FBI. I tell her I'll take it under consideration and, after a few more minutes, we hang up.

I look around at my messy apartment and, fearing I'll get permanently glued to the couch, I get up and walk over to the piano. It's close to ten now and Ramirez won't abide my practicing for long but I might be able to get in a couple of Bach Inventions. It's actually good for me to have to play within earshot of an irritable neighbor. He seems to complain a lot more when I make mistakes than when I get through a piece with a minimum of flubbing.

I sit down, and, failing to heed my teacher Mark Baxter's command to play twenty minutes of scales before doing anything fun, I launch into the first Invention in C.

I get through it smoothly, which is no great feat since I've been working on it for seven months. I'm about to try a more difficult piece when the phone rings again. I get up and walk over to the caller ID box, again hoping to see Attila's number there. *Florida*, the box announces, not bothering to tell me the caller's name though I know it's Ed. My heart rate accelerates. I pick up the phone.

ED BURKE/SAM RIVERMAN

21.

Radiance

I study Lucinda from across the breakfast table. She's looking down at the *Racing Form*. Her hair is hanging in two lank black curtains. Her nose is twitching as if an insect has flown in and is buzzing through one of her nostrils. It occurs to me that this isn't what I'm supposed to be thinking of a woman I've bedded on two consecutive nights. I ought to be seeing a glow around her. But there's no radiance coming from this girl and I don't think Lucinda actually even likes me much. We're just both lonely.

Suddenly, she gets up, goes over to the oven, pulls open the broiler door, and removes two pieces of maimed toast. She smiles as she deposits these on my plate. I stare down at the charred bread. She stares too and, after a moment, finds a knife and scrapes off some of the blackness. It still doesn't look appetizing.

"Thank you, that's lovely," I say. "Sure you won't have some?"

"I'm sure," she says.

"You're gonna ride Mike for me this morning, right?"

She looks at me. Her nose twitches again. "Sure," she says.

As I take a bite of charred toast, I reflect that something is obviously wrong with me. I know there are men who make sport of screwing women they're not that fond of, but I'm not one of them. I ought to be screwing the woman I do like. Ruby.

"What are you thinking about?" Lucinda asks me. Her dark eyes have gotten small.

"Ruby," I say flat out.

"Ruby? Who is Ruby?"

"Sort of my girlfriend," I say, immediately regretting it.

"Oh," she says.

"She's not officially my girlfriend. Lives up north." I backpedal a little.

"Well that's lovely," Lucinda sneers.

"I'm not trying to disrespect you, Lucinda. You asked what I was thinking about and I told you. I should have told you about her sooner. I wasn't sure how much you wanted from me. We're both just lonely, right?"

"Thanks a fucking lot," she says, pushing her chair back and standing up.

"Hey, Lucinda, I'm sorry," I say, but she's stormed into the bedroom and slammed the door shut behind her.

Moments later she emerges with her clothes on. She doesn't look at me.

"Lucinda, I'm sorry," I say weakly.

"Fuck you, Sam Riverman," she says, walking out the front door.

And now I feel like total shit. Treating people badly just isn't necessary. I hesitate for a minute, unsure of what to do. If I go after her she might think I care. Of course, I do care slightly. Just not that much.

I put my shirt on and go out the door. There's no sign of Lucinda. I don't know where she could have gone since she doesn't have a car. I go back for my car keys and, a minute later, I'm driving out of the complex. Within a few moments I see her, walking briskly along the side of the road. I pull alongside her and roll down the window.

"Hey, Lucinda, get in the car."

"Fuck you, Sam Riverman," she says, and keeps walking.

"Lucinda, come on. It's not that bad."

She stops walking, puts her fists on her hips, and looks at me.

"You're a creep," she says.

"No, not really. We should have talked sooner."

She looks like she's considering reaching into the car and ripping my head off. Then her fury turns to a pout. A coquettish gesture I wouldn't have guessed was in her repertoire.

"Come on, get in," I say.

She stands pouting a moment longer then comes around to the passenger side and gets in.

"Why were you such a jerk to me?" she asks.

"I'm sorry, Lucinda, I wasn't trying to be a jerk."

"Well, you were!"

"I'm sorry."

"Okay," she says. Her eyes are so sad.

"Come back to the apartment with me while I get ready then I'll give you a ride to the track?"

"Yeah," she says, "okay."

I pull the car back onto the road, make a U-turn, and head back to my apartment.

A HALF HOUR later I've showered and dressed and fed Cat. Lucinda has spent the whole time at the kitchen table, reading the *Racing Form*.

"You ready?" I ask her, picking my car keys up off the table.

"Yeah," she says darkly.

I feel like if I try talking to her she'll reach in the kitchen drawer, get a knife, and stab me. So I say nothing.

She is quiet during the ride to the track. As we pull into the backside, I ask her again about giving Mike's Mohawk a workout later that morning.

"Yeah, I said I'd do it," she answers bitterly.

"Okay then."

"I'll be ready for him around nine," she says.

I drop her near Jack Jenkins's office, where she's meeting with the trainer to talk over a few horses he wants her working. She looks at me briefly, says nothing, and walks away.

Lucinda's hoopla has put me behind schedule. I'm half an hour late feeding my three horses and they look depressed. I think of the horse joke: A horse walks into a bar. Bartender says, "Why the long face?"

My horses' faces all look longer than usual.

I go into the feed room and prepare their grain.

I let them finish eating then I muck the stalls, clean the waterers and feed tubs, and start grooming Mike.

I've long finished wrapping and tacking up Mike's Mohawk and there's still no sign of Lucinda. It would probably be a good idea to find a new rider for my string but I've already made the poor girl feel like shit, no need to add to it. Particularly since she's hypersensitive about her riding skills.

By the time nine-thirty rolls around, I'm feeling frustrated. My horse needs his work and the girl did say she'd ride him. I go walking off to look for her and am storming around, eliciting curious looks from grooms as I poke my head in at various shedrows. I'm about to turn and head back to my barn when I see Sebastian Ives, a groom who worked for me in my previous incarnation as an assistant trainer up at Belmont. He's walking a liver chestnut horse in front of a very well kept barn. I duck my head to avoid his noticing me. He knows I'm a Fed and though I look different, Sebastian and I worked side by side for four months and he might well recognize me just by my walk. Just as I'm passing him, he stares right at me. I quickly look away.

"Hey!" the thin black man calls after me.

I keep walking, feeling shitty about it because I liked the man a great deal. From the looks of it though, he's doing just fine. Don't know whose outfit he's working for but the shedrow seemed very classy.

I go back to my barn and find Lucinda sitting in a plastic chair she's pulled over in front of Mike's stall. She's a little dirtied up from riding and has her hair pulled back in a ponytail. She's drumming her long fingers on the plastic chair.

"Hi. I was looking for you," I say, glancing down at my watch.

"Here I am," she shrugs.

"So. Mike. I want you to do a mile with him. I had the chiropractor work on him yesterday. His back should feel better."

I notice that Lucinda's giving me a skeptical look.

"What?" I ask, "plenty of people swear by it. Thought I'd try it. Seems to have helped."

"You gonna call the animal communicator next?" she sneers, referring to the occasional "horse psychics" who circulate at the tracks.

"Wasn't planning on it," I reply, a little wounded because the thought had crossed my mind. "What's the matter, Lucinda?" I ask, looking into her hardened eyes, "and don't tell me you're just mad because I have a girl up north. You didn't ask me anything. I didn't lie to you."

At first, her face tightens and she looks like she's going to hit me, then, she softens and lets out a small sigh.

"What is it?" I ask.

"I don't know. It's everything. Nothing is going right. Then finding out you're into someone other than me, that didn't help." She shrugs and seems so vulnerable.

"Well," she adds, "why don't I go get on that horse of yours."

I look at her for a minute, feeling a mixture of things. Wishing I could help her but not knowing how. Her face is set now, trying to tell me she's okay.

We get Mike out of his stall and, in what feels like amiable silence, head over to the track. Fists of cumulus clouds have invaded the pure blue of the sky.

I GO TO the rail and focus my binoculars on Lucinda and the gelding. Mike actually looks okay out there. He seems interested in his work and he's moving nicely, like maybe the chiropractor did help him.

I watch the pair start cantering and, after about a furlong, shift into a higher gear. They're going along nicely when suddenly I hear people shouting. I put my binoculars down for a minute and scan around. Then I see it. A loose horse, coming up right on Lucinda and Mike. I put my binoculars back to my eyes, trying to see if Lucinda knows yet. She can doubtless hear the horse but I'm not sure if she knows he's riderless. The loose horse comes up to Mike's rump and, to my horror, starts nipping at my horse's hind end. I see Mike shy toward the rail. I panic. I don't think Lucinda has faced anything like this since coming back from her accident and I feel my stomach knotting. I focus on her face, but I can't see enough to read her expression. It seems like she's keeping herself together though. She's slowing Mike down and it looks like she's calm even though the loose stud colt is still nipping at Mike's ass.

To my relief, an outrider finally catches the unruly colt and gets him away from Mike. In a few more moments, Lucinda has pulled Mike up and is trotting over to the rail.

Lucinda steers the gelding over toward me, and, as she comes closer, I see that she's grinning ear to ear.

"Hey, you okay?" I ask.

"I'm great," she beams.

"Yeah? You handled that well."

"I know," she says. "I got my nerve back." Her face is more open and relaxed than I've ever seen it.

"So you did, girl. So you did."

Lucinda hops down, tells me she'll see me later, then walks toward the grandstands. Probably going to make rounds, make sure the whole backside knows what happened to her out there and how well she handled it. I lead Mike back to the barn and find he's none the worse for the wear, even seems a little livelier than usual, like his misadventures made him feel important. Humberto grunts at me, "You okay, buddy?"

"Yeah, we're fine," I tell him, not sure how he could have already heard about the incident. Humberto briefly looks from me to Mike and back. Then he turns and heads to the tack room. A moment later, he's got the salsa blaring.

BY LATE AFTERNOON, I uneventfully finish up the rest of my horse chores, take care of a little Bureau business, and finally come home to have a long soak in the tub. Cat perches on the closed toilet seat, occasionally dipping a paw into the bathwater as if testing its temperature for me. I sink down low into the water, letting it come all the way up to my nose. I feel like several tons have lifted off me. Lucinda is going to be all right. It's unlikely I'll sleep with her anymore and it's even more unlikely that she'll care. I inadvertently helped her get her nerve back and there's a good chance that's all she wanted.

I decide to try calling Ruby.

22.

When the World Stops Spinning

I woke up and turned over on Ava's bumpy couch. My body hurt like hell. I'd taken a spill off my boss Carla's pony horse the day before and though I hadn't been knocked unconscious, I was damn sore. Which is probably what woke me. That or being worried about Ava lurking there. She'd done this about a week earlier. I'd woken up and felt someone's eyes on me. It was pitch black but off in a corner of the room there was a slight glow and, as my eyes focused, I saw that Ava was standing there. She was wearing a fuzzy white bathrobe that seemed to glow in the darkness of the room.

"Ava?" I called out.

She said nothing and I started wondering if I was hallucinating.

"Don't worry, Ben," she said eventually.

"Worry about what, Ava?"

"Nothing is wrong," she said, which I didn't understand one bit. I hadn't asked her if anything was wrong.

"I'm a little sleepless," she added, taking a few steps toward me.

"Oh yeah?" I said, sitting up and bunching the blankets around me.

Ava came and sat at the other end of the couch. I didn't say anything. Neither did she. She just sat there staring down at her bare feet as if they surprised her.

"Can we talk?" she said after a few moments.

"Sure," I said, though in truth that was about the last thing I wanted. "Talking" consisted of Ava complaining about the world—and my listening. I'd mentioned Darwin to her a few times but she'd never seemed very interested. She preferred to rail on about her estranged jockey husband or the indignities of the job market—even though I'd never seen her actively look for work.

"How you doin'?" Ava asked me as if we'd just bumped into each other on the street.

"I'm doing fine, I guess," I said, trying not to act like I thought she was a total lunatic.

"You're comfortable here?"

"Sure," I said. "I appreciate your hospitality." We'd come to an arrangement. I was giving her seventy-five dollars a week for couch privileges. I would have preferred to sleep in a stall in the barn, but Carla wouldn't allow it. So I'd agreed to rent Ava's couch. She needed the money, I needed a place to shower and sleep.

"You're a man that was made to take care of things," Ava said then, out of the blue.

I squinted at her in the darkness.

"You're destined to look out for powerless animals," she continued. "It's good you're working at the track like this. Some people don't treat their horses so good, you know."

"Yeah?" I said.

"Sure, those big-shot trainers, most of 'em got enough money they can afford to go easy on a horse when something's bothering it. And most of the working-class humps are in it 'cause they love horses and they wouldn't do anything to hurt their charges. But there's a nefarious element, you know. People that go running sore horses when they know damn well they're about to break down. "

"Yeah. I know that," I said, wishing she wasn't talking about it and wondering why she was. The *nefarious element* as she called it was something I'd picked up on as soon as I'd set foot on the grounds back at Laurel Park. I knew there was some not-so-nice stuff going on, but I'd managed to steer clear of anything like that. Nancy Cooley had been a good lady who gave a shit about her horses, and my current employer, Carla Friedman, is well intended too. If she ever ran a sore horse, it would be because she didn't know any better.

"It bothers me," Ava said then.

"Can't say I like it any either," I told her. I was beginning to feel a little nervous, wondering why she was bringing this up, wondering if somehow she knew about what had happened back in Oklahoma.

"You've probably seen my husband by now. Attila Johnson? He's an apprentice?"

"I've seen him around, yeah," I agreed.

"You know why I'm not with him anymore?"

"No idea," I said, praying she wasn't about to spout out intimate details I didn't want to hear.

"Well, technically we are still married. But not for long. That man did some bad things to some nice horses."

I frowned and felt my blood stir. I was sure I didn't want to hear this.

"Held some horses back in races. Now I hear it's getting worse."

"What do you mean?" I asked in a whisper.

"I mean I hear he's maybe going to start doing worse than hold them back. Help some find their way into accidents. Fatal accidents."

"How's a rider gonna do that?"

"Oh, you'd be surprised," Ava said.

"Why are you telling me this?" I asked her. At which point she'd just shrugged, gotten up, wished me a good night, and headed on back to bed, leaving me to toss around, worrying over what her jockey husband was up to.

The whole thing had been eating at me all week long and I'd found myself keeping an eye on the jockey. But I hadn't noticed anything out of the ordinary. Yet.

MY BODY IS aching now and I'm not sure I'm going to be able to get back to sleep. I check the alarm clock propped on top of the TV and see that it's three already and I've got to head to work in another half hour. I shuffle into the bathroom to urinate and, as I'm coming back out to the living room, Ava appears in the hall.

"Can't sleep?" she asks.

"My body hurts," I say. "I guess I'll go in to work a little early," I tell her, just for something to say.

"Carla must love you for coming in to work early." She smiles.

"She likes me okay," I say. "Excuse me," I add as I walk past her to the living room where I start getting my things together.

I take my work clothes into the bathroom and put them on. Once I'm dressed, I go peer inside Grace's room where Crow is curled up at the end of the kid's bed. I make a little noise in my throat and eventually the bum lifts his head and looks at me.

I call to him softly and he reluctantly hops down off the child's bed and follows me. Ava has gone back in her bedroom, I guess, and, without further ado, Crow and I leave the house.

My car has definitely seen better days—probably in the eighties—and is protesting the cold. I finally get it started and uneventfully drive to the backside of Belmont.

I make my way over to the barn and am greeted by a few snorts and whinnies. My equine friends are awake and ready to eat. I tie Crow up near the tack room and he shoots me a filthy look, probably wondering why I tore him away from the comforts of Grace's bed in order to come here and lie in the cold dirt.

I get all eight horses fed quickly and, since I've got at least a half hour before Carla gets in, I take the opportunity to go over to Robert Cardinal's barn and say hello to Darwin. By now I've made friends with most of the people Cardinal has working for him and even Sammy, the security guard who lords over this area of the backside, knows not to think twice if he sees me lurking. I walk directly to Darwin's stall.

My colt has his head hanging over the top of his door and he nickers as I come close. I feel my heart melt as the little guy points his ears forward and shakes his head at me. Even if he only remembered me slightly in the beginning, Darwin's definitely come to know me in these few weeks I've been working at Belmont.

I go over and start scratching his cheeks, mindful not to get my face too close to his since he's hungry and pretty excitable this time of day. If I had any sense, I wouldn't mess with him at all until he's had his grain.

"Hello?" I suddenly hear a voice behind me. I turn around and find Robert Cardinal standing there, looking at me.

"Oh, hi, Mr. Cardinal," I say.

"What you doing here?"

"I'm just visiting with Darwin," I say. Even though all Robert Cardinal's employees are used to seeing me around here, Cardinal himself probably doesn't know about how I visit the colt every day.

The old trainer is frowning and seems on the verge of saying something but then changes his mind. He shoves his hands deep in his pockets and turns to walk away.

"Mind you don't get bitten. He's a mouthy one," the trainer says.

For a minute I stare after him. Then I go back to scratching at Darwin's cheeks—the whole damn world could stop spinning and I wouldn't notice it.

A FEW HOURS LATER, I've done most of my morning work and Carla is in her office chain-smoking and yelling at owners on the phone. I decide to take a little journey over to Henry Meyer's barn to snoop. Ever since Ava told me how her ex is up to no good and maybe on the verge of hurting horses, I've been keeping an eye on him. For the last week or so I've made it my business to learn all the little creep's habits. Which sometimes isn't that easy in light of the fact that there's a big guy with a shaved head that shadows the jockey everywhere. A fact I reported to Ava. A fact that seemed to disturb her. Though not nearly as much as hearing about the small black-haired girl that Attila is unquestionably smitten with. I actually thought Ava was gonna lose it completely when I told her about the girl. She claimed she already knew about it but I wasn't sure this was true. She didn't eat any dinner that night, went into her room and didn't come out and I was left to feed the child. I didn't mind. Grace is actually a nice kid.

The thing that was worrying me now was I'd heard Robert Cardinal was going to put Attila on Darwin in a race later that week. I couldn't think of any reason why anyone would want the apprentice doing something to hurt Darwin but you never know. I had to see to it that the guy did not ride my horse. This might be a tricky thing to pull off. But it would have to be done.

BIG SAL

23.

Vicious

I wake up with the most vicious hard-on I've had in months. My wife is asleep next to me, flat on her back with her mouth half open. I don't think she's the cause of the extreme morning hard-on though. More likely the little exercise rider got into my dreams. I've got half a mind to go hunt that girl down right now at four in the morning, hold her personally responsible for my physical condition but I've got this wife. If she wasn't such a head case, I probably wouldn't be getting exercise-rider hard-ons.

I turn over on my side and nudge Karen. She doesn't move. I pull the covers back and run my hands over her chest. She moans a little but not really a sexy moan. Used to be she loved to wake up and find me inside her. Maybe she still does.

I reach between her legs, feeling her heat before putting my mouth on her.

"What the fuck?" my wife says, suddenly waking up.

"Morning, baby," I say.

"Get away from me, Sal."

"Karen," I say in a soft voice, "I thought you wanted to make another baby." I'm willing to do anything right now, including knocking her up against my better judgment.

"Fuck you, Sal," she says, getting out of bed.

I watch her storm out of the room. After a moment, I go into the bathroom where I jerk off with a vengeance. Picturing Layla the exercise rider.

"Feel better?" Karen asks spitefully when I emerge from the bathroom.

She's grudgingly making coffee. Her mouth is drawn down in anger.

"I don't understand you, woman."

"Don't 'woman' me, Sal."

"What do you want me to do to you, Karen?"

"Just drink your fucking coffee and leave me alone," she says, violently hitting the coffee pot's On switch before storming out of the kitchen.

I sit at the table, waiting for the coffee to brew and wondering what my wife is brewing.

A half hour later I leave the house without saying another word to Karen.

I get in the truck, put on some Beethoven, and drive to the motel to pick up Ruby and the jockey. I start thinking maybe I'll pull Ruby away from the jockey and bend her ear about my wife problems awhile. Ruby never offers much in the way of advice, but she listens just fine.

I leave the truck running as I go to knock on the motel room door. Attila opens up immediately. He doesn't look like he's in a good mood. Must be a mood virus going around.

"You guys ready?" I ask the jockey.

"I'm ready. Ruby's gone."

"What do you mean gone? Where'd she go?"

"Back home. We weren't getting along," he says in a flat, quiet voice.

"Oh," I say. "Sorry about that," I add.

The jockey shrugs. "Give me one minute," he says. He turns back into the room where he grabs his down jacket and a bag.

We walk over to the truck in silence.

"You don't have to do this anymore, Sal," he says once he's settled in.

"Don't have to do what?"

"Watch my back. Ruby's not keen on me right now. You're her friend. You don't know me from a hole in the dirt."

"A hole in the dirt?"

"I mean I'm nothing to you."

"I never heard that. 'A hole in the dirt.' Isn't it supposed to be a hole in the ground?"

"My mother liked to change expressions around," he says in the same quiet, flat voice.

I feel badly for the guy and wonder exactly what he did to invoke Ruby's wrath.

"That's a Southern thing, I bet," I say then, trying for a cheerfulness I don't feel, "playing around with words and all. Must have been nice growing up in the South."

Attila is looking at me like I've got three heads.

"It was okay," he says after a minute. "What about what I said, Sal? You don't have to do this."

"Like I told you and Ruby before, I'm out on Disability right now and if I stay home I'm just gonna sit on the couch popping pain pills. This is a much better way for me to spend my time."

"How come your back's not bothering you now?"

"It only acts up when I gotta work," I say, laughing. "Besides, I slipped it to the wife pretty good this morning. Loosened me up some."

Attila looks a little grossed out and I can't blame him. I'm not sure what possessed me to say that when it's not even true.

We drive in silence the rest of the way.

I park the truck and walk with the jockey over to Robert Cardinal's barn. Attila's riding a couple for him this morning before doing some of Henry and Violet's horses. I hang around as Attila talks to the trainer, getting his instructions. I walk next to one of the grooms as Attila and another exercise rider head over to the track. I'm just thinking about how, between Attila's mood and Ruby's not being here, this is gonna be a pretty lousy day when something weird happens.

A guy with stringy long hair suddenly starts talking to Attila. The guy's asking the jockey about some horse named Darwin. Attila is frowning at him and doesn't seem to know who the guy is. I walk a little closer, not liking the feel of the whole thing.

"What's up, Attila?" I ask him as I fall in stride with him and the weird-looking guy.

"Nothing," Attila says.

The weird-looking guy scowls at me then suddenly skulks off in the other direction.

"What the fuck was that?" I ask.

"I don't know who the hell that guy was. You know who that is, Larry?" Attila asks the groom.

"Works for that crazy broad Carla Friedman. You know, the one works her horses in a western saddle."

"So what's he want with me? Who's that horse he's asking about?"

"Three-year-old Robert got in last month. Robert told you about him. I think he wants you riding him. We got him running maiden special weight in a coupla days. That guy's like obsessed with the horse. I guess he's a little soft in the head."

Attila is frowning, looking confused. I have a funny feeling in my stomach but am not sure what to do about it. We reach the track and Attila gets on his first horse. I take out Karen's binoculars and focus them on my charge. Nothing happens though. He works the colt then gets on another one. The sun starts to come up, burning away the fog lingering at the edges of the track. Horses gallop and flow, the sound of it like pretty thunder. Once in a while, I think about my wife and the way she shoved me away. When this gets me feeling too fucked up, I think about Layla and my mood improves.

By nine, Attila's talking to Henry Meyer, getting instructions about a filly Henry's going to put Attila on for the first time. Just as I'm thinking it's gonna be pretty fucking dull keeping my binoculars on the jockey for another half hour or so, something very nice happens.

Layla comes over to huddle with Attila and Henry.

I actually find myself looking up at the sky to thank God or the gods or whatever the hell is up there.

She looks adorable in her bright orange safety vest just like Attila's. She has her blond hair tucked up in her crash helmet. Actually, she could pass for a boy the way she's dressed. A cute boy, but a boy. I find myself getting excited just looking at her. I'd like to pick her up and carry her over to the nearest bale of hay and peel off every single layer of her protective clothing. Henry Meyer's got other plans for her though. He decides at the last minute he wants her riding the filly he was going to try Attila on. This worries me since I've been hearing about what a head case the filly is. But it's not like I've got any say in the matter. Attila stays at the rail with Henry as Layla gets up on the filly's back and steers her onto the track. Since Attila's right here where I can see him, I allow myself the pleasure of focusing my binoculars on Layla as she trots her mount along the rail. I savor an extreme close-up of the girl's face, watching her mouth become a pink button as she concentrates.

A few moments later, Layla's got the filly going full steam, working alone close to the rail. As they breeze along the backstretch of the track, my eyes play tricks on me. I see the filly suddenly crumble and go down sideways.

"What the fuck!" I hear Henry say nearby and I realize my eyes aren't playing tricks on me. The filly is down.

Chaos breaks out as riders pull their horses up and both the equine and human ambulances speed over to the site of the accident. I follow Henry as he goes running onto the track.

It's not a sight anyone should have to see. The filly is on her side, the whites of her eyes are showing and she's panting horribly. Layla's entire body is pinned under the horse.

Someone standing near me throws up. I feel my knees get weak and I slowly sit down in the dirt.

I suppose I've gone into some sort of blackout and lost track of time because suddenly Attila is sitting next to me, saying something.

"Huh?" I say to him.

"Never mind," he says somberly.

I look over to where the disaster was but now the filly has been moved into the horse ambulance and there's no sign of Layla.

"Where's Layla?" I ask Attila.

"She's gone, Sal. Her skull was crushed. You saw."

"I did?"

"That's what happened to me first time I saw a rider down like that. I can't remember it to this day. But Layla's dead, Sal. The filly might make it though."

"What?"

"Someone shot the filly. Missed her heart though. She's alive. But she crushed Layla and killed her."

"Oh my God."

"We gotta get up, Sal. Gotta get off the track."

Attila is standing now and he reaches down and takes my hand. He pulls me to my feet and puts a hand on my back, forcing me to walk forward.

THE NEXT HOUR goes by in a blur of cops and officials. I make my statement to the cops, telling them that no, I didn't see anything out of the ordinary. They ask me what I'm doing here at the track and I tell them I'm thinking of buying a horse. One cop scoffs, the other looks interested. They finish with me and I start walking. Not even sure where I'm going. Eventually, I find myself back at Henry's barn. I don't know where Henry is, but I find Attila there. He looks terrible. I probably do, too.

"We have to talk," he tells me.

"Talk," I say.

Attila looks around nervously. "Let's take a little walk," he says.

We walk away from Henry's barn, veering down a muddy path near a manure pile. Attila starts talking, telling me he's sure it was him the shooter was after. Of course I knew this on a subconscious level but didn't want to think it. The guy is responsible for that lovely young woman's death.

"We were wearing the same thing, Sal," he tells me, "she was on the filly I was supposed to ride. It was me they were after." He's not looking me in the eyes. Probably knows what he'll see there.

"You tell the cops this?" I ask the jockey.

"Course not."

"Why the fuck not, Attila? An innocent girl is dead. I'm gonna tell them," I say, restraining an urge to grab him by the shoulders and shake him.

"You don't have to, Sal. I'm quitting."

"Quitting what? Being a target?"

"I'm not gonna ride anymore. It's too fucked up. I'm gonna ride Jack Valentine in the fifth race today and that's it. I'm out."

"Good," I say, feeling disgust for the man, "but I'm still telling the cops."

"Just let me ride this race, Sal. Then you tell anything to anyone. But I promised Violet I was gonna win this race for her. You gotta give me that."

I stare at the small man. I still feel contempt for him but, for some reason, I feel like I have to grant him this. I don't know why. Truth is, I should fucking kill him.

I don't say anything else to the guy. I just walk toward the parking lot to get my truck. I don't know where I'm gonna go. Doesn't matter.

I slip a CD of Bach concertos into the machine and turn the volume to its highest level. I stare ahead.

24.

Half Naked

A terrible ripping sound wakes me. I sit up in bed and see that it's just Lulu, annoying me by ripping a brown paper bag she's pulled out of the trash. The minute I lay eyes on her, she stops and looks at me guiltily. I throw back the covers and put my robe on, which is exactly what Lulu was hoping for. I have a pounding headache and my mouth is dry, like I was on a drinking binge in my dreams. I walk into the kitchen and start preparing the cats' meat. It's not until I'm scooping vitamin powder into the bowls of food that I start to remember last night. Attila running through the parking lot half naked, just to save me a few steps.

I look at my kitchen clock and see that it's already close to nine and Attila's day has long started. He's probably on a horse. Probably thinking about his wife. I'm not sure when or how I started getting the idea that he's still hung up on his wife but now that this notion has come to me, it won't leave.

After drinking two cups of very strong coffee, I push Attila out of my mind and mull over last night's phone conversation with Ed. I think I detected longing in his tone as he detailed the progress of his three modest racehorses and prodded me here and there about my whereabouts, probably having sensed I had something going with another man. As of last night, I really don't know if I *have* something going with another man, so I didn't volunteer anything. Ed and I talked amicably for about fifteen minutes and then hung up, vowing to stay in closer touch. I'm tempted to call him right now. To pour out the story of Attila. To tell Ed exactly how badly I miss him. Instead, I decide to shower, get dressed, and show up early for work.

As I leave the house, I light my first cigarette of the day. I blow smoke rings up to the pale sun as I walk.

I GET TO WORK and find that my boss, Bob, has gone on a cleaning spree and the little museum is a mess. Display cases have been pulled away from the walls, pictures have been taken down and my boss is on all fours, polishing the floor.

"Bob, what are you doing?" I ask.

He pauses, looks up at me from behind his pink-hued glasses, and grins ruefully.

"Place was filthy."

True enough but that's never bothered him before.

"I thought we were going to open early today," I say. "What if people come up here? The place is a mess."

"It's okay, we'll stay closed."

"And you're going to make me *clean*?" I ask, horrified.

"No no, wouldn't dream of it, dear girl. Unless you want to volunteer."

"Not particularly," I say. Bob knows that, as a teenager, I worked as a maid at a hooker hotel in Sunset Park. There were a lot of unpleasant surprises while cleaning sheets and toilets used by prostitutes and their clientele. The experience forever soured me on heavy-duty cleaning.

"You want to go home and shack up with your jockey, huh?"

"His name is Attila and no, actually, I don't. He's at work. At the track. And I'm not sure how much more shacking I'll be doing with him."

"Oh?" My boss pauses and looks up. "What happened?"

"I don't know," I shrug.

"You don't want to tell me."

"No, I'm just not really sure what's going on. It seems like it's ending."

"All right. I'm here if you need an ear. But you don't have to hang around. Go home. Play the piano. Do something useful. I'll give you a half day's pay, since I did tell you to come in."

"You will?" I'm astonished since our humble museum doesn't generate a lot of cash and I've never known Bob to be unabashedly generous.

"Yeah. Go on," he says.

I do as I'm told.

I walk down the creaky old stairs and out onto Surf Avenue. I look around, suddenly not sure what to do with myself. The sky is low and the streets are bleeding slush.

I know I should tend to myself. Shop for food, get some exercise, and call Mark Baxter to schedule a piano lesson, *anything*. One of the things I miss about being an active drunk is that life was simpler then. All I ever had to worry about was the next drink. If I ran out of food, I drank. If my laundry was dirty, I drank. If I broke a leg, a heart, a fingernail, I drank. If I felt personal turmoil and discontent over the way of the world, I drank. Now, I don't drink. And it's the endless and banal self-maintenance that sometimes gets me down more than anything.

I start walking to the water. I park myself on a boardwalk bench and fish a cigarette from my pocket. A man suddenly appears to my right and says hello. He's not carrying his boom box and it takes me a few moments to realize it's Rite of Spring Man.

"Hello," I say, smiling at him.

"Mind if I join you?" he asks.

"Not at all," I say, though in truth I'm not quite sure how I feel about it. I've never exchanged more than a few words with the man and I've liked it that way. He's a romantic figure to me and I don't want to ruin that. But I don't want to be rude either.

"Your man friend is okay?" he asks me. "No more people tryin' to drown him?"

"No, no one else has tried to drown him," I say. "But I'm not sure he's okay."

"What's wrong with him?"

"A lot," I sigh.

"Tell me about it," he says. He sees my hesitation. "I'm not gonna go repeating your troubles to anyone. I barely ever talk to people. You know me, I got my music. Most of the time, that's enough."

I look him in the eye. It's hard to tell how old he is. Maybe forty-five. He's got an in-between black man's complexion. Neither dark nor light. Though he's over six feet and has some meat on him, his face is small, the features delicate and almost pretty. He has enormous eyes and a mouth that curls up at the edges. His hair is cropped short and he's wearing a nice dark wool overcoat.

I don't know if it's his good taste in overcoats or the fact that it's unlikely he'll repeat what I say to anyone, but I find myself spilling the whole story to him.

"I knew your man friend had to be a jockey," Rite of Spring Man says when I reach the end of the tale.

I feel deflated. I've told him the whole story, from meeting Attila to finding out he probably has a price tag on his head, to the debacle last night. And all he has to say is that he knew Attila was a jockey?

"My name is Lionel, by the way," he adds.

"Ruby," I say, still feeling a bit upset with him.

"That's quite a story, Ruby. But I knew you were a girl with a story. Never mind this jockey business. That's bad enough. But you're carrying a lot of other things around too."

"I am?"

"We all are. Some more than others. You, you've got sad eyes. You got joy in you too. I'm not saying you walk around moping and spreading misery all over but you got some serious sad. And I don't think you and that jockey gonna make it fly."

"What makes you say that?"

"The way you talk about him. You admire him. But you know it ain't long for this world."

"I do?"

"Maybe not," Lionel backtracks. "Listen, I know next to nothing about what makes people stick together. I'm just telling you my hunch."

"Oh," I say. "And what should I do? Call the cops just to try and protect him from himself? The only thing he really loves is horses. I don't want to put his riding career in jeopardy."

"No, I don't guess anyone would want to do that." Lionel shakes his head. "I don't know what you should do, girl. That's why I got out of the world."

"What?"

"That's why I live like I do. In that shitty SRO over there on Seventeenth Street," he says, motioning in the distance. "I couldn't take it anymore. The decisions and the maintenance and the difficulty. I never found my way in the world but I love music. I work a little here and there, but mostly, I just listen to music."

"Where's your boom box?" I ask since it's the first time I've seen him without it.

"Somebody stole it."

"That's awful."

"Don't go offering to buy me a new one."

"Oh," I say, "I don't think I was going to."

"That's good. I don't want it to be like that with you and me. Chances are, we ain't gonna talk again much. I'll wave at you when I see you and maybe you'll give me that pretty smile of yours but we ain't gonna hang out much 'cause I don't do much hanging. I wouldn't want that nice distant acquaintanceship ruined by your having bought me a new boom box. I can work. I'll get a new one."

"Okay," I shrug.

"You're gonna be all right, Ruby," Lionel says as he stands up. He pulls his overcoat tighter around himself, smiles, and then walks off.

I stare after him for a moment. Eventually, the wind kicks up and throws sand in my face.

I walk down the beach all the way to Brighton where I go into a diner and order pancakes. The waitress is tall and fair. The skin is pulled tightly over her broad face and her eyes are tiny and light blue. She seems to dislike me. She violently scratches my order into her pad then turns away. There aren't too many other customers in here right now. Two old guys in hats picking at a plate of fries. A teenaged girl eating an omelet. The surly waitress brings my pancakes and slams the check down in front of me, as if daring me to order anything else. I douse the pancakes in syrup and dig in. The comfort food isn't particularly comforting though. I finish my meal, leave an excessive tip because the waitress was mean to me, and get up and walk. I go to the water again. The sky looks like it's aching. I don't know if it's from being in proximity to where Attila was nearly drowned but I'm suddenly having a bad feeling. Sal's out at Aqueduct with Attila but that's not reassuring me much. I turn my phone on to try reaching Sal, but before I dial his number, I find that there's a message. It's Sal telling me to call him, that it's urgent. My stomach seizes up. I dial Sal's number but it goes straight to voice mail. I then try Attila's cell phone with the same result. Although I have bad knees and can't do much running, I break into a fast jog, heading for home.

By the time I get back to my place my knees hurt and my stomach is in knots from running on a full stomach but it's the least of my worries. The cats, who came to greet me at the door, seem aware that something is wrong. They keep out of my way as I press the Play button on the answering machine. Another message from Sal. Again, I try his cell phone. Still nothing. I have to go to the track.

I run into the bedroom to put on warmer clothing. I'm just getting my red down jacket out of the hallway closet when the phone rings. I race over to get it on the second ring.

"Yes?" I answer breathlessly.

"Ruby?" says a female voice.

"Who's this?"

"Violet Kravitz."

"Oh, hello."

"There's been some unpleasantness at the track," Violet says.

"Unpleasantness? What?"

"Murder," Violet says quietly.

"What?" I feel like I'm going to vomit.

"Layla, an exercise rider. She was murdered during morning works."

"Oh," I say, feeling relieved and then immediately guilty for my relief.

"I nearly scratched Jack from his race. I feel very strangely about running my horse on such a terrible day. However, Henry thinks we should run."

"He's probably right," I offer, still not sure what any of this has to do with me and half expecting worse news to be forthcoming.

"You're not working today?" Violet asks.

"No, my boss sent me home."

"That's good."

"How so?"

"I'm calling because I understand that you and Attila have had some sort of disagreement and I assumed you weren't planning on coming to watch the race. I can't say that the atmosphere here is particularly good but I would like to see you and I'd like it if you were here to cheer Jack on. The horse was so fond of you and I admit to having small superstitions. I feel your being there would help him somehow."

"I'm actually on my way," I tell Violet. I'm aching to tell her exactly *why* I'm on my way. I bite my tongue though.

"That's wonderful," she says, sounding genuinely delighted. "You'll come find us on the backstretch then? We'll be in the receiving barn. I'll leave your name at Security."

"Thanks, Violet, yes, I'll be right there. Oh, and have you seen my friend Sal?"

"The big fellow? Attila's friend?"

"Yeah, him."

"I saw him earlier, yes. He was with Attila after this morning's terrible events. I haven't seen either of them in a while though."

"All right, I'll be there soon, Violet, and thank you."

I hang up and realize that the only way I can conceivably get to

Aqueduct quickly is to take a car service. I put a jacket on, check that the cats have fresh water, then throw money, keys, and cigarettes in my pocket and leave. I glance over at Ramirez's door and wish it were open. I don't know that I'd tell him what I'm up to, but just having a "Hello, lady" from him would give me strength. The door is closed though and there aren't any sounds emanating from his apartment. I go down the stairs two at a time and jog over to the car service on Mermaid Avenue. There are two cars parked outside the tiny storefront, waiting for something to do. A lively Dominican man ushers me into his beat-up white Lincoln Town Car and I tell him my destination.

"You playing the ponies?" he asks with interest.

"No, I mean yeah, maybe, but I'm going to see a horse I know in a race."

"Oh yeah? You got a hot tip for me, girl?"

This makes me wonder. Do I? Will Attila ride well?

I tell my driver to bet Jack Valentine in the fifth.

BEN NESTER

25.

Runaway

I stare at the little guy knowing there's a chance I'm not going to see him again for a long while. Darwin's groom, Petey, is mucking some stalls out down the aisle. He nodded at me when he saw me heading over here. I feel okay about Petey. In the time I've been watching him, I've seen he's come to really give a shit about Darwin. Maybe not the way I do, but I know he'll see to it nothing bad happens to the little guy. Though Petey can't do anything to keep the colt safe on the track. It's up to me to take care of that. Which means I might not be seeing much of Darwin anymore.

Darwin reaches his head over the stall guard, trying to bite at my pockets where he knows I've got peppermints for him.

"Hey, no biting," I tell him, tapping him on the forehead a little. He pins his ears at me. I frown at him. Eventually, he puts his ears forward again. I scratch under his chin and feed him a couple of peppermints, watching him roll them around on his big tongue.

After a long while, I run my hand down Darwin's face one last time and then walk away. I don't turn around even though I can feel him looking at me.

I'm back at Carla's shedrow going over some tack I've got hanging on a hook in the aisle. I'm just getting some gunk out of a bit when I hear a loud noise and I look up to see a horse tearing toward the barn. I frown up at the sight and it takes me a minute to realize it's my boss, Carla, on a runaway and that he's taking her back to his stall. Before I've had time to think, Carla is ducking, trying to flatten herself against the horse's neck as he shoots for his stall. The stall door is closed and the colt bangs right into it then starts rearing.

"Nester!" Carla screams, sounding genuinely terrified.

I come within a few feet of the flailing horse and start grabbing at his reins. He's snorting and crazed and can't figure out which way is up. I've got to get hold of him before he hurts himself and my boss.

I try to put myself inside the horse's mind to send good thoughts there. The horse calms down a little bit. I reach for the reins. Carla's still screaming which isn't helping any. I pull the horse's head toward me but he spooks and tries to rear again. I send him more calmness and in that one moment of quiet, Carla gets her feet untangled from the stirrups and hops down.

"Jesus," she says, collapsing right there in the dirt.

The horse, a two-year-old named Soft Demon, is terrified and still trying to pull away from me.

"Don't do it, buddy," I tell him. "You're gonna hurt yourself and you won't like that one bit," I say.

He suddenly stands completely still, his big eyes and labored breathing the only sign of his chaos.

People have gathered around, some of them having seen the start of the event up in the paddock where Carla was trying to give the colt a schooling session, though why she *rode* the poor colt in the paddock I don't know. I thought she was just going to lead him around and show him the sights there. Carla gets to her feet and people start asking if she's all right. I open Demon's stall door and lead him inside. I stand at his head awhile talking to him and at first he just keeps looking around, expecting something terrifying to suddenly appear in his stall. After a long five minutes, he finally puts his head down and rubs against my chest. The terror has abated. I start taking the tack off him. He's wet with sweat and I've got to walk him off but I don't want to risk taking him out of his stall again with all the brouhaha going on out there. I feel myself getting angry at the rubberneckers and, as I let myself out of the stall, I glare at them. Carla is evidently enjoying a moment in the sun over it all, holding court, recounting the event. This annoys me. I clear my throat: "Folks, please move along, I got a scared horse I gotta walk off."

At first Carla looks at me like I'm a fool, but eventually she starts nodding in agreement.

"He's right," she says, "we need some quiet here."

Which is when I notice the big bald guy. The one that's always hanging around that jockey husband of Ava's. His is one of at least six faces staring at me, though what the hell he's doing here I couldn't tell you. I thought I saw the guy get in his truck and drive away when I was tagging after Attila two hours ago. The guy was upset about the girl dying on the track and I'd watched him yelling at the jockey—seeming to hold him somehow responsible. I had also felt like the shooter was after the jockey—who'd been dressed the same as the girl exercise rider. I wished the shooter *had* offed the jockey—then it wouldn't be my problem anymore. Now though, I've got even more problems. Once I do get the jockey out of the way, I figure I have to find that shooter. After all, he almost killed a horse.

The onlookers start leaving, but the big bald guy keeps standing there, looking at me. I look right back at him to the point where it's getting weird. Just when I'm about to say something to the big guy, he turns and goes away.

I've got a lot of thoughts clouding my head but I need to get Soft Demon cooled off, so I keep the thoughts away and go back into the colt's stall. I put his halter on and run a stud chain under his lip. I lead him outside and start walking him. He snorts a little at Crow, who's tied up outside the tack room, but on the whole, the colt is back to his normal self. I match my pace to his and we walk, my right foot hitting the dirt at the same time as his right front hoof.

ATTILA JOHNSON

26.

The Layout of Eternity

It can all turn on a dime. Two days ago I had hope. The blizzard had stopped, I was about to get on a horse, and I had a romance going with a very attractive woman. I knew some folks were ticked off that I was refusing to hold horses back, knew maybe there'd be consequences, but meeting Ruby had made me want to clean my slate. I never suspected how severe the consequences would be.

Right now, I'm sitting in a far corner of the grandstands where no one would think to look for me. I've got a watch cap pulled down over my telltale pale hair and I'm wearing a thick overcoat to disguise my smallness. And I feel pretty goddamned small. It's forty-five minutes till the first race and I have to get to the jocks room soon, but I needed to be alone first, to stare at the track, to attempt to clear my head. All around me, Aqueduct is coming to life. Bettors are arriving swollen with hopes and jocks are going into the jocks room and owners are wondering if this is their day and trainers are cautiously optimistic and horses are being led from their barns and I just don't care about any of it, can't feel any of the adrenaline and beauty coursing through me because Layla is dead and it should have been me. By now, I'm sure the unlucky sniper has learned of his mistake and is hunting me. And Layla is hopefully off somewhere, her soul transported to a calmer place. I'm not sure what I think about the potential for afterlives and souls but in all likelihood, I'll be getting a tour of the layout of eternity very soon. I'm not planning to hold Jack Valentine back this afternoon. I'm going to give him my all.

Harsh wind is blowing over the track and up into the grandstands. I shiver and sink deeper into my overcoat. An old man in a down jacket has taken a seat a few rows in front of me. He has a hot dog which, by now, surely must be frozen. I don't know what he's doing out here when there's ample room in the heated part of the grandstands. He probably just doesn't like people. Is a loner among loners. He spreads the *Form* on his lap and bites into his hot dog. Out on the track infield the tote board starts flashing odds. The man in the down jacket crumples up his paper hot-dog plate and throws it to the ground. I'm incensed. I once heard a song lyric saying something to the effect of I *can be condemned to hell for every sin but littering*. I hate littering. I want to kill this man for littering.

With this thought, I get up from my seat. I walk past the litterbug and shoot him a disparaging look. He looks right back at me. He has dead eyes in a face the color of pollution. If I do make it through this day alive and find some way to place myself in the world, I won't have to look into the dead souls of the more degenerate gamblers anymore. There are plenty of respectable horseplayers and race fans but for every one of them there are two droolcases who barely even see the horses and certainly don't think of them as the noble creatures they are. I've heard these types call horses pigs, blood clots, and of course, the ever popular *nag*. It's these people who are the real nags and ought to be forced to gallop thirty-five mph on one leg with blood pouring out of their mouths.

As I walk toward the jocks room, I remember telling Jim, the racing secretary, that I'd stop in and say hello. His wife is friends with Ava and the four of us used to grab dinner sometimes. Now I never see the guy. I make a quick detour but Jim's in the middle of a thousand things so I don't stay very long. A few minutes later, I go into the jocks room. There is a smell of sweat and mud. The bright sound of men's voices rising and falling.

The TVs are on, some showing regular TV, others showing the odds for the first race. I sit in a chair and pick up a copy of *The New York Times*. I stare at it as the riders for the first race get ready to go out to the paddock. Time passes. I feel curiously blank as I stare at the newspaper's type. It blurs before my eyes and then turns to horses. The ink is galloping.

I look up at the TV. The riders are getting astride their horses and being led to the track. The horses are skittering, preening, spooking. I feel each horse's heart beat inside my own. Tears come to my eyes.

RUBY MURPHY

27.

Bad Lady

By the time the driver drops me at the Aqueduct backside entrance it's only an hour before the first race goes off. I pay the driver, thank him, and get out. By now, I've worked myself into a frenzy of worry and there's a sheen of cold sweat on my forehead. I keep seeing the image of Attila in his towel, sprinting through the motel parking lot. It makes me sick with guilt, but guilt isn't what the bad feeling is about. I don't even know what the bad feeling is about. But it's bad.

I walk into the tiny security office.

"You here for Kravitz?" a gentle-voiced matron asks.

"Yeah," I nod. I don't suppose there are many un-credentialed visitors to Aqueduct on a bleak weekday like this.

"Nice lady," the matron says, and suddenly I'm not sure if she's talking about Violet Kravitz or me. For a moment, I tangentially think of Pattahbi Jois, the ashtanga yoga guru, an eighty-something-year-old Indian man whose workshops I have taken on occasion. He is fond of calling his students "bad lady" or "bad man," reserving the much coveted "nice lady" or "nice man" for some particularly excellent execution of a pose. I once earned a resounding "bad lady" for being alarmed when he came over and adjusted my balance in headstand. He kept nudging my legs forward and I felt like I was going to topple over and break my neck. I fought against his adjustment and was called "bad lady"—to the delight of my friend Jane who was practicing just to my right.

Bad lady has a bad feeling, I think to myself as I pin my credentials to my down jacket and walk toward the receiving barns. Not even the smells and sounds of the backside can do much to improve my bleak state of mind. I'll probably feel better once I lay eyes on Attila and assure myself he's in one piece. Maybe I'll even relax and enjoy some races.

I reach the receiving barn and begin walking down the aisle, looking for Jack Valentine. It's slightly embarrassing because there are so many bay horses that I stop in front of a few different stalls mistaking their inhabitants for Jack. I go all the way down the aisle before finally seeing a long bay face that looks intensely familiar. My recognizing the big gelding is aided by the fact that Violet Kravitz is standing at Jack's side.

"Ruby!" Violet smiles but it's a sad smile, still clouded by the day's events. She comes out of Jack's stall.

"Hi, Violet." I find myself hugging her which is surprising because I'm not a big hugger. I try but I grew up in a family where demonstrativeness was reserved for animals. As a result, my sister and I are slightly hug-shy.

"I'm sorry about what happened this morning," I tell Violet.

"Yes. It's tragic." Her lovely pale eyes are a world of sadness. "I'm very thankful that you've come though, Ruby. It helps."

I have no idea how my being here could help anything but I'm pleased that she feels this way.

"Attila is quite glum. I'll understand if you need to keep your distance from him, but I'd bet it would cheer him considerably to lay eyes on you."

I doubt that. I shrug.

"Where is he?" I ask casually.

"I think he's in the grandstands," Violet motions in the direction of the track. "He likes to do that sometimes before going into the jockeys' room. I think it centers him to sit gazing out at the track."

"Oh," I say, feeling slightly miffed. This is yet another thing Attila never told me about.

"Well, maybe I'll go look for him," I tell Violet.

"I think you have someone to say hello to first," the lady says, indicating Jack Valentine who has his head hanging over his stall guard and is staring at me intently.

The horse looks like an eager puppy. I walk over and extend my palm for him to lick. He does this slowly and thoroughly. With my free hand I scratch between his ears. Violet stands to the side, beaming, as if she'd made him herself.

For a few lovely moments time stands still and I am utterly transfixed by the horse. Reality intrudes eventually. I tell Violet I'll see her after Jack's race. For a moment she looks forlorn. Then she nods, and turns to forage for something in a trunk she has sitting in front of Jack's stall.

THE WIND IS ANGRY as I head into the grandstands to try finding Attila. Or maybe it's just me. The grandstands are almost entirely empty. I see just one old man in a down jacket, staring at the tote board.

I go back inside and over into the clubhouse. It's not exactly packed but the heat has been cranked and it's toasty, almost homey in here. I wave at Johnny, my favorite teller. Johnny's a sad soul. We talk sometimes and he always asks me about myself but rarely reveals anything about himself. I nearly fell over when he told me he was once a jockey. I don't know why. I guess I expect retired jockeys to do something more glamorous than being a teller. But for most of them, once their riding career is over, there aren't that many options. A few go on to work for trainers or become trainers themselves. Some become jockey agents. Others end up selling real estate or drinking the rest of their days away. I guess being a teller makes sense. I've even met a few down-on-their-luck trainers who hold teller jobs for a while till things pick up. I wonder momentarily if I should become a teller, but then I remember that I don't like handling money.

I walk by Nathan's where the first batches of fries are just getting cooked. The clubhouse feels cheerful as the fans start filing in and the place comes to life. It's forty minutes to post time for the first race. Attila has to go to the jockeys' room soon and presumably, once he's in there, he'll be safe. But I'd really like to get a look at him now to calm myself down.

I detour into the enormous women's bathroom. Sadie is sitting at her post in a stuffed chair near the mirrors. A white apron covers the front of her blue smock. Her jet black hair is pulled into a severe bun on top of her head. She nods at me but doesn't offer a smile. Those are reserved for the women who hit it big and come in to tip her lavishly. Since there aren't many women at Aqueduct, there aren't many women hitting it big. Sadie doesn't get to smile much.

As I emerge from the bathroom, Attila walks right by me. He's got a watch cap on and has his coat pulled up close to his chin. This is his idea of incognito. I'm about to accost him when I notice a strange stringy-haired guy walking just a few steps behind Attila. Normally, a strange stringy-haired guy at a racetrack wouldn't be cause for alarm but I've seen this guy before. It seems like I've seen him close to Attila before.

I follow them both. Attila seems to be heading to the racing secretary's office. The stringy-haired fellow follows until Attila goes inside the office, at which point the guy turns the corner and lurks there looking hesitant. I'm just a few feet away from him but he doesn't seem to have noticed. I pretend to be absorbed in the tote board as I try figuring out what the hell to do. My thinking process isn't working very well and I find myself walking up to the guy without any idea of what to say.

"Aren't you Fred?" I accost the man.

He looks like he's seen a ghost.

"What are you talking about?" he asks. His eyes are watery and worried. His mouth is pulled into a straight line, even when speaking.

"You're Fred, right? Didn't I meet you last week?"

The man's eyes dart around. Clearly I'm interfering with his stalking of Attila.

"I'm not Fred," he says finally. He's gazing at me firmly now. "We have something to talk about though," he adds.

All my alarms go off at once. I glance at the racing secretary's door to see if Attila is emerging. He's not.

"Why don't we go over there," the guy says, motioning toward the far wall of the clubhouse where the elevators and emergency exit stairs are.

"Whatever for?" I ask, trying to keep a light tone.

"Trust me, you want to talk to me. It's to do with your boyfriend."

I doubt that any of this is good. But I have to know. Who is this guy? Why is he shadowing Attila?

I follow him over to the stairs. He pushes through the door marked Exit and we are in a quiet stairwell.

"Now," he says, producing a gun and leveling it at my heart, "I would like you to come with me."

For a moment all I feel is lightheadedness. Then the fear comes.

"Don't scream," the guy warns. "I have no qualms about shooting people."

I keep quiet.

28.

The Girl

Carla drives the horse van and I follow in my car as we head over to Aqueduct where we're running a nice claiming filly in the ninth race. My boss didn't understand why I wanted to bring my car so I told her I had some errands to run after the races and left it at that. I have Crow with me too since I may not be able to get back to Belmont to retrieve him later. I follow Carla in through the backside entrance and over to the receiving barn. I leave Crow in the car as I help Carla unload the filly. She's a fairly bombproof filly and unloads without fussing. As soon as the filly is settled in her stall, Carla tells me I'm free for a few hours. She seems to be brewing something with Lalo, a groom who works for Shug McGaughey and who happens to have some horses in the stalls right next to our filly. I've noticed my boss getting buttery around Lalo for a few days in spite of the fact that I'd previously thought she batted for the other team. Lucky for me, Carla's fixation on the groom makes her want to hang around the filly's stall doing all my work and freeing me to hunt for the Jockey. I walk past the stall where Henry Meyer's got Jack Valentine, the horse the Jockey is riding in the fifth race. I see Meyer there, in the horse's stall, taking some shipping wraps off the horse's hind legs. No sign of the Jockey though.

I wander over to the track and then into the clubhouse. I walk slowly. I don't have a clear plan, just a mission.

Post time for the first race draws close and I still haven't seen hide nor hair of the Jockey. Truth is, I'm not sure how I'm going to take care of matters but from what Ava told me, Robert Cardinal's planning to have the Jockey work Darwin tomorrow. Time is of the essence.

As I head toward the jocks room, luck falls my way. I see him, just coming through the turnstile between the grandstands and the clubhouse. He's got a hat on and looks like he's attempting to travel incognito but I'd have picked him out five miles away and wearing a wig. He walks right by me. Once he's a few feet past, I follow him. He's apparently not going to the jocks room though. He veers to the right and walks into the racing secretary's office, closing the door behind him. I walk on a few paces and then park myself to the left of the door. The frustrating thing is that I still do not have a clear plan in my head. I've got a little gun Ava gave me, and she has helped by telling me what to do and where to take the Jockey. She gave me keys and directions to a little house upstate that belongs to a friend of hers. I can bring the Jockey up there until Ava sorts things out and can prove to the cops that Attila is no good. Providing I can ever get close enough to the man to capture him.

I try to quiet my mind but it's a tornado in there. Then, the Girl approaches me. The Jockey's girlfriend. It's obvious she doesn't know who I am or exactly what I'm doing. She may have noticed me following the Jockey but that is all. I manage to lure her to the exit stairs. She is quite gullible. Once I have her there on the cement landing, I take the gun from my jacket pocket and point it at her. She looks terrified.

"Don't scream. I will hurt you," I tell her in a quiet voice.

Her skin looks gray. She doesn't scream though.

I walk behind her, nudging her ahead of me down the stairs. I stay slightly to her left, with the gun in my right hand but pressed so closely into her back that it can't be seen. Not that anyone is looking. It's a slow day at Aqueduct and we pass few people as we walk out into the clubhouse parking lot.

The Girl is being good, keeping her mouth shut. We make it to the lot where I've got the Chevy parked and I tell her to get in the backseat. Crow, my slut of a dog, immediately starts licking the Girl. I have to order him into the front seat. The Girl looks baffled.

"What do you want?" she asks me.

"Don't worry about it," I tell her.

She pleads with me as I get the rope out of my glove box and start tying her hands. I put the gun to her temple and that quiets her.

"Please don't do this," she says after a few moments of silence.

"I'm not gonna hurt you," I tell her. "Just shut up, all right?"

I bind her hands and as I lean down to find a rag to gag her, she screams. I put my hand over her mouth and she sinks her teeth into it. I shove her away and clutch my bleeding hand. Though Crow is looking from me to her and back, he hasn't seen fit to come to my rescue and I mentally curse him. Usually, anyone makes one false move toward me and Crow is on them like a bad dream.

"Don't do anything like that again!" I yell at the Girl, looking into her huge frightened eyes. For a moment, I almost feel badly for her. Then I gag her, pat her down, and find a cell phone and forty dollars, which I take for safe keeping. I leave the half pack of cigarettes I find in her pocket though I can't tell you why. I cover her with an old blanket I've got in the backseat for Crow, before getting behind the wheel.

"We're gonna drive a coupla hours. You'll want to get comfortable."

I get back into the front seat and put the car in drive. It occurs to me to go leave a note for Carla but then I might run into her and have some explaining to do. I figure she'll get by without me. She won't be happy about it but she'll get by.

Crow has settled into the passenger side of the front seat and I pat him with one hand as I start driving out of the backstretch, my cargo quiet and still in the backseat.

29.

Last Ride

It seems like entire days have passed by the time I start changing into my silks for the fifth race. I move slowly, deliberately, knowing it's the last time I'll do this.

I notice Santarez, one of the particularly unscrupulous young riders, giving me the once-over. I don't know why he's eyeballing me and, to be honest, I don't give a flying fuck.

We file out of the room and into the paddock. Henry and Violet are standing at the mouth of Jack's saddling stall. Violet seems to be talking to the gelding as Henry pulls his legs out, ensuring there isn't any flesh trapped under the girth.

As my fellow jockeys stand in the center of the walking ring, talking to owners, I go over to greet my mount. Jack is an exceptionally kind horse but I'd be fussing over him even if he were a cantankerous prankster since he's the last horse I'll ever ride in a race.

Violet and Henry both greet me and Violet steps aside as I go to rub Jack's face. I'm surprised when Jack stands perfectly still, letting me scratch his cheeks. I don't think I've ever known a three-year-old that would stand so quietly ten minutes before a race. His eyes droop half shut and he moves his head, indicating that he wants me to scratch his chin and jawline. Jack has a soulfulness that you barely expect to find on a fifteen-year-old school horse, never mind a three-year-old racehorse. I lose track of everything as I stand there, taking in the smell of the horse. I even shut my eyes for half a second, remembering the first time I touched a horse, how the smell reached a place in my heart. Who knew it would come to this?

I take a deep breath, trying to push the gloom away.

As Sophie leads Jack out of his stall, I crane my neck to look at the spectators. I'm vaguely hoping to spot Ruby even though I don't truly want her to be present should anything terrible befall me. I don't see her anywhere. The faces all belong to the typical dead-of-winter Aqueduct crowd. Middle-aged and old men. Men clutching newspapers and tip sheets. Men with angry faces, fat faces, lonesome faces. Men who rarely taste happiness.

The paddock judge calls for all riders to go to their horses and Henry gives me a leg up. I feel Jack's massive body igniting. We walk out onto the track to meet Juan and his pony horse. Jack nuzzles the pony's neck. Normally, Juan and I would be chatting but there's nothing normal about this afternoon. Juan's eyes look puffy. I imagine he's been mourning Layla whom he's known for several years. It seems ludicrous that Layla's dead and I'm here, alive and on a horse, a fine, big-hearted, talented horse. Juan unsnaps the leadshank and I steer Jack into the chute, unaided by the assistant starter. Jack stands perfectly still as the other colts and geldings file in with varying degrees of irascibility.

A few seconds later, the bell goes off and Jack breaks perfectly, flying straight out of the gate and immediately finding his stride. At seven furlongs, this race is a furlong longer than what he's used to running but not long enough for him to dawdle. I see that Ricky Fisher has sent his colt, a second-time starter called Bed of Nails, to the lead. I position Jack neck and neck with Santarez's horse, a compact chestnut with a lot of white markings.

When I'd watched a tape of Jack's last race—a six-furlong race three weeks earlier—I'd seen that he'd been left to lag at the back of the pack a little too long. By the time he came on, there wasn't enough ground left and he ended up third. I won't let that happen today.

"Keep at it, guy," I tell Jack, giving him his head a little more. I feel the gelding pulling strength from his core as his massive lungs take in air and distribute it through his body. More than anything though, I can feel Jack Valentine's willingness.

To our right, a gray long shot named Golden Gizmo has caught us and there are now three of us across the track. A length in front of us, Ricky Fisher's mount is kicking clods up into all our faces and my goggles are covered in mud. I pull up my first pair of goggles, having a few good moments of visibility before the second pair also gets dirty. I notice Ricky Fisher pulling farther ahead of us and, at the same time, Santarez's horse, who seemed full of steam, suddenly starts giving in. To my right, Golden Gizmo begins struggling. I can hear his breathing getting choppy and his jock, an old-timer from the Maryland circuit, is beating on the poor colt who just doesn't have anything left in the tank.

Ricky Fisher has now pulled almost four lengths ahead of us and it'd be a relatively simple proposition to just leave him there. The man who threatened me yesterday failed to tell me which horse I was supposed to let win. If it was indeed Fisher's horse, then the horse doesn't need much help. It would require a monstrous effort on Jack's part to get ahead now.

Jack is by Compelling Sound by Seattle Slew and this lineage is nothing to shrug at. His ancestry kicks in now and, just when I thought he was done for, he finds another gear. I feel him dropping lower to the ground as his massive heart pumps. He switches leads, gaining a length on Fisher. I see the jock turn to look over his shoulder at us. Then I am blinded as a clod of dirt gets kicked in my face. I pull my third pair of goggles up. Jack's strides are monstrous. From nose to tail he is one fluid line of power. He gains on Fisher's horse. I can't hear the announcer or the crowd or anything other than my own blood rushing in my ears and the thunder of the narrow but powerful horse underneath me. Then I feel Jack tiring. It's the last furlong and though I tried to let him know he had to go a little farther than last time he's weakening.

"Not now, fella," I say, "not yet. Give me one more burst and we're there, Jack." I lift my hands ever so slightly. One of his ears flicks in acknowledgment and I feel him surge once more.

We're now neck and neck with Ricky Fisher's horse.

Jack surges again and flies ahead just as the wire comes.

I stand up in the irons, letting Jack know it's over and he's done it.

I feel tears in my eyes again and I let them flow as I coo at the horse. His ears are forward now.

I turn him around and start cantering back to the winner's circle a little sooner than I normally would. I want to cut it short and get off the track where I'm so vulnerable. I don't imagine a sniper would take a chance in a crowd like this but you never know.

Sophie meets us near the winner's circle. She is beaming as she reaches up and shakes my hand then pats Jack's neck and kisses him on the nose. The gelding is tired but proud as he lets Sophie lead us. I see Henry and Violet, both glowing, both radiant. I lean forward on Jack's neck, studying the intricate network of veins, taking in the smell of a tired but triumphant thoroughbred. My last time.

SAM RIVERMAN/ED BURKE

30.

At Sixes and Sevens

I can't say I'm sorry to see the state of Florida becoming smaller beneath me. As the plane gains altitude and the city of Ft. Lauderdale recedes, I feel lighter. Chances are, I'll be back soon, but I'm damn glad to have been called up to Belmont where the Bureau operative is in over his head. An exercise rider is dead, a filly is injured and, according to the operative, there's more where that came from.

My boss didn't call me till late yesterday afternoon. I'd just come home to take a break before evening chores and I was feeling good. After seeing Lucinda's exhilaration over her cathartic incident aboard

Mike's Mohawk, I'd decided the time was ripe to have a talk with her. I had successfully ended things without causing her any evident flickers of pain. I'd come home, fussed over Cat like some sort of lunatic, and was debating whether or not to call Ruby again. We'd actually had a good talk the previous night and though she hadn't divulged that she'd been knocking boots with some other guy— hadn't even really told me what she'd been up to at all—I felt like the thread between us was stronger. But I was afraid of jinxing things by calling her again. I jumped halfway out of my seat when the phone I was staring at with so much concentration started ringing.

It was just the office calling. I was pleasantly surprised when they told me I was needed up there and should find someone to look after my horses while I came to New York for an indefinite period of time. I'd rushed back to the track, found Roderick, and offered him an overly generous amount of money to feed, muck out, and walk my horses. It didn't seem to strike him as odd that I was suddenly abandoning my string. Maybe this was customary behavior for inexperienced claimer trainers with too many irons in the fire.

I stood for a few minutes with each of my horses, feeling shitty about leaving them, particularly since Karma Police was supposed to run two days later. But I didn't guess he'd mind. As long as the horses got fed and walked a little they'd be okay. Not fit, but okay.

I went back to my place and booked a flight for Cat and me for early the next morning, then packed up my laptop and some clothing. I soaked in the tub for a while, mulling over the whole Ruby situation, wondering what would happen once we were face-to-face again. I kept thinking I should call her but something prevented me. I'd wait till I landed at JFK.

I tried to get to bed early but found myself tossing and turning. Got up and watched three back-to-back reruns of *Law and Order,* a bit disgusted to find that two of them were newer episodes and featured the unappealing blond assistant DA as opposed to one of the tough brunettes. Eventually, I slept. A little fitfully. Waking up earlier than I needed to. I got to the airport well ahead of schedule and sat in a brightly lit doughnut shop, sipping coffee that tasted like old tires.

There's nothing but blue sky and ocean outside the plane window and I feel better than I have in many weeks. Since there's no one in the seat next to me, I reach down and pull out Cat's Sherpa bag, bringing it to my lap. I open the bag a few inches and look in. She shoots me a withering glance. I stick my hand in and scratch her neck until I finally get a purr out of her. Satisfied, I put the bag back under the seat and start to tangentially think of the racehorse Sherpa Guide, a cocky little bay gelding that Ruby's been obsessed with since watching him break his maiden a few years ago at Belmont. The horse caught her eye in the paddock that day and she bet him. And won. She followed his career and was probably the only one who had ten bucks on him to win in an undercard race on Belmont Stakes day a while back. Sherpa went off at 34–1 and ran four wide to come on like gangbusters in the last furlong of the race, winning by a length and a half over a horse named Personable Pete. Ruby has tried to be there for every one of Sherpa's races. She takes his losses personally and frets during his layoffs. Once, she was cheering him so vigorously during a race that a stranger standing nearby asked her if she owned an interest in the horse. I grin to myself as I think of the little picture of Sherpa Guide that Ruby has taped to her fridge. This soothing thought helps me doze off and I wake as the plane begins its descent into the homeland.

AS I STEP out onto the curb to catch a shuttle over to the car rental place, the wind hits me and my breath catches in my chest. I feel a wave of anger—at the cold gray sky, at the vicious wind, at the bleakness that is New York City in late winter.

I rent a nondescript compact car and head toward Long Island. I get myself a room at the less-than-lovely Boulevard Motel just a few blocks away from the track. Cat is pretty upset with me when I finally open the Sherpa bag and invite her into the garishness of the motel room. She seems to scowl as she looks around, taking in the pressed-wood dresser, the fluorescent lighting, and the bedspread printed with pink flowers. Eventually, she deigns to hop out of the bag and go sniff at the food and water I've put down for her. I stare at her as I take my phone out and dial Ruby's number. The answering machine comes on. I start talking, telling her I'm unexpectedly in New York. Asking her to call. I try to keep my voice level. I dial her cell phone but I'm forwarded to her voice mail. I leave the same message. I put the phone back in my pocket and start wondering where she could be at nine in the morning. I suppose I don't want to dwell on it.

I watch Cat lap water from a plastic cup and, when I'm sure that she's comfortable and has suffered no adverse effects from the plane ride, I bid her adieu, lock the door, and reflect that I am in all likelihood the only FBI agent who travels to his assignments with a cat. Last time I checked I didn't even *like* cats. I walk to the non-descript car, get in, and drive.

SPRING HASN'T EVEN thought of putting its touches on New York yet, but the entrance to the Belmont backside looks inviting all the same. Feels like home. A little less so when I pull up to the gate and a young security guard scowls, removing any trace of attractiveness from her face, and asks me my business.

"My name should be on your sheet. Sam Riverman," I tell her. She looks down at her clipboard.

"Okay, go," she says, waving me on without looking at me.

I haven't been gone long but I realize I've already gotten used to the friendlier environment of Florida.

I park the car and start walking over toward the barn area. Before I've reached the first shedrow, the sounds come. Radios, hooves against cold dirt, buckets banging into wooden stalls. The Belmont backside population has been thinned by winter, with the heavy hitters gone south or west. Those left behind have settled in, grinding their teeth and bearing the cold.

I find my way to Jim Radcliffe's barn where Carmelo Jimenez, our operative, is posing as a groom named Carlo Sanchez. The first person I see at Radcliffe's shedrow is a sturdy but slightly stooped Latin man leading a sleepy bay mare.

"Hi, I'm looking for Carlo," I say.

"You found him."

"Oh." I'm genuinely surprised. The man *really* looks like a groom. "Carlo Sanchez?" I double-check.

"Yep. And you're Sam Riverman," Carlo says.

Carlo is a weathered man in his mid-forties. He has a pencil mustache that doesn't belong on his thick-featured face.

"Got a minute?" I ask.

"Sure. Let me just put this girl away."

I make myself comfortable on a tack trunk in the aisle while Carlo finishes up with the mare. I note that our operative has found a good outfit to work for. Though I don't know much about Jim Radcliffe, it's obvious the man runs a tight ship. Everything in the shedrow is tidy, clean, and color coordinated in maroon and yellow. I feel a sudden stab of anxiety wondering how my three claimers are faring down at Gulfstream this morning with only Rod to tend to them. I'm about to take out my phone to call Rod when Carlo materializes before me and indicates that I should follow him. He leads the way to the tack room and shows me in, pulling the door shut behind us.

"This is okay?" I ask, a little surprised since it doesn't seem like the most secure place to talk.

"Fine," he assures me. "Radcliffe isn't coming in till afternoon and no one else will walk in with the door closed, they know I come in here to make phone calls. They think I've got a hot mama tucked away somewhere." Carlo smiles faintly.

He indicates a chair and tells me to make myself comfortable. He flips a bucket over and sits on it. He brings his enormous calloused hands to rest on his knees then looks up at me with an almost mischievous expression. "I got the job done about two hours ago."

"How's that?"

"Got it on tape," he grins.

"Got what on tape? I'm not up to speed with the situation here. You were bugging this Nick Blackman individual?"

"Oh yeah. Bugging him. Dude couldn't have been more stupid."

It surprises me to hear *dude* issue from Carmelo's mouth.

"What happened?"

"Talked in his car. Seemed to know we had his barn office wired but didn't seem to think we'd get his car. Took a ride with his boss, Davide Marinella. You heard about Marinella?"

"Yeah. Sure, I read the file. Bookie, mob, et cetera."

"And proud racehorse owner. Which was his downfall. Guy got fucking sentimental about his racehorse. Tried having the race fixed. Little allowance race with a bunch of nobody riders in it. Got to most of the riders except Jasper Lee who don't bend that way, and Attila Johnson, a bug boy. From what I'd heard, Johnson was crooked, but I guess he all of a sudden got a conscience. He won't play ball. They try to take Johnson out right in broad fucking daylight on the track yesterday morning during works. Got some girl rider instead. All this just so Marinella's lousy horse could have a chance in a race. Un-fucking-believable. But this Attila Johnson, he rides the race of his life and wins it."

"You got all this on tape?" I ask, incredulous.

"Nah, that I pieced together. What I got on tape this morning was Marinella telling Nick Blackman he's gotta get rid of Attila, that the guy's a loose cannon. Apparently they'd been trying to scare Attila for a few weeks with little incidents but it hadn't done the trick. So Marinella tells Blackman he's gotta help him take Attila out. *On tape.*" Carmelo grins.

"Now we got warrants coming and most of it gets wrapped up today. I'm not having anything to do with it from now on. They want to keep me useful, so I'm not blowing my cover. I'll keep working for Radcliffe another couple weeks so it seems unrelated when I quit."

"And what do I do?" I say, feeling left out.

"I guess it's back to the sunshine state for you, friend. Check in with the office." Carmelo adds, "Maybe they want you up here a few days before you go back."

"Right. I'll do that," I tell him.

"It's a bitch, huh?" he says apropos of I don't know what.

"Yeah," I shrug. "Good work," I add, even though I feel left out and a little bitter about having taken this trip north for no good reason.

I walk away from the shedrow feeling at a loss until I remember Ruby mentioning some burgeoning friendship with Violet Kravitz, the wife of Henry Meyer. I stop the next hotwalker I see, asking if he knows where Henry Meyer's barn is. The guy just shrugs. I ask a few more people until someone finally points me in the right direction.

It's nearing midday now but the sun hasn't won its battle with the steely cloud bed and the wind is working overtime.

I find Meyer's shedrow but it's deserted. Lunchtime I guess. I go to what I assume is the door to the barn office and knock, not expecting a response.

"Yes?" a female voice answers. I open the door and find an elegant gray-haired woman sitting at a desk, looking immensely guilty about something.

"Oh," she says, visibly relieved, "who are you?"

"I'm a friend of Ruby Murphy's?" I venture, smelling smoke and noticing a half-extinguished cigarette sticking out from under the woman's boot.

"Oh!" The woman looks pleased. "Where is that girl?"

"I was going to ask you. Are you Violet Kravitz?"

"Yes I am, and you?"

"Sam Riverman," I say, extending a hand.

"Oh." Violet seems disappointed.

"I'm afraid you've caught me smoking, Sam Riverman. My husband prohibits such recklessness," she says cheerfully. "Please don't mention it to him."

"Wouldn't dream of it."

"Nice of you, Sam. Now tell me what brings you here looking for Miss Murphy?"

"She'd mentioned spending time with you. I happened to be on the backside visiting a friend. Thought I'd see if you had Ruby secreted away in here since I haven't been able to reach her."

"I haven't been able to reach her either, actually, but since I

haven't seen hide nor hair of Attila, I'm assuming the two have reconciled and disappeared together."

"Attila?" I say with a sinking feeling.

"Oh, you don't know Attila?"

"No, I'm afraid I don't. He's a rider though, isn't he?"

"Yes, he's a rider. And the paramour of our Miss Murphy
though I had the distinct feeling the liaison wasn't long for this
world. But now I'm gossiping with a complete stranger. I hope you
won't think poorly of me."

"No," I say, feeling sick.

"You look dejected. Have I blundered horribly? Are you a suitor
of Ruby's?"

"Oh . . . I don't know," I say, making a helpless gesture.

"I'm a motor mouth," Violet Kravitz says, visibly shaken. "I've
blundered."

"It's really all right," I say, trying to silence the woman before
she divulges more unwanted information. "I should get going, it
was nice to meet you."

"Likewise, Sam Riverman, and if I do see Ruby I'll certainly tell
her you were asking after her."

I nod, smile anemically, and walk away.

I go back to the parking lot and sit in the nondescript compact
car for several long minutes. I feel paralyzed by my confirmed suspi-
cions. I have been gone for months and I'm particularly lousy at
communicating my feelings so I suppose it's only fair that Ruby has
taken up with someone. All the same, I feel kicked, and particularly
incensed to learn she's been sleeping with a crooked jockey with a
hit out on him.

I drive back to the motel. I let myself in and find Cat sleeping
in the middle of the bed, not even deigning to open an eye.

I sit down in an uncomfortable brown chair and stare at the
dirty carpet.

31.

Caught

At first, I was so scared I was sure I was having a heart attack. My chest felt tight and I couldn't breathe. I kept hoping that we'd pass by someone I knew as we walked from the clubhouse into the parking lot. It didn't happen though and I asked him if he was sure he had the right girl. After all, he hadn't called me by name. He ignored the question. The way Attila's world had been crumbling, I'd been half expecting something like this to happen, but I wasn't sure what purpose my being kidnapped would serve.

When we reached the guy's car he unceremoniously shoved me into the backseat. There was a white dog in the car and the animal started licking me, much to my captor's chagrin. The guy scowled at the dog, sharply told him to get in the front seat, then started tying up my hands. I looked right into the guy's eyes as he did this. He had light brown eyes clouded with trouble. His hair was longish, stringy, and dark. He was probably in his mid-twenties. He looked almost gentle, easily frightened. So I screamed. His hand flew over my mouth and he shoved me backward. I sunk my teeth into his hand. He found a rag on the floor and stuffed it in my mouth. Then, he searched me, finding my cell phone and taking it. He also took the forty dollars I had in a front pocket but returned the half pack of Marlboro Lights to my coat pocket. I wanted to tell him I desperately needed a cigarette but all I could manage from behind the gag was a horrible moaning sound that he chose to ignore. He shoved me under a dog blanket in the backseat of his car then started driving.

Between bouts of panic I thought about a whole lot of things as I lay under the smelly dog blanket with a gag in my mouth and my bound hands losing circulation. I thought about dying. In a surprisingly level-headed manner. I hoped that if it happened it wouldn't hurt and someone would look after my cats. By age twenty-five I had begun announcing to my mother, sister, and friend Jane that I wanted to be buried in a nice graveyard with a tree and an old gravestone. People could conduct experiments on my body, transplant my organs, use my skin cells, whatever, so long as what was left of me went in a hole in the ground. My loved ones thought me mildly macabre for thinking about things like that at so young an age. Now I was hoping it hadn't been prescient.

I thought about Attila too. And about Ed. Wishing Ed would save me. Hoping Attila wasn't in even deeper trouble than I was in now.

After we'd been driving for about twenty minutes, the guy pulled over, got out, and came to take my gag off. It was like he'd been thinking about things while he was driving and decided he should have asked me a few questions.

"Where is the jockey?" he demanded.

"I have no idea."

"Where!" he barked, shoving the gun toward me. I noticed that it was a tiny, almost feminine-looking gun.

"I don't know! The last time I saw him he was at Aqueduct."

"But where would he go after that?"

"I have no idea. And I don't know what good I'm going to do you."

"Please be quiet," he said, pushing me back down and putting the blanket over my head.

He got back in the front seat and started driving again.

I waited a few minutes and then tried calling out a few muffled questions. He hadn't put the gag back in, so I thought I could be heard from under my blanket. I asked if he expected to get a ransom for me and if so from whom. I suppose I was nervous enough to seem casual as I told him that none of my friends or relatives have any money and that I'm of little or no monetary value to the world at large. By that point I wasn't truly fearing for my life anymore. He told me to shut up and that he wouldn't hurt me as long as I didn't try any *funny stuff*. He said it just like that: *Don't try any funny stuff.* As if reading from a bad script. I asked him if I could call my neighbor to feed my cats. He ignored me and when I asked again, he said no.

Eventually, I just lay there, under the blanket, trying to stay calm. I managed to lull myself into a sort of dark reverie that was akin to sleep. I woke up when the car's motion changed and we came to a stop. I had a throbbing headache and a dry mouth. My captor came and helped me out of the backseat. We were in the country. There were pine trees and snow. The air was cold and clean smelling and I could hear what sounded like a little stream running nearby. Ahead, there was a small white one-story house, and about a hundred yards back a little wooden cabin. As the guy told me to walk toward the cabin, the dog trotted at his side. It was almost bucolic seeming for a moment. Then my captor pulled some keys from his pocket, unlocked the padlock on the cabin door, and nudged me inside. It was just one big, dirty room and the floor felt unstable. There was nothing in it other than a sagging cardboard box and a chair with a broken back. An odor of mold and dust thickened the air.

"I need to pee," I told my captor. This seemed to alarm him. He'd apparently never been here before either. He joined me in looking around the little room and discovering that there was no toilet in evidence. The cabin had two windows that overlooked the stream. I could hear it rushing out there and the sound was making matters worse.

"We'll see about that when you tell me where to find the jockey."

"I told you, I know about as much as you do. The last time I saw him he was walking into the racing secretary's office at Aqueduct. Which I assume is far from here. Where exactly are we?"

"I don't think that's any of your business," the guy said, looking around nervously, as if there might be a sign announcing our location.

"Okay, so don't tell me, but the fact remains, I have got to go to the bathroom."

"All right," he said, "I'll find something." He turned and went back outside. I was planning to make a run for it when I heard him padlock the door. I stood there, cold and scared, my hands throbbing from the rope. The dog was still in the room with me. We stared at each other. He was a cute dog. Mostly white. Shaggy hair. Some kind of mutt.

He panted a little.

I started eyeing the windows. They didn't seem particularly secure and I was figuring I could kick them out pretty easily but, before I'd had time to get any further with this plan, my captor was back.

"Here," he said, setting a bucket on the floor.

"Great," I smirked. I had the sense that he felt bad about it, that, in spite of the fact that he was doing fairly unpleasant things to me, his heart wasn't exactly in it. He untied my hands and I rubbed my wrists.

"I'm gonna leave so you can use that in privacy," he said, motioning to the bucket, "and then I'm gonna be boarding up these windows."

"Oh," I said, deflated.

He called to his dog, then went back out. I heard him locking me in. I stood hesitating, not particularly keen on peeing into a bucket. It seemed I had no choice though. I pulled my pants down and squatted. It was a relief.

I'd barely rezipped my pants when the guy appeared outside the biggest window. He had a giant piece of plywood that he fitted over its exterior. Pretty soon he was pounding nails into the wall, imprisoning me.

I took my pack of cigarettes out of my coat pocket. I lovingly lit a cigarette and inhaled deeply. Though I'd been trying to cut down, this didn't seem like the time to be hard on myself.

I could smell my own urine in the bucket, so I carried it to a far corner and covered it with a piece of moldy linoleum that I peeled off the floor. I thought about how miserable horses get when their stalls are dirty and for the first time I really understood. The guy pounded another sheet of plywood over the second window, but it wasn't big enough to shut out all the light.

I went over to look through the contents of the sagging cardboard box that was nudged against one of the walls. There were a few tattered children's books as well as a hardcover copy of Balzac's *Père Goriot*. I gratefully picked it out and opened it. The first third of the pages were missing but the rest was there and I felt ridiculously elated. As if finding two-thirds of a book I like was a sign that all would soon be well. I kept digging through the box and felt a flush of adrenaline as I found a rusted old carpet knife. Clearly the psycho wasn't experienced at kidnapping or he'd have looked through this box. I put the carpet knife into my pants pocket and looked around. There was a shaft of light in one corner of the room, so I sat down on the cold floor, pulled my coat around me, lit another cigarette, and started reading *Père Goriot*. For a time I was actually transported to Balzac's world. As I read, I kept picturing Balzac's face as it looms out from the monument on his gravesite in Paris, which I'd visited once years earlier. Somehow, thinking of Balzac's face made me feel better. For a while. Then I got really cold and scared and time refused to move.

My captor doesn't strike me as the person in charge of whatever is going on. Maybe the person in charge has already found Attila. I picture Attila's face. His close-set vivid eyes. I think of how mean I was to him at the motel the other night. How suddenly everything in me had shut off as quickly as it had opened when we first met. I wonder at my own sanity. I pray that Attila is okay. I cry.

32.

If Wishes Were Horses

I'm sitting in the living room with the TV on but I'm not seeing the screen, the living room, or anything other than a vision of Karen with her spandex workout pants rolled down over her shelf ass. I keep replaying the scene in my mind, but it's not getting me worked up. It's just making my heart break. Her note is there, on the coffee table, right where she left it. I've looked at it but I haven't actually touched it. As soon as I saw it there, I knew what it would say. She's gone. She's taken Jake and they've split.

"*. . . for a few days or until I sort things out.*"

I have no idea where she is. Probably not at her mother's since she can't stand her mother. Karen's got a couple of girlfriends but she's always kept me away from them, like her relationship with the girlfriends is a thing I'm not allowed to sully. Not that it's sexual or anything. Just that Karen likes her boundaries. She even likes the word *boundaries* and abuses it left and right. If I want to fuck her in the bathtub, there's a *boundary* involved. My getting in the tub with her would violate the *boundary* of her being alone with her body. And maybe all these *boundaries* should have been a red flag. I don't really know if you're supposed to have quite so many *boundaries* in a marriage. In fact, right now, I don't know fuck-all other than I got in late last night and felt like hell and now I feel even worse. It had been a rough day what with witnessing Layla's death. Seeing that made me lose it a little and I'd gone off to think things through. I wanted to kill that jockey, but, eventually, I got to feeling bad about the poor jerk and went back to the track to try to keep an eye on him. I watched as he actually won another race. Afterward, I half expected that whoever had taken out Layla that morning would do the same to Attila. But no. I saw him go into the jocks room unmolested, then I saw him come out and I guess he was done riding for the day, he had his street clothes on. He went to the parking lot, got in a car I didn't know he had, and drove off. I left it at that. Then I went to AA. Sat listening to the complaints of newcomers and the wisdoms of old crooked-nosed guys that have been sober forty years. Though I don't usually go in for that kind of thing, I went to dinner with a bunch of people. Some Italian place on Thirteenth Street in Manhattan. We were in there half the night. Just shooting the shit the way a bunch of drunks do. Eating. Drinking Cokes and soda water. I didn't tell anyone exactly what was going on with me, just said I had some troubles with the wife. One of the old-timers told me to just be patient. I figured maybe he was right. I'd give Karen some space to be crazy in and then maybe eventually she'd come around to liking me again.

BY THE TIME I got home, it was late, almost one. Sometimes Karen stays up watching old movies but not this time. She was in the bedroom, apparently asleep. I tried shaking her a little. I wanted her to wake up and say good night. She didn't move though.

I slept in late. When I got up and went downstairs, I saw the note.

I don't know what she thought. What made her decide to leave when she did. Maybe she thought that I was out whoring all night.

And now I have no idea where to find her or why she left and I'm staring at the TV screen, trying to think of something to do. Eventually, I decide to call Ruby. I dial her home number from memory but of course nothing's ever that simple. She's not there. I leave a message then go to the hall to get my cell phone from my coat pocket so I can look her cell number up. No luck on that one either.

I glance outside and see that it's started raining hammers and nails.

For once, the weather agrees with my mood.

I put my jacket on and go outside. It's a lot warmer than it's been and the rain is melting what's left of the snow. It's a damned mess out there.

I get in the truck, start the engine, and put Beethoven on at full volume. The truck has become the only place that's really mine anymore. As soon as Karen moved into my house eight years ago, she started redecorating and changing everything around and, over time, it got to be her house, not mine. Now I don't feel that comfortable there.

It's Beethoven's Third Symphony and after a while the relentless fucking cheerfulness of it starts making me see red. I take the CD out and listen to the rain pounding down on the truck. Eventually I start driving. I head toward the Woodland Motel. I don't really expect to find Ruby there and, if he has any sense, Attila will have moved to Tahiti. But I don't think of Attila as someone with a lot of sense.

I knock at the door to room eight and nothing happens. I go to the motel office, a tiny room with a metal and glass booth where presumably the front desk person sits, shielded from untoward clientele. The booth is empty though and there isn't any kind of bell to ring. I call out a few times and eventually, an enormous white woman comes lumbering in. She's so big she can barely squeeze through the door and has to turn to the side to fit. She has unnatural-looking black hair, some of it done up in little crooked braids, the rest hanging in greasy curtains. She's wearing bright red lipstick and has drawn in dark black eyebrows the way crazy ladies always seem to, a sort of Joan Crawford look with the eyebrow pencil going way beyond where there could have been any actual eyebrow. She wouldn't have been a good-looking woman under any circumstances but at her weight she's downright scary. Plus, I figure, she's got to be insane. No one in her right mind would do that eyebrow thing.

"Yeah?" she snarls, showing me the brown stuff stuck between her front teeth.

"Room eight, Attila Johnson, you know where he is?"

"Ain't nobody in room eight."

"There was yesterday. Short blond man?"

"Oh yeah," she says, looking a little animated now. "He's gone. Guess you'd say he checked out."

She bursts into a horrible laugh that makes her body jiggle.

"What?" I say, pulse accelerating.

"He split, mister. Left his key in the room at least and, of course, his girlfriend had paid for the room ahead of time. But he's gone."

"Oh," I say, relieved. "All right, thanks." I turn and walk away, feeling her staring at my back.

I DON'T KNOW why but now I'm determined to find Attila. I drive to the crummy little house where he rents the basement. I double park the truck and am about to walk down the three steps to his door when a woman's voice calls out: "Can I help you with something?"

I look to my right and notice a middle-aged woman standing in the doorway.

"I'm trying to find Attila," I say, forcing out a smile. She looks at me like I just crawled out of a sewage pipe.

"That makes three of us," she says, putting her hands on her hips. "I'm looking for him because I need money for the electric bill and that nice wife of his was by yesterday looking for him too."

I knew Attila had a wife, but I thought they'd long been separated. Or at least that's what he'd told Ruby. I felt myself swelling with a protective feeling for Ruby.

"Okay," I shrug at the matron. "If you see him, tell him Sal was looking for him."

"Sal? That's Italian?" she asks, cocking a judgmental Irish eyebrow at me.

"Egyptian," I say, turning my back to her.

AS I PULL UP to the security gate at Belmont, I realize that the temporary parking sticker I'd been issued while chauffeuring Attila around expired yesterday. The security guard isn't in a friendly mood and won't let me through, so I ask her to call over to Henry Meyer's barn. Violet answers the phone and, to my surprise, says she'll come get me. As involved as Henry and Violet are with their horse lives, I wasn't even sure they'd remember me by name, much less come fetch me. The security guard seems peeved, like she was hoping I wouldn't be granted access. I pull my truck to the side and sit waiting for Violet. Ten minutes later, the good lady appears.

Before I have time to stumble out any explanation of what I'm doing here or why, Violet gives me a cheerful hello and watches as the security guard issues me a pass and a parking permit.

I offer to drive Violet back to her shedrow and she gratefully accepts, hopping into the passenger side of the truck. She's wearing a huge red rain poncho but some of her hair has gotten soaked and is dripping onto the seat of my truck.

"I'm sorry about the puddles," Violet says.

"Not a problem. Thanks for coming to get me. I guess you wonder what I'm doing here."

"Oh, I never wonder what anyone is doing at the racetrack." She smiles.

"Oh no?"

"I fell in love with all racetracks the first time I set foot on one. I understand when someone suddenly wishes to be at the track."

"Oh," I say, though I don't feel like any deep love of the track has anything to do with my being here, don't in fact know if I even like being at the track. I ask Violet if she's heard from Ruby or Attila but she has not.

"And certainly everyone is looking for Attila," she says. "It has been quite a day."

"Oh yeah? What else happened?"

"That cretin Nick Blackman was arrested is what."

"Nick Blackman? Who's that?"

"Crooked trainer. Ran his horses into the ground. He was evidently following orders from a Mafia person," Violet says. "I'd long heard there were Mafia connections in racing but I'd really never seen evidence of such a thing." She shakes her head. "I'd also heard rumors about Attila, but I chose not to believe them. It seems he put himself at risk by winning the race on Jack Valentine."

"Really?" I say, although that much I know to be true.

"Oh yes. The FBI was here. As well as dozens of police officers. You didn't think poor Layla's death would simply get swept under the rug now, did you?"

I tell her that no, I suppose I didn't.

"You go park the truck and then come to the office," Violet instructs me. "I'll tell you the rest."

I do as I'm told, dropping her at the barn then parking the truck. As I walk back to the shedrow, the rain starts coming down harder, punishing me. For what, I'm not sure.

Five minutes later, Violet has installed me in the most comfortable chair in the office. I don't know where Henry is but one of the grooms comes into the office and hands Violet a towel.

"Thank you so much," Violet says, bowing slightly to the guy. I can't imagine grooms get bowed to all that much, but this guy seems used to it.

Violet starts drying her long gray hair as she gives me details of the day's events. I'm more than a little startled to hear her utter Uncle Davide's name. I try keeping my face blank. I don't want to have to explain to Violet how it is I know Davide Marinella, my friend Johnny, the bookie's, uncle. Davide is known to everyone, including the FBI, as Uncle Davide.

"It's always the way with these Mafia people though," she says. "They've always got names. I'm sure this reprehensible Davide man is not in fact anyone's *uncle*."

I shrug. The truth is, he's uncle to a dozen or so of Johnny's brothers, sisters, and cousins. According to Violet, Davide's downfall came in trying to fix that little race Jack Valentine ran in. All just to give his horse a chance. Stupid if you ask me. And surprising. I just wouldn't have thought Uncle Davide to be stupid. Shows how much I know. Just about zero.

"And, as a sad punctuation mark to these dark events, it appears Jack Valentine chipped a sesamoid bone. It will take him months to recover and we're probably just going to have to pension him on a farm somewhere or sell him off as a pleasure horse prospect."

"I'm sorry, Violet, that's a shame."

"It's sad, yes," she agrees, "but that's horses."

I ask her a few questions about horse injuries, finding that in fact I am quite interested in all of this and on some level maybe racing really is getting in my blood. Which must be how I've somehow ended up here, sitting in a racing stable office at three P.M. on a Friday afternoon with rain coming down in rivers and a forty-something-year-old woman darting out of the office anytime someone walks by so she can try to cadge cigarettes. I don't know if the entire backside of the track has been asked not to give Violet Kravitz cigarettes or if the collected lot of them have given up the habit, but no one seems to have a cigarette and Violet is getting increasingly fidgety. She doesn't seem to have any actual work to do and we've tried and failed to reach Ruby several times, so finally I suggest I give her a ride to the store to get some cigarettes.

"Certainly not, Sal." She is indignant. "I am not going to buy cigarettes. What do you take me for?"

"Sorry, I just thought, well, I thought you wanted a cigarette."

"One. Not twenty."

"Okay. Sorry. I take it back."

This makes her laugh.

"You still haven't told me what's brought you here on this unfortunate afternoon, Sal."

"Just needed to hear someone other than my head talking at me," I shrug.

"Well, should you need an ear, mine is in perfectly good working order," she smiles.

"Thank you, Violet, that's nice of you," I say, meaning it. "You need a ride somewhere or you staying here?"

"Henry will be back soon. I'm going to wait for him here and do a little work," she says, indicating a stack of paperwork on the desk.

"All right then, Violet. Thank you for keeping me company."

"For tales of murder."

"Yes. All of it. Thank you," I say, and I find myself bowing to her just as she did to the groom.

I get back to the truck and put Beethoven's Third back on because suddenly I can tolerate a little good cheer.

I DRIVE OVER to Brooklyn and to the North Side, in the direction of Johnny's candy store, wondering if it'll even be open or what will be going on. I pull into a spot half a block away and am debating about whether or not I feel like going in there. For all I know, the feds have the place wired. I'm sitting staring ahead when I get the best idea I've had in a very long time. It occurs to me that my son Jake's violin teacher, Marilyn Levy, lives right around here somewhere and that Jake happens to get his violin lessons at four on Fridays. It's now four-forty-five. If Karen's really trying to hide from me, she probably hasn't taken Jake for his lesson. On the other hand, she's so religious about my son having to learn to play the fucking violin, you never know. She might just figure I'd have forgotten about the lessons and their location.

It takes me a couple of minutes of driving around to remember which block it is, but finally I find the little brownstone on North Sixth Street. There's a spot right in front. I pull in and wait. At five minutes to five, my wife strolls onto the block. She looks so good. It takes her a minute to notice my truck and when she does, her eyes get big and I see her hesitate. I jump out of the truck.

"Sal, what the fuck are you doing here?" she spits.

"Come on, Karen," I say.

"Come on what?"

"Let's talk."

"I have to get Jake."

"Sure. I'll give you both a ride home and then you and me talk."

"Are you kidding me?" She is so angry she actually comes closer, putting her face just a few inches from mine. She's turning red from head to toe.

"Karen, I'm not sure how I've made you so damn mad but I'm sorry about it. Please come home."

"Just like that? Months of relationship crimes and I'm just gonna go, 'Oh, okay, I'll go home.' No fucking way, Salvatore."

Wow. Salvatore. Now I know she's mad.

"What relationship crimes?"

"You're off gallivanting with that fucking Ruby slut. You bring her home to fucking dinner, Sal, that's what. And then you claim she's got some boyfriend and you're off at the track helping her boyfriend? I don't think so."

"What's Ruby got to do with this?" I ask, genuinely shocked. "Her boyfriend was in a bad spot. I tried to help."

"Oh right. Yeah. Sure. You think I'm fucking stupid? You think you can just go bang the nearest slut and I don't mind 'cause you're putting food on the table and big TVs in the living room? And you ain't gonna be putting nothing nowhere if you don't go back to work, Sal."

"Karen, honey, I got a bad back."

"You got a bad dick is what you got."

Now I'm offended.

"Karen, listen to me," I say, putting my hands on her shoulders.

"Don't touch me," she hisses.

"Karen, I love you. I think about you constantly. I want to make love to you five times a day. I don't understand you at all but I love you. Will you marry me?"

This seems to stump her.

"What?"

"Will you marry me?"

"I already made that mistake, Sal."

"I want to do it over, Karen. I want to marry you again. I want you to tell me everything you think. I want to know everything."

Her mouth is open a little and she's quiet. I've genuinely surprised her.

"I gotta go get Jake," she says after a few moments.

"Get Jake. Then come home and talk to me."

"I'll have to think about that," she says, turning her back to me.

I watch her walk up the stoop and ring the violin teacher's doorbell.

She looks so fucking good. And what's more, she's my wife.

ATTILA JOHNSON

33.

Dead by Yesterday

I'm awakened by a terrible wheezing sound. I sit up on the narrow lumpy bed but my eyes won't open and my head is throbbing. I rub my face and start breathing deeply. The wheezing sound is getting louder. I finally pry my eyes open. My vision is blurred as I look around, trying to find visible evidence of the horrible sound.

I throw the thin blanket back, stand up, put my boxers on, and walk into the hall. The sound seems to be coming from the room next to mine. I put my ear to the door and bingo. The wheezing is coming from the entrails of room three at the lovely Sea Breeze Hotel in Coney Island.

Suddenly, the weight of my head against the door makes it swing open and I nearly fall into a darkened room.

"What the fuck?" a raspy voice asks.

"Sorry," I say into the dimness. "I got lost." I realize this sounds ridiculous.

The wheezing grows louder then a light comes on and I'm face-to-face with the source of the terrible sound. He's a thin old man sitting in a straight-backed chair. He's yellow all over and his eyes are lost in folds of drooping wrinkled flesh.

"What the hell you doin', fucko?" the thin man asks.

"I'm very sorry. It was an accident. Sorry to have intruded," I say, backing into the hall. The man is wheezing even louder now and looks like he's about to keel over.

"Are you all right, sir?" I ask, even though it's obvious he isn't.

"Mind your beeswax, fucko," he says.

I walk back into my room, fantasize briefly of punishing the old cruster for calling me fucko, and then decide his life is punishment enough and besides, at this point, I *am* a fucko. A no-good has-been. I'm nearly thirty-five years old and my distinctly lackluster riding career is over after five wins, five seconds, and eighteen thirds. I've got two grand in the bank and a crummy rented basement apartment. The woman I thought I might fall in love with has disappeared, my wife is insane, and my daughter probably hates me. I *am* a fucko.

The filthy carpet is cold under my bare feet so I get back in bed, pull the blanket over my head and ponder what possessed me to come to this rancid hotel. I had a notion I'd run into Ruby by staying here, just a block from her place. She'd once pointed the Sea Breeze Hotel out to me and told me she'd spent a night here long ago, before she'd moved to Coney. I figured if she could stomach it, it wouldn't be all that bad. I was wrong. The place is the worst kind of dive and what's more, I haven't been able to find Ruby. I've called, I've rung her buzzer, I've even run into Ramirez, the grouchy neighbor, but he didn't know where she was either. And now I've had a fitful cold night and been awakened by the old wheezer next door. Though if I think about it, it's all icing on the cake since I expected to be dead by now.

One thought that's kept my instinct for self-preservation alive and well is my daughter, Grace. I'm not sure I trust Ava to stay sane enough to properly raise our daughter and I dread to think what would happen if my drunken father somehow got custody, or worse yet, Ava's rigid right-wing parents. I start obsessing over the whole thing and it occurs to me to write out a will and attempt to assign custody to someone I trust. I spend a few moments contemplating this but the only person I can think of is Violet Kravitz and I can't quite picture the lady's reaction to being willed a child. It seems if she wanted one, she'd have gone ahead and had one.

I eventually get out of bed and put my clothes on. They don't smell all that good but I'm afraid to go back to my apartment to get clean things. I probably shouldn't even be within miles of Coney Island since whoever is trying to do me in has tried doing it here. But the fact is, I have no idea what to do or where to go. I suppose I could go back to North Carolina. I've got a few friends there. I could probably get work on a horse farm. Eke out an existence— but little more. Life without racing isn't much of a life and I'm too old to start from scratch.

None of these thoughts serve to cheer me or make the dank hotel room less dank. I throw water on my face, run my fingers through my hair, then put my jacket on and go down to the front desk to return my key to the rail thin black woman at reception. She says nothing as I hand her the key and thank her.

I've completely forgotten about the car and probably wouldn't have remembered until much later had I not walked right by it. I bought it yesterday afternoon before going to ride my last race. I figured if there was any chance of my staying alive, I'd need a car. I'd known for a while that Pepe, one of Violet and Henry's exercise riders, was trying to sell his Gremlin. The car is bright orange. Not the most anonymous car in the world but cheap and available on short notice. Pepe wanted two grand for it but I got him down to twelve hundred. The thing will probably die after fifty miles but it's better than nothing. I unlock it and get in. I still have no idea where I'm going. I take my phone out and try Ruby's various numbers once

more for good measure, not really expecting her to be there. I start
wondering if she's suddenly packed up her cats and left town.

I put the phone away and stare at the gray silence of Surf
Avenue. I've never seen it this sleepy and contained and I remember
pictures Ruby showed me of this strip a hundred years ago. The
wide dirt road was lined with amusements and horse carriages.
Happy people strolled, wearing clothes that now seem so restrictive
and formal but must have been considered sportswear at the time. I
wish I could go back and live in a time when horses were everywhere and people didn't leave one another.

I feel another bout of tears coming but I'm tired of crying, having cried more in the last twelve hours than in the collected thirty-
four and three-quarters years of my life.

I pull the Gremlin out of its parking space and drive up onto
Surf Avenue, making a left onto Ocean Parkway.

Next thing I know, I'm pulling up to a storefront lawyer in the
middle of a Hasidic neighborhood off Ocean Parkway.

A very young woman is sitting at a desk in the front room. She
seems quite surprised to see a walk-in client in spite of the fact that
a sign outside indicated that such clients were welcome. I guess I
don't fit the bill for their regular clientele, all of whom, judging by
the three people seated in the waiting area, are Hasidim.

I explain to the young woman that I'd like to draw up a will.
She looks at me crookedly and I'm not sure if she thinks I'm an
absolute nut case or if she has some sort of eye problem. She asks
me to take a seat and I do. The magazines all appear to be in
Hebrew so I just sit, staring at my hands. For some reason, I haven't
examined my hands in a long time, and as I notice now how old and
battered they are I simultaneously think of Ruby's nicely made
hands that her piano teacher has convinced her are stubby. I suddenly want to kill the piano teacher.

About a half hour later I'm ushered into a cluttered back room
with a drop ceiling. The lawyer is a man named Saul Victory who,
as it happens, doesn't seem to be Hasidic at all though I suppose he

might be a less rigid Hasid who doesn't go in for all the dark suits and hats and exotic hair configurations.

"A will?" Saul Victory says after offering me a seat.

"Yes," I say.

Saul Victory doesn't seem to think it's a strange request. In fact, he's a rather nice man and becomes extremely animated when I tell him I'm a jockey.

"Ah," he says, getting a dreamy look, "how I miss that horse, Point Given."

"Yes. There's a lot of that going around. Speculation about what he could have done as a four-year-old. He was a very good horse."

"He was a gangster," Saul Victory exclaims, pounding his fist into a pile of papers on his desk. "I'll never forget the way he looked on Belmont Stakes day with that crazy mask on his face— What do you call that mask?"

"Blinkers?"

"Yes, his crazy blinkers and the way he walked. He walked like Muhammad Ali. That horse was a gangster."

I can't say I ever really thought of Point Given as a gangster, but okay. I don't have the heart to tell old Saul here that my racing career is as over as Point Given's. As we get through the business of drawing up a will, I let him keep chatting about some of the horses he's watched race. He is, with good reason, vigorously enthralled by Funny Cide and smitten with Azeri. He even mentions Ruby's favorite horse, Sherpa Guide.

An hour later and several hundred dollars poorer, I walk out of Saul Victory's office feeling a little lighter.

And then a strange thing happens.

I have a very strong urge to see my wife.

The idea is so shocking to me that I pull the Gremlin over to the side of the road and sit for several minutes trying to think through this surprising urge. But I can't see straight or think straight. I need to see my wife.

I start driving to Queens.

Soon enough, I'm in front of the house. The crummy two-story vinyl-sided house. I don't know how we could have expected to be happy in a vinyl house. I remember trying to talk Ava into holding out until we found a brick house. She wouldn't though. Wanted to settle somewhere the second we landed in New York.

I pull the Gremlin into the driveway.

I walk up the two steps to the front door and knock. Nothing happens and I'm almost relieved. This can't possibly be a good idea. Then, just as I'm about to turn and get back to the Gremlin, Ava comes to the door. She's wearing a white fuzzy bathrobe and her hair is up. It occurs to me that she's beautiful.

"Attila?" she says, unsure.

"Hi, Ava."

"What are you doing here?" she asks, dangling her arms loose at her sides.

"I don't know," I shrug. "Is Grace here?"

"You came to see Grace?"

"No, mostly I came to see you. But I miss Grace."

"What are you really doing here?" she asks, narrowing her eyes.

"I don't know. I miss you."

"Damn straight you miss me. I didn't trust you to realize that though."

"Huh?"

"Oh just come in and shut up."

"Okay."

I follow my wife inside our vinyl house.

34.

Compelling Thunder

The sky has gone mad and a massive storm is drumming at the windows of Ava's friend's cottage. Crow is lying on the blanket I've put down for him and he keeps putting one paw over his face, as if protecting himself from the thunderstorm. I'd like to just lie down next to him and put my own paws over my face and hope for it all to go away, but it's not that simple.

I'm sitting on the lone chair in the place. There's a futon in one of the two bedrooms but I've only taken small naps now and then. I have to keep my vigil. The girl is locked in the cabin behind the cottage and, although I boarded up the windows, she could still conceivably find a way out if I don't pay attention.

The rain is coming harder and one of the windows starts leaking. A crash of thunder lets loose and Crow howls, compelled to add his song to that of the sky.

Ava has loaned me a cell phone and I take it out of my pocket now, trying Ava's home number for what seems like the thousandth time in the last twelve hours. Again, no answer. I haven't talked to her since leaving the track, when I called to tell her about the change of plans and how I'd had to take the girl instead of the jockey. She'd seemed a little surprised by this, but told me to go ahead and take the girl upstate. Ava was supposed to call again though and she hasn't.

I get up and go into the little bathroom with its ancient blue tiles. I relieve myself and look out the bathroom window toward the cabin. I suppose I have to feed the girl now. I go back into the kitchen and look into the fridge where I've put the few groceries I bought back in Queens. When I open the package of sandwich meat, Crow comes running over and starts doing a dance. When that fails to make me feed him, he jumps straight into the air, then lands and chases his tail. It's pretty impressive. I give him a piece of bologna. I make a sandwich for the girl, tuck a bottle of water under my arm and then tell Crow to follow me outside. We both trot through the little yard between the house and the cabin, trying to dodge the raindrops that are falling and turning the snow to slush. I have to put the sandwich down so I can pull my keys out of my pocket and I issue a threat to Crow not to eat the prisoner's sandwich. It takes me a minute to unlock the huge padlock and I manage to get pretty wet.

As I push the door open, I find her standing there, staring at me.

"Please," she says, "my cats need to be fed, please let me call my neighbor." She's obviously pretty worked up about it, has her face all bunched up and there's no color in her lips. She'd tried this one yesterday afternoon, on the ride up here, piping in every twenty minutes or so about her cats. I figured it was just a ruse but now I'm starting to wonder. She does look like a girl who'd have cats and, to my chagrin, Crow continues to feel drawn to the girl, is in fact nuzzling her right now as she pets his head.

"Crow!" I call out to the disloyal dog.

"It's fine," the prisoner says. "I like dogs," she adds, entirely missing the point, which is that I don't like my dog kissing up to strangers.

"I'd like for you to imagine you're in my shoes," the girl says now. "You're trapped somewhere and your dog is at home, starving. If the positions were reversed, I'd let you call a neighbor to have them feed your dog."

She stares at me so hard I'm convinced she's trying to bend my mind. I stare right back at her, feeling torn—on the one hand worried about her damned cats, on the other hand picturing Darwin and how, however indirectly, this girl could have impact on his well-being.

"Please?" the girl says. She looks down at Crow then back up at me, adding another *please*.

"How about you eat something and we'll think about it," I say, offering the sandwich.

She stares down at the sandwich in much the same way she was staring at me a few seconds ago.

"What is that, meat?" she asks.

"Yeah, pastrami and bologna."

"Thanks, but I'm a vegetarian," the prisoner says. "I don't eat anything with a face."

This takes me by surprise and I look down at the sandwich in my hand, suddenly picturing a face on it.

"This doesn't have a face," I say.

"At some point it did."

I can't really argue with that even though deli meat is so far removed from animals that it practically is vegetarian.

"So," I say, feeling like a complete jerk, "you definitely don't want this?" I indicate the sad-looking sandwich, even though I know the answer and, in fact, wonder if I'll give up meat. Up till now, I'd always thought vegetarians were just pale people who liked being difficult. But this *face* thing has freaked me out.

"No, I'm not going to be eating that," the girl affirms.

"Mind if Crow has it?"

"I don't know if processed meat is good for him," the girl says, sort of sternly. "I feed my cats raw meat."

Christ.

"But go ahead," she adds, "he's probably used to it."

I can't believe this girl, this prisoner, is making me feel like shit about what I feed my dog.

I pick the sandwich up and stuff it into one of my huge pockets. I reach for the bottle of water and give that to the girl. She takes the top off and drinks loudly.

"Thanks," she says, after draining half the bottle.

I remove my gun and the cell phone out of my other pocket and though I'm not actually pointing the gun at the girl, she takes a step back and turns paler than she already is.

"Oh, sorry," I say reflexively before remembering that yes, I should be pointing a gun at this girl, particularly right now.

"I'm going to let you call this neighbor of yours, but at the slightest hint of asking for help or letting him know where you are . . ." I let the sentence trail off and I wave the gun at her a little, trying to act like it means nothing to me to use it. And it wouldn't have meant anything to me to use it earlier in the day, when I so clearly saw this girl's jockey boyfriend as an immediate threat to Darwin. But things are a little different now. Though I don't want her to know that.

"Thank you," the girl says softly.

"Number?" I ask, keeping the gun pointed at her with one hand while preparing to punch the numbers in with the other.

She recites the number and I dial. It rings once and I hand her the phone, bringing the gun very close to her face. I watch her blink several times.

"Ramirez," she says into the phone, "it's Ruby."

I can tell the guy is asking her where she is and I carefully watch her face.

"Don't worry," she says, "I'm fine but I won't be home for a while. I wonder if you could please feed the cats until I get back."

Her voice sounds pretty tense but she's not up to any direct funny business that I can see.

"Don't worry about it," she's saying. "Please just feed the cats, okay?"

At that I snatch the phone away from her and hang it up and I'm worried now, feeling like a jackass because surely the neighbor can have the number traced.

"That was bad," I say, bringing the gun closer to her face. "You sounded upset."

"I didn't say anything to make him suspicious," the girl says, "though maybe the way you snatched the phone away and hung it up might get him wondering."

"Don't be a smartass, girl," I say between my teeth. "This isn't a game."

"I'm aware of that. Even though I don't know what the hell good having me here is doing you."

"You mentioned that. But I don't think you know your own value. That jockey of yours is pretty crazy about you."

"Not anymore he's not, and anyway I don't know what you want from him. He's a powerless person, you know."

"And powerless people take it out on helpless innocent animals."

"What?"

"You know what I mean."

"I do? No, I don't. What are you talking about?"

The girl looks genuinely puzzled.

"Your boyfriend is up to no good."

"I'm not sure what kind of 'no good' you mean."

"I don't need to discuss this with you," I say then because I feel myself getting sucked into this girl and her deranged point of view.

I turn my back to her, call to Crow, and go out the door.

She's protesting as I lock her back up and walk away.

I get back into the main house and start walking around in circles in the living room. Eventually, I try Ava again. At last she answers the phone.

"Ava. What's going on? I've been trying to call you. I'm up here. In Saugerties."

"I know, Ben, thank you. I'm sorry."

"Don't be sorry."

"But I am. It's not necessary. The plan is off."

"What?"

"Attila isn't going to do anything to your horse. Or any horse."

"I don't know what you're talking about."

"I misled you, Ben. I'm sorry."

"What?"

"I was upset with Attila and wanted to teach him a lesson, but I'm afraid there was never any danger of his actually harming a horse. Or harming anything at all."

"This is crazy. What's going on here, Ava?"

"I'm sorry, Ben, forgive me. You can release the girl. There's no point in any of this."

"You've got to be kidding me."

"No, Ben, I'm not."

"I don't believe you, Ava. I'm not letting this girl go."

"Ben, you have to. Kidnapping is against the law."

"It wasn't my idea."

"I realize that. But I was wrong. I led you to believe Attila would harm your horse but it's not true."

"I just don't believe you, Ava."

"Ben, you must. It's true. Let the girl go."

"I will not. And that guy's going to jail. I don't care what I have to do to bring attention to it. I know these things. I know what he's planning."

"Ben, please!" Ava is begging now. I hang the phone up and then turn it off.

Outside, the rain has let up and the thunder is distant.

Crow lies down on his blanket and puts his face on his paws.

RUBY MURPHY

35.

Crawling

I'm curled under the filthy quilt I found in the cardboard box. It's very cold in here and I'm starving, which doesn't help. The tips of my fingers have gone numb and I'm dizzy. It's gotten dark out and there's no electricity so I had to stop reading. I finished *Père Goriot* this morning and devoted the afternoon to reading through the children's books that were in the box. There weren't any delectable

Dr. Seusses but I did find a copy of *Charlotte's Web* and a nice book of fairy tales. Pretty weird to be reading *The Princess and the Pea* while some nutjob is holding me prisoner in a cold cabin in the woods and is trying to feed me bologna. To the psycho's credit, after finding out I'm a vegetarian, he did bring me an orange and two pieces of white bread—which I inhaled—but now the acids from the orange are eating through my mostly empty stomach.

I don't know if it's physical discomfort or the onset of some form of confinement-induced psychosis but I find that I just can't wait anymore. I have to take some sort of action. I have the carpet knife and I certainly considered trying to jab at my captor but a carpet knife doesn't hold much of a candle to a gun. I would have to take him by surprise and there just hasn't been any way to do that.

I throw back the quilt and begin pacing the floor, listening to it creaking in protest. After a few minutes of this, I begin noticing where the floor is sagging badly. I jump up and down in one spot, feeling it give. I could probably jump right through but I'm not sure what's underneath the cabin. I kneel down and start picking at a corner of one of the linoleum squares covering the floor. It's slow going until I remember my carpet knife. I begin slicing into the stuff, ripping up the squares. Beneath the linoleum are old rotting floorboards. I start kicking at one of these. It gives after a few kicks and I get my whole foot through. I stamp some more until I've made a large hole in the floor. I get down on my belly and peer into the darkness. I can't see anything but I can smell the cold dark earth below. I reach down and I can just touch the dirt with the tips of my fingers. There's enough space for me to get in there and crawl, but I'm not sure if I can actually crawl to freedom or if I'll just be trapped under the cabin. It's not like I have anything to lose though so I push my whole torso through and climb down. I am soon on my belly, under the cabin. It's pitch dark and I'm sure there are monstrous insects down here if not rats. Thinking about it makes my heart start pounding too fast. But it's either crawl through this or go back up into the cabin and await my fate. Neither seems an appealing prospect.

36.

Long Shot

My wife's thighs are more generously fleshy than the last time I was between them. She's put on a few pounds, which is probably the only reason I am here. At her thinnest, she is craziest. At this weight, which I'd wager is about one-twenty, she is usually okay, because she has enough meat on her bones to keep her connected to earth but not so much that she feels and acts leaden.

It's shocking to taste her. It has been three months, but it feels like as many decades. And if someone had told me this morning when I woke up to the horrible wheezing sound of a dying old man that I'd be making love to my estranged wife a few hours later, I'd have told them they were crazier than Ava's ever been.

Ava is wiggling her hips and moaning in pleasure and for a moment I think of Ruby and a spear of guilt shoots through me. I was on the verge of loving her, but I probably never could have crossed over that precipice because of this woman, this savage, this moaning she-beast Ava who is in my blood just as I am in hers. My wife shakes in orgasm and I pull my head away and am about to enter her, to descend softly into her world, when the phone rings.

I jump to my feet.

"Attila! Calm down! It's just the phone, come back here."

"No. They're after me," I say, panicked, already looking for my clothes.

"Baby, if anyone is really after you, they're probably not going to call first."

"Answer it, Ava, please."

"You want to talk to your assassin?"

"Just answer it."

Ava reaches over and picks up the phone.

She listens then waves her hand at me, signaling that it's nothing to worry about.

I go into the bathroom and throw water on my face. I stand naked in front of the mirror, looking at my torso. The muscles that will be of no use to me now. The muscles that will never again know what it's like to hold back a thousand pounds of thoroughbred for the first half mile of a route race, the muscles that will probably turn to Jell-O now that their purpose has been taken from them. I can hear Ava, still talking on the phone. I walk down the hall to look at Grace's room. It doesn't look like a little girl's room. It's bare and tidy, the only decoration a huge poster I gave her of the race-horse Cigar. On the dresser is a little toy stable with some plastic horses arranged in order of size. Next to these there's a bobblehead doll of the great race mare Xtra Heat. I'd never before noticed that my daughter's only toys were representations of horses. There are no dolls or stuffed animals. It occurs to me that I don't know my daughter at all anymore. I'm not sure when she turned into the creature who would inhabit this formal, minimalist room. I feel my chest tighten but I also feel relief just to know I'll see her soon.

"Baby," I hear Ava calling me.

I walk back into the bedroom.

"Who was that?"

"It's a long story," she says, looking sheepish, "and not necessarily one you will like. But I'll tell it to you later. Please get on top of me," she says, reaching for me.

"What, Ava? What have you done?" Between the false lightness of her tone and her evident urge to get me preoccupied, it's clear that she's done something bad.

"Just come here," she ventures.

"No, Ava. Tell me," I say, sitting at the edge of the bed.

"I thought I had to do something drastic to get your attention."

I don't like the sound of this.

"What? What have you done?"

"That awful girl," she says, thrusting out her bottom lip.

"What awful girl?"

"That little rat-faced girl you've been fucking."

"What! What have you done to Ruby?"

"Well, nothing. I just got someone to take her somewhere. I wasn't going to have him hurt her or anything . . ."

"Ava! What the fuck have you done?"

I'm shaking her by the shoulders now and she starts crying.

"Don't shake me, Attila," she protests weakly. I can already tell she wants nothing more than to confess. She mutes her sobs and begins spilling the story. She evidently convinced a dim-witted groom that I was out to hurt horses and that the only way to get me to stop was to kidnap me, and failing that, kidnap my girlfriend. I feel my blood pumping through my head. I am dizzy and furious.

"So you tried to have me drowned, Ava? And you had Layla killed? What are you fucking nuts?" I'm screaming at her and feel very close to killing her. She's sobbing and protesting that no, she doesn't know anything about anyone being killed or my nearly being drowned or any of it and I keep shaking her by the shoulders as she sobs. After many long minutes of this, something shifts and I sense that her protestations are genuine, that my wife is indeed insane but she did not try to have me killed nor was she involved in Layla's murder.

"Who the fuck is after me then?" I ask rhetorically.

She doesn't answer me, she just stares ahead. She's not sobbing anymore but tears are still sliding down her cheeks.

I pace.

"And so this guy has Ruby in a cabin up in the boondocks somewhere and won't let her go?"

Ava nods.

"Is he going to hurt her?"

She shrugs.

"Ava, this is very serious, we have to call the police."

"And say what? I had someone kidnapped but now I want to call it off and the guy's wacko and won't back off?"

"You should have thought of that sooner, Ava."

"I couldn't think. I needed you," she says, and in that moment I feel a great confusion. I feel the entire history of me and Ava passing through me, the repulsion and attraction linked so closely they nearly choke each other, just as we have nearly choked each other with passion and sickness.

"We have to go get her then," I say. I start putting my clothes on. My wife continues to sit on the bed. She is naked. Her small breasts look sad against her unearthly pale skin. Her face is still wet with tears, her blond hair is tangled.

"Get dressed, Ava. Now."

She gets up and walks slowly to the closet. I watch her methodically put on simple cotton underwear, jeans, and a white sweater.

A few minutes later, as I frantically pace the length of the living room, Ava gets on the phone and makes arrangements for Janet, the beady-eyed woman who takes care of Grace, to pick our daughter up at school. Ava is being quite rude to Janet, but I've noticed that Janet seems to take some sort of pleasure in being barked at by my wife.

I say nothing to Ava as we go out to the Gremlin. Ava makes little cooing sounds over the funny-looking little car and I ignore her. She has the damnedest way of acting completely normal and nonchalant under the direst of circumstances.

We get in the car and pull out into traffic. It becomes evident that Ava doesn't really know how to get up to this cabin in Ulster County.

"Haven't you been there before?" I ask her, frustrated.

"Of course I have. It's my friend's cabin," she says, a bit mysteriously, probably trying to provoke me into asking *what* friend.

"But you don't remember how to get there?"

"I took the bus."

"Ah," I say.

We stop at a gas station where I buy a road atlas and where Ava takes an extraordinarily long time in the bathroom, emerging very sullen looking. I know she wants me to ask what's wrong, to have me coax an improved mood from her, but this isn't a time for games. I feel my insides churning over the harm I've brought to Ruby.

The Gremlin sputters forward on the thruway and I pray that it will make it up there. I don't really care what happens once we've gotten there and rescued Ruby from Ava's lunatic kidnapper. But we must make it there.

We are both silent for a long spell. I am turning things over in my mind. Ruby. My wife. What could have driven her to do something like this? Eventually, I start talking to her.

"Have you been having a bad time, Ava?" I ask her, trying to inject my tone with an empathy I don't quite feel.

"What do you mean?" she asks, pivoting her head toward me.

"Have you been feeling unwell?" I ask softly, as I stare at the road ahead, peripherally taking in the bleak late winter landscape of brown grass and naked trees.

"Are you being ridiculous, Attila?" Ava asks sharply.

"What do you mean ridiculous?"

"Don't tippy-toe around me. You're asking if I've been particularly nutso lately and the answer is yes, I have. I have missed my husband and it has done bad things to my containment device."

"Your containment device?"

"My body. My brain chemistry. You know me, Attila. You know that change affects me unfavorably."

"That's not true, Ava. And half the time you were the one instigating major changes. Like sleeping with other people."

"Let's not discuss that."

"Why not? You've *kidnapped my girlfriend*, Ava, and let's not forget that the only reason I ended up in someone else's arms was you, your behavior. And I don't just mean your sleeping around. You are mysterious, Ava. For years you have kept yourself hidden." I glance over at her. Her lips are parted. She looks very young and terribly sad.

"She's really your girlfriend? You tell people that?" she asks with a pout.

"She's a very kind and good person. We never discussed exactly what we were to one another. But I don't want her hurt. I have already hurt her."

"You have?" she asks, hopeful.

"I have. Because I could never be hers. Not completely."

"Because of me?" she asks, a note of triumph coming into her voice.

"Something like that," I say. I feel myself gripping the steering wheel tighter.

She knows that all will be restored between us. The love and hate, the passion and sickness. For better or for worse, we are bonded.

BY THE TIME we reach the outskirts of Saugerties, night is falling. For the last half hour I've been unable to speak. I've kept my eyes on the road but this hasn't prevented the images from coming. Images of Ruby. All the good that she represents. It was meeting her and feeling her faith in me that caused me to clean up my act and stop holding horses back. Sure, I'd been feeling like shit about it for a long time, but it was Ruby who made me want to come clean. It was Ruby who guided me to winning that last race. And I've done nothing but bring her harm. A sick feeling spreads through my stomach like ink in water.

"There," Ava says, indicating a steep driveway, "it's there."

I pull in and negotiate the winding, ill-paved way. Tall trees stand vigil all around.

We pull up to a small white frame house. A light is on inside and, no sooner have we gotten out of the car, than a man emerges from the house. I've seen him before. At the track. I never forget a face. Particularly not this one. It's not the most distinguished face but it's troubled. He has worried eyes, a full but tense mouth and a long fringe of dark hair. He is holding a small gun which he has aimed at us.

"Ben," Ava says to him.

"What do you want, Ava? What's he doing here?" He motions at me with the gun.

"I tried to explain, Ben. I'm sorry, I misled you."

"I don't trust you."

"Rightly so, Ben," I try intervening. "Ava doesn't always know what she's doing," I say, at which my wife gives me an icy look.

Ben does not look appeased.

"Where is Ruby?" I ask him.

"She's fine," he says.

"She's in the house?"

"She's there. Out back, in the cabin." He motions behind the little house. "But you're not going to see her until I have some assurances about my horse."

"Who is your horse, Ben?" I ask him softly.

"You know who my horse is. You were gonna ride him. And hurt him."

"I don't know who your horse is, Ben. Can we please come in and talk?"

The man hesitates. His mouth is half open. His worried eyes are searching us.

"Yeah," he says eventually, "all right. You go first," he adds, indicating that we should walk in front of him. He follows, herding us with his gun.

We enter through an empty kitchen. A white dog appears and looks at Ava.

I walk ahead into a small living room and as I turn back around, I see Ava making a very stupid move. She is reaching for the gun in Ben's hand. As she does this, the dog shows teeth, growls, and lunges for Ava's leg.

"Fuck! Get him off me!" Ava screams but the dog's teeth are sinking into my wife who starts hitting the dog on the head.

"Don't touch my dog!" the lunatic screams, bringing the gun right to my wife's temple.

"Get him off her!" I implore the lunatic.

Ava is grabbing at the dog and then, time stops. The lunatic issues one more warning and then *shoots my wife in the head*.

I watch in horror as life drains from Ava's body and she falls to the ground.

The dog still has his *teeth in her leg*.

"Stop it!" I hear her voice before I see her. Ruby. She has suddenly materialized from behind the lunatic. He flips around, startled. The dog is also startled and at last lets go of my wife's leg. I crumble down to Ava's side as both the dog and the lunatic rush over to Ruby. I grab Ava's wrist but there is no pulse. My next thought is for Ruby. The guy now has his little gun jammed up against Ruby's temple. I spring to my feet.

"Stay there," the lunatic orders me in a deadly serious voice.

I freeze in my tracks as my mind races, frantic. Then the dog goes over to Ruby and begins licking her hand. This distracts the lunatic who looks down at the dog. As he does so, I lunge for him and Ruby skirts away. It all happens so quickly. I am barely aware of any movement from the guy and then I feel an explosion in my chest. I see a great splash of impossible brightness. I feel myself falling.

I try to sit up but I can't. I am choking. I watch my fingers scrabbling at the floor. I don't know what they're reaching for. The lunatic is bending over me. He looks worried. He is saying something. I look past him. At Ruby. Her eyes meet mine. My body is on fire as it never has been and I realize that in a few seconds I will die.

Ruby bends over me. I want her to run. I want her to be safe. I try to tell her this. To run. To hide. And then I find myself telling her to ride. In my twilight it's what matters. This girl who has horses in her just as I do. This girl should ride. I try to convey this. I'm not sure that any words are coming out. I suddenly see a great wash of faces. My daughter. Violet Kravitz who I hope will look after my child. Ava. Ruby. And the horse, my last ride, Jack Valentine. I rekindle the feeling of giving the big gelding my all. Of winning at long odds.

All my life, I have been a small man but now, at last, I am gargantuan.

37.

Ride

"*He's dead,*" I keep repeating as I cradle Attila's head. It's as if I'm trying to make myself believe it. I have never held a dead person's head in my hands. A dead person I have been intimate with. A person with whom, at least briefly, I entertained the idea of sharing my life. "*He's dead,*" I say again, aloud.

Just a few feet from Attila's body is the body of a woman I assume to be his wife. She went quickly and her face isn't contorted in pain or expectation of death. Attila on the other hand looks agonized. His bright blue eyes are open and there is a memory of pain in them.

As the psycho stands near me, staring, I reach over and close Attila's eyes.

Though there's no reason why the psycho shouldn't kill me as well, I am not afraid. I feel a sob come up from deep inside me but I force it back down.

"How did you get out?" the psycho asks me now.

"Doesn't matter," I say. He seems to consider this and then decides that in fact I'm right. It doesn't matter.

"You killed two people." I look up at him.

"It was an accident," he says, actually seeming remorseful. "They tried to hurt my dog."

I have no comeback for this. I have no comeback for anything.

"I have to go now," the murderer suddenly announces. Making

it sound like he's got to go to the store or perform some other mundane task rather than flee the scene of his crime.

"You tell them it was an accident," he says, frowning at me. "Those people tried to hurt my dog." He gestures at the bodies and begins backing out of the room.

I keep my mouth shut. It's not like I have anything to say anyway. It occurs to me to ask where he's going. But I don't. Doesn't seem like he knows. I watch him slap his thigh, calling to his dog. The dog glances back at me once, as if apologizing, and then they are gone. I continue my vigil, crouched near Attila's body.

I'm not sure how much time passes before I finally stand up and look around for a phone. There are two empty jacks but no phone. My body feels like it weighs more than an entire ocean but I force it to move. I walk in circles in the living room for a while, then crouch down by Attila once more. I lean over and kiss his cheek. It is already slightly cool. I hesitate and then trace his lips with my fingers. With his last words he kept trying to tell me something. To run, I think, but it also seemed like he was saying *ride. You have to ride*. I don't know what this meant. Ride a horse? Our last good moment together was in fact when I was riding Lucky out at the Hole. Maybe this is what Attila was thinking of. I will never know. And realizing this makes me sob again. More time passes. I start thinking about moving again. About getting out of here. It feels wrong to leave him here but I can't see what choice I have. I walk out of the house and start heading down the dark, steep driveway. I come to a road. I look left and right but see no lights. I begin to walk. When I hear a car, I put my thumb out. The car passes by without slowing down. Another one follows a few minutes later with the same results. About ten minutes later a truck appears. The driver slows down. I walk over to the passenger side and get in. The driver is a heavy-set middle-aged white guy. At first he's very cheerful, maybe thinks I'm going to show him a good time. I disabuse him of that notion. He takes me to the nearest police station, in Saugerties. He wishes me luck as he leaves me there. I don't think luck can help me now.

38.

Falling

She's lying on her side with her knees tucked toward her chest. Her face is smooth and childlike in sleep. I'm afraid to move and disturb her so for a long time I stay beside her, propped on one elbow, watching her sleep and marveling that she can look this peaceful such a short time after walking through the mouth of hell.

It was just dumb luck that I was able to help her at all. When I couldn't find hide nor hair of her that day at the track, I started getting worried. I was sick to my stomach after learning about her and the jockey, but some instinct was telling me my girl was in trouble and I had to squash my hurt pride and help her. I was supposed to be checking in with the office and then getting myself back down to Florida to tend to my string and keep things going there but I didn't. I went looking for Ruby.

I called all her phones to no avail. Under the guise of helping him find the man, I got Carlo to give me Attila Johnson's address and vital statistics along with a photo. I didn't want my face to show anything so I didn't look at the picture of Attila Johnson until I was alone. In it, he was standing near a barn. He was staring into the camera, unsmiling. His eyes were a little hard, but he had good features. A shock of boyish white blond hair made him look younger than he was.

I drove to the address Carlo had given me for Attila. A nosy landlady nearly called the cops on me when I went asking her to let me into the guy's basement apartment. She examined my badge at length and eventually let me in. She flicked on the overhead fluorescent, then stood in the doorway watching me.

"I'll be all right, ma'am," I told her. "I'll let you know when I'm done." She hesitated for a few moments then reluctantly went away.

There wasn't much to see. A narrow twin bed, a pressed-wood dresser, a miniature fridge, a hot plate, and a scale. I went through the dresser drawers. There were a few pieces of clothing, none of these in very good shape. In the closet was one navy-blue suit. It was very small. I got an image of Ruby touching the man who'd worn this suit. I sniffed at the suit, wondering if I'd smell her on it, but it just reeked of mothballs.

I looked through the trash. An empty container of protein powder and a very brown banana peel. I shuffled through a stack of *Daily Racing Form*s near the bed. I sat on the bed. I wondered if Ruby had slept in it.

I went into the bathroom. The medicine cabinet held one crusty toothbrush and a jumbo-size bottle of generic ibuprofen. The guy was out of toilet paper.

The apartment didn't contain traces of Ruby or of anything other than a depressing life.

I closed the door behind me. The landlady was standing on the porch, waiting.

"Thank you, ma'am, I'm done."

"Find anything?"

"No, ma'am," I said. "Have a nice day."

I got back in the car.

Carlo had told me that Attila had a kid and an estranged wife whose address I'd jotted down. I nosed the car into traffic and drove.

It was a narrow two-story house flanked on both sides by houses that were identical save for the color of their vinyl siding. This edge of Queens had clearly been the victim of a particularly aggressive vinyl-siding salesman. The guy—and it had to be a guy—had come through, spreading ugly uniformity in his wake.

I rang the doorbell but nothing happened. I knocked. When

that failed to yield results, I tried the two neighboring houses. No one was home. Finally, I picked the lock on the wife's house. I could get in trouble for it, but I can't say I cared.

The door opened into a narrow hallway. To the right a small living room and ahead, a kitchen. The kitchen windows looked out over a tiny concrete yard. There didn't seem to be any animals or indications of happiness. The living room held an orange couch, a rocking chair, and a large television. There was a bookshelf holding more porcelain knickknacks than books. On the far wall there were pictures of horses. Two of them were win photos from Aqueduct. Two horses I'd never heard of but the rider was Attila Johnson. He looked happy. I wondered if he still was.

Upstairs were two bedrooms. Not a lot of cheer in either one, though one of them was obviously a child's. The bed was small. The dresser was made of pink plastic. On top of it sat a collection of plastic horses.

I made my way back downstairs, reset the lock, and let myself out.

I sat in my car for a few minutes then decided to go by Ruby's. It was rush hour and it took me nearly an hour to get to Coney Island. The day was still gray and the wind had gotten meaner.

I parked the car on Mermaid Avenue, and, as I headed over to Ruby's, I took my phone out and tried calling her again. The machine came on. When I reached her building, I picked the downstairs lock and climbed up the narrow stairs. I knocked at her door and then at the neighbors'. No one seemed to be home anywhere today. I picked Ruby's lock too.

Ruby's cats were waiting at the door and the big one let out a hunger cry as soon as I came in. The air inside the apartment smelled stale, like no one had walked through it in more than a day. The cats started milling around my legs, screaming at me to feed them. I walked into the kitchen and looked in the fridge. There was a packet of raw meat there. I fed it to the cats. I noticed their water bowl was dry and I started to feel a little sick. It was totally uncharacteristic for

Ruby to have left her cats unfed and unwatered. Something was very wrong.

I was trying to figure out what to do and what to look for when I heard something in the hall. I threw open the door and there was the neighbor, Ramirez, with his girlfriend, Elsie.

Ramirez frowned and looked behind me, seeing if Ruby was standing there. Elsie looked me over head to toe and a few different emotions crossed her face. Finally, she asked what I was doing there.

"Looking for Ruby," I said. "When's the last time you guys saw her?"

"What you doin' in her apartment?" Ramirez asked.

"I had to let myself in. I'm worried about her. I'm trying to figure out where the hell she is."

"Ain't none of your business," Ramirez said.

"She's got a new man," Elsie added.

"Thanks," I winced, "I heard. But that new man's in a bad spot and I think he brought Ruby into it with him."

"She's in trouble?" Elsie ventured, looking to Ramirez.

Ramirez shrugged, "I ain't seen much of her since you been away. She called me yesterday though, right before I went to pick you up at the airport. Asked could I feed her cats and I actually forgot"—he hung his head a little—"I didn't think about it too much, I was on my way out, but she didn't tell me where she was or why. She was a little rude too, hung up on me."

"When was this?" I asked.

"Yesterday," Ramirez said, hanging his head again.

"Didn't say where she was calling from?"

"Nah. Some cell phone though. Number came up on the caller ID. Wasn't a number I'd seen before."

"So it's still on your caller ID box?"

"I guess," Ramirez shrugged and, after a little nudging, invited me in to look at the number on the box.

I put in a call to Carlo to have him trace the number. Told him it pertained to the jockey. He said he'd get on it and call me back. I guess neither Ramirez nor his girl wanted me in Ruby's apartment.

Elsie brewed up some tea and begrudgingly asked what I'd been doing with myself. In spite of being eaten with worry, I found myself telling Elsie about Gulfstream. About Clove in particular. I watched Elsie warm to me as I detailed Clove's story. Not that I was telling it to win points. I loved that mare and I loved talking about her to anyone who'd listen. What's more, it took my mind off Ruby.

Eventually Carlo got back to me. Ruby had called Ramirez from a cell phone belonging to Attila Johnson's wife. They were still working on tracing where the phone had been when Ruby had used it.

I figured I'd overstayed my limited welcome by then and I was about to head back to the motel when Ramirez's phone rang.

The man stared at the phone like it was a weapon.

"You mind answering that in case it's her again?"

"I don't know that number," he said, indicating the caller ID box.

"May I?" I said and, without waiting for an answer, picked up the phone.

"Hello?"

"Hello?" It was her voice.

"Ruby? Are you all right?"

"Who's this?"

"Ed."

"Ed?"

"Yeah, remember me?" I said, somehow finding it within myself to attempt a touch of levity in what was a distinctly unfunny situation.

"Where's Pietro?"

"Who?"

"Ramirez, where's my fucking neighbor, Ed," she said, hysteria coming into her voice.

"Right here, Ruby, he's here, but where are you, are you all right?"

"No, I'm not."

By then Ramirez had taken the phone away from me and it wasn't until one hour and fifty-odd minutes later, when I had driven the compact car at breakneck speed up the New York State Thruway to retrieve my girl from the Saugerties police station that I got any details of what had happened to her.

I found her sitting in a chair in the main hall of the station, holding her head in her hands, looking down at the floor. She seemed so tiny.

"Ruby," I said softly.

She glanced up. Her face was so pale it was nearly blue. Her eyes were rimmed red from crying. She looked into my eyes for a second then bent her head back down, as if it weighed too much to be held up.

"I'm sorry," I said, sitting down next to her. I could hear the police scanner bleeping from an office down the hall. We sat in silence for ten minutes. It was a low-key police station. No one was brought in while we were there. Eventually, I went to speak to the captain. The man seemed to be in shock, too. Murder in Saugerties was uncommon. Particularly a murder that attracted the FBI. Some of my cronies had already come and talked to Ruby. They were up at the house now, looking at the crime scene.

I LEFT RUBY to her thoughts as we made our way to the car and began the trip back down to the city. I thought maybe we'd pass the whole time in silence but about an hour down the thruway, she started talking.

"He was a good man," was the first thing she said.

"I'm sure he was," I said, though I didn't really believe it.

"Really. He was. I can't believe he's dead."

"I'm sorry you had to see that."

"Both of them," she said.

I still wasn't clear on exactly what had happened or why, but Ruby had been kidnapped by a deranged man who was after Attila Johnson. The man had locked her away in a cabin and boarded over the windows. She'd escaped by making a hole in the floor and crawling out from under the cabin. Then she had witnessed her lover and his wife being murdered.

"I didn't know what to do," Ruby said, speaking in a small flat voice. "I just let the guy walk out. He walked out and opened up his car door, called his dog. He had a dog. Then he just drove away."

She didn't tell me what she did then, but I had a feeling she had stayed in there with the bodies awhile. Saying her peace to her murdered lover, I suppose. I don't know. There wasn't a phone in the place and she'd started walking along the road until someone picked her up and gave her a ride to the police station.

"He was in trouble, Ruby," I told her when she'd finished talking. "He'd been holding horses back and then all of a sudden he got a conscience about it. Attila got on the wrong side of a guy we've had an eye on for years. Guy had his fingers in everything. Prostitution, drugs, but ironically, he wasn't doing anything crooked in racing. Owned a few horses but it was on the up-and-up. Apparently this was one thing he did for the love of it. Only he didn't have much luck with his stock. His horses didn't win races and I guess something like that doesn't sit well with that kind of guy. He got tired of playing it straight. Resorted to what he knew. Paid off some riders, threatened others. Attila didn't go for it though."

Ruby asked what her kidnapping had to do with any of it.

"We don't know that yet," I told her, immediately feeling weird about the *we,* like I was in some club she wasn't part of. "The Bureau I mean," I corrected. "They haven't got all the pieces yet."

She didn't seem to notice the correction.

"Ben Nester, the guy that grabbed you, he was just a groom working for some very small-time trainer. They got nothing on Nester. No idea how he ties in. Yet."

She didn't say anything then. I wanted her to ask me more questions. She didn't though and I wasn't going to push it.

It was close to dawn when I got her back to Coney Island. The edges of the sky were lightening, slowly pushing the night away.

Ramirez and Elsie were standing in the hall as we came in. Ruby said a few words to them then excused herself. She opened up the door to her apartment, walked in a few feet, then bent down to pet the cats. I stood in the doorway watching her. After a while, she made her way to the couch and sat down. She hefted Stinky, the big cat, into her lap and cradled him. She was staring ahead.

"Should I make you some breakfast?" I asked her softly.

"I don't have any food," she said.

"I could go get something."

"I don't care," she said.

That hurt. I knew she didn't mean anything by it. Just that I was the last thing on her mind right then.

I told her I was going to the store and went out. The sky had a lot of pink in it now but Coney Island was still asleep. I went over to Mermaid Avenue. Most of the shops wouldn't open for hours but there was one open bodega with a cop cruiser parked in front of the place. Though the practice of selling pot, dope, or coke from tiny Puerto Rican–run grocery stores was long extinct in most of Manhattan, it still went on in the outer boroughs. This particular bodega must have done something to piss the cops off if they were blatantly watching the place. Charged them for lunch maybe. I glanced at the boys in blue and went in. I was surprised to find a carton of eggs that hadn't reached its expiration date. I picked up a container of juice and some bread and butter and jam.

The wafting smells of my cooking didn't animate Ruby much but she shoveled down a few mouthfuls of egg. I had about a decade's worth of things I wanted to tell her but they'd keep. When I felt that staying any longer would be an outright intrusion, I told her I was going to head out.

"Okay," she said.

"I'll see you soon?" I asked but she didn't answer. I didn't push.

I CALLED HER the next day and in a flat voice she informed me she was fine. I didn't ask if she wanted to see me.

I started thinking through things. I didn't want to go back to

Florida. I wanted to see my horses, train them, race them, but I didn't want it all taken from me just weeks or months down the line. The Bureau had been able to get me a legitimate trainer's license and I didn't see why one couldn't be issued to me on my own. I'd passed the trainer's test. I'd even won a race already. Quitting the Bureau to train horses wasn't necessarily a levelheaded, logical decision but horse people aren't known for their level-headedness.

Two days after going up to rescue Ruby from Saugerties, I went into Headquarters and gave notice. No one really seemed to give a shit. There was too much going on. Terrorist alerts. A war-happy monkey for president. I proposed to buy my three claimers off and my boss, a not-so-friendly guy named Greg Langdorf, said he'd let me know. He seemed to think I was a bit soft in the head. I didn't think that highly of him either.

No one at the Bureau seemed surprised by my announcement. The only one who had anything to say about it was Lenny, a guy I'd gone through the academy with.

"How will you live?" he asked me.

"What do you mean?"

"You're not gonna make any money," he said.

"Thanks for the vote of confidence," I smirked at him.

"Hey, just stating the facts."

"I don't have a lot of overhead. And I soured on the Bureau a while ago. More than that though, I need to be around horses."

Lenny didn't really get it but I figured Ruby probably would. If I ever saw her again. For now, I decided I should just give her a lot of space. A few weeks' worth.

I had just come back to the motel room to pack my things and head back to Florida to close up shop. My cell phone rang, and Cat, exhibiting a new neurosis, growled at the sound. I felt like growling at it myself until I saw the incoming number: Ruby's.

At first she screamed at me. I'd never heard her outright angry. But I was sure hearing it now. I started grinning. I was glad she couldn't see it. That would have made her even angrier.

I threw some food in Cat's bowl then got in the car and drove to Ruby's. Fast.

I don't know what I'd expected, but she looked great. Her strength was back.

"You look great," I said, venturing to peck her on the cheek.

"I do?" She seemed genuinely surprised.

"Yes."

We sat on her couch. We looked at each other.

"I feel weird," she said.

"I would imagine so," I said.

"I don't mean about Attila. I just feel sad about him. He didn't deserve that. I meant I feel weird about you."

"Oh," I said.

"I've missed you," she said in a very small voice.

"Oh?"

"Yeah. A lot," she said.

It occurred to me that she had a funny way of showing it. But I didn't mention her taking up with a crooked jockey.

"Attila just happened. I didn't know where you and I stood. And he just sort of walked into my life and I let him. But it deteriorated as suddenly as it came on. I think it was over. And now of course, he's dead."

"I'm sorry, Ruby."

"It's not your fault."

"No, I mean about not communicating better. I was, I *still* am crazy about you. I thought about you constantly when I was in Florida."

"You did?"

"I did."

"And now you're going back to Florida."

"No."

"You're not?"

"Well, I am for a short time. But I'm coming back here. I've quit the Bureau."

"What?"

"Had to do it. It was just luck that I got two horse-related jobs in a row. Soon I'd be sent somewhere undesirable to do something repellent on behalf of a government I no longer wish to serve. I got horses in my blood and I need to tend to that."

And the other thing I needed to tend to was her. The girl was in my blood as surely as those horses were. I leaned over and kissed her. I thought I would taste her grief. But I didn't. She'd absorbed it already, contained it inside herself, in a place that wouldn't taint what was between us.

I LOOK DOWN at her now. She's still lying on her side with her knees tucked up toward her chest. There's a breeze coming in from one of the windows she opened to welcome an unseasonably warm day. Her hair is falling in her face and I reach over to push it away. She stirs a little and opens her eyes. I kiss her.

BEN NESTER

39.

Ether

Crow lies down next to me and rests his head on his paws as the train pulls out of the station. All around us, people are speaking French. It's sort of soothing to not understand them, to be surrounded by something melodic and incomprehensible. I'm inclined to like France. In the few hours I've been here, I've noted that dogs are treated like royalty. And so it is that Crow is sitting next to me on the train, being given full rights.

It's the middle of the day and the train is half empty. Two seats ahead of me are three high-school-aged girls discussing something in lively voices. To my right is a man in a business suit speaking with a woman in a red dress. The woman says very little. The man sounds like he's trying to talk her into something. As the train picks up speed, Crow sits up and looks out the window, watching the French countryside slip by. We're not far from Paris, passing through suburbs but they aren't bad looking. Even generic apartment houses seem more attractive than their American counterparts.

In a half hour, we'll be in Versailles. I have no idea what I'll do once I'm there, but I have to go. My mother had always wanted me to go to her hometown of Versailles, Kentucky, but I can't do that now. I figured maybe Versailles, France, was the next best thing. Not that I knew that's where I was going that day when I accidentally killed the jockey and his wife. I hadn't really meant to kill those people but they were trying to hurt Crow and I couldn't stand for that. Once I realized what I'd done, I knew I had to hide. I drove to Manhattan and me and Crow slept in the car. When I woke up the next morning, I figured people might be looking for me. I shaved off all my hair and decided to grow a beard. I even thought about dyeing Crow's off-white fur but I thought it might make him sick so I didn't.

I didn't have much money or ideas on how to get more. The one thing I knew was that I should go to Versailles. I went to a vet right then that first day in New York to find out what all I had to do to take Crow to France. I had to get him shots, a health certificate, and have him microchipped for ID purposes. I hated to have something implanted in his body like that but there was no way around it. I had to get a passport for myself too. Thankfully, I'd been calling myself Ben Nester for a long time, but that was just the name I'd been using since age sixteen when I'd decided to stop going to school and give myself a new start. Being Ben Nester hadn't turned out that well so now I would go back to being Carver Brown. The police, however, would be looking for Ben Nester. Carver hadn't ever done anything wrong and, besides, he had a birth certificate and even an expired driver's license.

I used most of what money I had left to get Carver Brown a rush job passport. But I still had to get a ticket to France.

I was dirty and broke, living in my car in one of the most expensive cities in the world. I was starting to feel trapped.

I figured I'd do one more thing my mother had always wanted to do. She had loved classical music and she'd always told herself she would go to New York one day and go to Carnegie Hall. Once I came along though, she didn't go much of anywhere. So I thought I should go for her. I didn't look that good and I only had sixty dollars. I left Crow in the car and went to the Turkish baths and got myself cleaned up some then I went up to Carnegie Hall. I wasn't even sure if it would be open or what would be happening but I got there at seven and there were people milling around everywhere. I couldn't figure out where I was supposed to buy tickets, so I was standing in the lobby, packed between all sorts of people and not knowing what to do, when an opportunity presented itself. There was a lady in a disgusting fur coat who had her purse dangling near me and the purse was open and I could see her wallet. So I just reached in and took it. I slowly made my way to the other side of the lobby. I was still packed in between many people and all of a sudden it was like the gods were making offerings to me. I found myself behind a man who obviously had a wallet in his back pocket. Someone else happened to bump into him and while they were all apologizing to each other, I took that man's wallet too. I made my way through that lobby collecting wallets like nothing at all. Totally effortless.

I'd never in my life been a thief, but I figured it was okay. It had started with the lady in the fur coat and people shouldn't wear dead animals.

Eventually, I found the place to buy tickets, only apparently the show was sold out. It didn't matter though, at least I'd set foot in Carnegie Hall.

I left.

I went back downtown to where the car was parked. Crow was particularly glad to see me, like maybe he'd sensed I was up to something that might have gotten me in trouble. He did some extreme licking of my face and hands, making glad sounds as he did it. I just closed my eyes and let him. When he'd settled down a little, I took the four wallets out of my coat and opened them. The first one only had forty-something dollars in it and a lot of credit cards but I didn't want to get caught by using credit cards. The second wallet had a hundred and something and more credit cards. In the third wallet, I hit the jackpot. It was a red alligator wallet I'd taken from the lady with the fur coat. The thing was filled with hundred-dollar bills. Over two thousand dollars' worth. The fourth wallet only had a couple hundred but that was fine. I had plenty now.

A few days later, Crow and I flew to Paris. All I had was a big backpack with two changes of clothes and my toothbrush. My seat turned out to be in the middle of a row of seats, packed in between two Frenchmen. They didn't say a word to me though and I spent the first few hours worrying about Crow being transported like luggage in the plane's belly. I had to drink a lot to calm down about it and then, thankfully, I slept.

When we landed in Paris, I raced to the special baggage area to retrieve Crow and he actually seemed okay. A little put out, but okay. I started trying to figure out how to get to Versailles, which is when I learned that dogs are royalty in France and can go anywhere. I just left Crow's crate by the trash at the airport and Crow and I eventually found the right train.

OUTSIDE THE TRAIN windows, the suburbs are becoming quainter. Old houses with beautiful slate roofs. Majestic ancient trees popping early spring buds.

The train pulls into the station at Versailles and for a minute I'm panicked, not really knowing where I'm going to go. Then I see signs everywhere steering the way to the château. I follow the signs, passing pretty old buildings lined with cafés and souvenir shops. A wide elegant boulevard leads directly to the back of the palace. It is imposing, an enormous stone structure that appears to go on for miles. I feel my mother with me as I approach. I know she's glad for

my getting to see something like this. Crow and I walk to the side of
the palace, over an old cobblestoned courtyard and to the back,
where the formal gardens stand. It's a cold day but there are thou-
sands of tourists in spite of this and at first I'm disappointed. It's all
so well kept and grand. A long series of vast terraces lead to a fountain and beyond it to a long canal. It's certainly big, but it's too man-
icured for my tastes. I walk though. Crow trots at my side. We head
down past the fountain, threading through packs of tourists and
happy couples. We walk along the broad canal for a bit and then, to
my right, I see a very long road lined with enormous old trees. We
turn down this road and the throng of tourists thins out, giving way
to people walking with kids and dogs. Then, to my astonishment,
we come to a field full of horses. Very well-groomed, lush-looking
horses. I don't know what the hell they're doing there and I want to
ask someone but I don't speak French. There's a sign up at the end
of the pasture, but that too is in French. I start reading it anyway
and I get the idea that there is some sort of equestrian school here
on the grounds.

I stare at the horses for a long while and, for the first time in
days, I let myself think of Darwin. I feel tears come into my eyes. I
know the little guy is probably fine, but I don't have any way to keep
tabs on him now and that breaks my heart.

I'm standing like this, staring into the field, trying to keep the
tears inside, when a woman starts talking to me. She's speaking
French and at first it doesn't occur to me that she's speaking to me.
Finally, she lightly touches my shoulder and I turn my head toward
her. She's a middle-aged woman with long brown hair tied back in a
ponytail. She's wearing a bottle green wool cape and she has a very
fancy-looking camera strapped to her neck.

She says something in French and I shake my head at her.

She tries some other language which, I suspect, is Italian.

I say, "No, I'm sorry, I only speak English."

"Ah," she says in unaccented English, "you are American? I
would not have guessed."

I am strangely flattered by this.

"Do you live here?" the woman asks.

"I'm thinking about it."

The woman smiles. She has the strangest eyes, brown flecked with bright gold. They're friendly eyes though, they hold no traces of contempt.

"Where are you staying in Versailles?" she asks.

"Nowhere. I just got here. I don't know. I was just walking and I saw these horses and had to stop and look at them," I say. "I love horses."

"Horses should be loved," the woman says. "I come here at least once a week to photograph them," she adds.

"I'd like to get a job taking care of these," I say.

"But you should," the woman says enthusiastically.

"I've worked with horses before," I tell her, as if she's interviewing me for the job.

"I thought so, yes," she says. "Your hands." She motions at my weather-beaten hands. Although they could just as easily look ravaged from almost any sort of outdoor work, this woman has apparently taken them for horse-work hands. Again, I'm flattered.

I smile, finding that I like this woman better than I've liked any human in quite a while.

"Of course there are stables just over there," she says, motioning vaguely ahead.

"Oh?"

"Yes. There's a school for the horse circus."

"Horse circus?"

"Yes, the dancing horses." The woman smiles.

"Maybe I'll go over and ask them for a job taking care of the horses."

"You should," the woman says. "It was nice to meet you." She adds then, "Good luck to you." She smiles, tightens her cape around her shoulders, and walks off.

I stand there, my dog at my side, staring at the horses.

40.

Grace

It's late morning and the Long Island Railroad train is mostly empty. I don't suppose there's much call for going to Floral Park at eleven A.M. on a Thursday in late March. Admittedly, I'm not particularly thrilled at the prospect myself. It's been difficult to be interested in much of anything these last weeks. The moment I start feeling a little bit better, I picture Attila again. When I'm not picturing his dead body, I'm remembering him full of life, running half naked through the parking lot of the Woodland Motel. And it breaks my heart again and again.

They've all been trying to rescue me. Violet all but forced me to go see Dr. Ray, an acquaintance of hers who's a shrink. I actually like going to sit in Jody Ray's well-appointed office over in Chelsea but I can't say that it's helped much. I've had three sessions with her but the images of Attila's and Ava's bodies are burned into my head and don't seem to be going anywhere anytime soon. Jane and her husband, Harry, have made it their business to try helping me too. The day after it all happened, they came by my place to try forcing some life into me. I hadn't found a reason to eat or get dressed yet when they called to say they were downstairs. I put my robe on and went to let them in.

They stood at the door wearing matching grave expressions. None of us said anything as we climbed up the stairs to my place. Ramirez's door was open and as we walked by he called out to me. I think he'd been keeping a round-the-clock vigil, expecting trouble.

"It's okay, Pietro," I told him, "it's my friends, Jane and Harry."

"All right," Ramirez said, coming to the door to make sure it was in fact Jane and Harry. I offered him a pale smile. He just frowned.

Jane and Harry and I went inside my place. The cats emerged from the bedroom to inspect the visitors. I immediately went back to the couch, where I'd been lying all morning.

"I brought muffins," Jane said, holding forth a paper bag.

"Oh good," I said.

"You look like you need one," Jane said, coming to sit at one end of the couch as Harry crouched down to pet the cats.

"I need more than a muffin," I said, making a vague stab at humor.

None of us did much laughing though. After about an hour, Jane persuaded me to get dressed and come with her and Harry to take a walk. Coney Island just looked flat and gray though.

After three days I started wondering why Ed hadn't called since the morning after he'd come to get me in Saugerties. A lot of feelings coursed through me—mostly anger at his apparent abandonment. It got to the point where I was angry enough to call him.

"*What the fuck are you doing,*" were the first words out of my mouth when he answered the phone.

"Ruby," he sounded like I'd punched him. Which, I suppose, I had. "Are you okay?"

"No. I'm not okay. Why haven't you gotten in touch with me?"

"I was trying to be respectful."

"That's what you call it?"

Ed was quiet. After a moment, it dawned on me that the man had no idea that I wanted him to call.

"I wanted you to call me," I said.

"Had I known, I would have. Can I come over?"

"Please. Yes."

He was at my place within twenty minutes. For a while, we sat quietly. He asked if I wanted to talk about Attila. I didn't.

Eventually, we went to bed and stayed there for a long time. Ed then stunned me by saying he was quitting the FBI and coming to New York to train claimers.

THE TRAIN APPROACHES Floral Park and my mood improves slightly. I'm about to see Ed for the first time since he left for Florida to pack up his little stable and return to New York.

I get off the train and start walking. The sky is blotched and gray. The air is cold, even though spring should be coming any minute now.

By the time I reach the backstretch entrance, it's raining lightly and my hair is moist. I don't have a hat or umbrella and I get soaked.

I reach barn fifty-four but there's no sign of Ed. There are horses but it's impossible to know if any of them are his. I walk closer and peer into the first stall, finding a big bay mare. She's friendly enough and licks my extended palm. I scratch her face a little and then move on to the next stall. Here, a small chestnut gelding shows me his hind end. I cluck at him a little but he's not in a sociable mood. I move on to the next stall where I find a big dark bay gelding, also with his butt to me. I try a tentative cluck and he pricks his ears forward and turns around. He has intelligent eyes and he bears a striking resemblance to Violet Kravitz's Jack Valentine. The horse comes over, sniffs at my hands then truffles at my head, rubbing his nose against my wet hair.

"So you found him," a voice says behind me.

I turn around to face Ed.

"Hey you," I say.

"Hey yourself." He pulls me into his arms. I close my eyes and sink into the hug.

"You found your friend," Ed says eventually, pulling back from me and motioning at the bay horse.

"What do you mean?"

"Jack Valentine. Or do all horses look alike to you?"

"Oh, I *thought* that was him. What's he doing here?" I ask, surprised. After winning his and Attila's last race, Jack came up with a chipped sesamoid bone in his left front leg. He won't race again, but he will eventually heal. I figured Violet would have already sent him somewhere for a layup.

"He's using my extra stall until you find somewhere to keep him," Ed says.

"What?"

"Violet wants you to have him," he says.

After a few seconds, I realize my jaw is hanging open. Then, I feel tears coming. I look from Ed to the horse.

"You do want a horse, don't you? You've always talked about wanting a horse. When Violet asked me about it, I figured it was a great idea." Ed is looking at me intently. All I can do is nod stupidly.

"He's on stall rest for a few more weeks, then you'll have to hand walk him a few times a day. After that, you're gonna want to let him grow up some. Eventually he'll make a great pleasure horse though."

Ed is patting Jack on the neck. "We'll find a way for you to board him somewhere cheaply, I promise," he says.

I walk over to Jack and start stroking his face. His eyes droop shut and he puts the edge of his muzzle on my shoulder. I can't quite believe this is happening.

When I can bear to tear myself away from Jack Valentine, Ed introduces me to his three claimers. One thing I can say about all three horses is that they seem intensely attached to their caretaker. Even the recalcitrant chestnut who wouldn't give me the time of day is demonstrative with Ed. The man certainly has a way with beasts. And with children too, apparently. After about an hour—most of which I've spent vigorously grooming Jack—Violet Kravitz comes by with young Grace Johnson. I had heard that Attila had left a will asking that Violet look after Grace—which gave me a shock since I hadn't realized that he truly knew his days were numbered. There have been legal complications over the child, but, thankfully, neither Attila's father nor Ava's parents really wanted much to do with Grace and it appears Violet and Henry will be able to adopt her. I've only seen the girl once, at Attila's and Ava's funerals, where she was standing with what must have been Ava's parents. She looked very pale and solemn, but she wasn't crying. I didn't get a good look at her then and now I'm startled to see a lot of Attila in her. I probably stare a little too intensely because she seems frightened of me and won't talk to me. She takes a shine to Ed though. She babbles at him nonstop as he introduces her to each of his horses, speaking of each one as if it were Man O' War himself.

Violet and I go into the empty room that will eventually be Ed's tack room. She wants nothing to do with my gratitude though.

"By accepting the horse you save me the trouble of spending weeks finding him an appropriate home," she says, waving a hand at me.

"Violet, he's a beautiful mover and he has a great temperament. I'm sure you could have sold him."

"To whom though? I can't let some stranger take my horse. Most people can't be trusted with a gentle horse like that, dear girl."

"I'm honored. And I'll take good care of him."

"Oh I have no doubt of that. What I do doubt is your condition."

"My condition?"

"How are you holding up?"

"I'm fine. I mean not fine at all, but fine. You know what I mean, don't you?"

"Yes," Violet sighs, "I'm afraid I do. I have no idea what to do with the child," she says in a low voice, peering outside of the tack room, as if expecting Grace to be standing there listening.

"But you seem great with her," I say, surprised.

"It's an act, Ruby, in fact I'm terrified. I'm not sure what Attila was thinking. Henry always claimed to dislike children and I certainly had never planned on having any. But what can I do? I cared about Attila and the child is an orphan."

"She seems like a nice little girl," I say.

"She's a very nice little girl. It's heartbreaking. She's the saddest, sweetest child you could ever meet. And I feel inept."

"That alone means you're fit to take care of her."

"What does?"

"That you feel inept. Only people who are trying very hard at something feel inept at it."

"I'm not certain that I agree with you but it's a nice thing to say, Ruby."

Violet reaches over and squeezes my hand.

We come out of the tack room and go stand in front of Jack Valentine's stall. The horse pricks his ears forward and looks at us.

"He's a keeper, all right," I say to Violet.

"Oh yes," she agrees, "and so is that man down there." She motions at Ed who is just emerging from a stall, Grace at his side.

"You hold on to him," Violet tells me.

I'm not sure if she's talking about the man or the horse, but I'll try to do right by both.

ABOUT THE AUTHOR

MAGGIE ESTEP is the author of *Diary of an Emotional Idiot* and *Soft Maniacs*. Her work has appeared in various anthologies and magazines, including the *Village Voice,* the *New York Press,* and Nerve.com. She is currently working on *Flame Thrower,* the next Ruby Murphy mystery, and hanging out at racetracks, cheering on long shots. She lives in New York City.

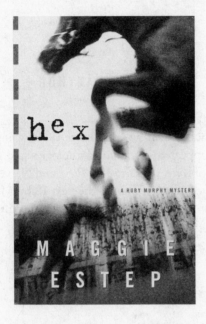

A *New York Times*
Notable Book
of the Year

HEX · 1-4000-4837-0 · $14.00 paperback · (Canada $21.00)

S taying out of trouble is a long shot when Ruby Murphy gets involved in horse racing's seamy underbelly—a dangerous world where nothing is as it appears and people and thoroughbreds seem to have remarkably limited life spans.

"There is about Maggie Estep's work a directness, a clear determination—a drive to cut through, to break through, to claw through—that is impressive."
        —A. M. HOMES, author of *In a Country of Mothers*

THREE RIVERS PRESS · NEW YORK

Wherever books are sold · www.crownpublishing.com